St
T

A Clara Fitzgerald Mystery
Book 27

By
Evelyn James

Red Raven Publications 2023

www.redravenpublications.com

Storm in a Teacup is the twenty-seventh book in
the Clara Fitzgerald series

Other titles in the Series:
Memories of the Dead
Flight of Fancy
Murder in Mink
Carnival of Criminals
Mistletoe and Murder
The Poisoned Pen
Grave Suspicions of Murder
The Woman Died Thrice
Murder and Mascara
The Green Jade Dragon
The Monster at the Window
Murder on the Mary Jane
The Missing Wife
The Traitor's Bones
The Fossil Murder
Mr Lynch's Prophecy
Death at the Pantomime
The Cowboy's Crime
The Trouble with Tortoises
The Valentine Murder
A Body Out of Time
The Dog Show Affair
Worse Things Happen at Sea
A Diet of Death
Brilliant Chang Returns

Chapter One

Outside the window, the wind was blowing loose rubbish down the road, and bending the bushes and shrubs in peoples' gardens. A handful of tiles flew off Mr Taggerty's roof and shattered on the pavement, narrowly missing Tommy Fitzgerald who had made the regrettable decision of taking the dogs for a walk shortly before the fierce storm blew in.

Clara watched him arrive home from the safety of the parlour. Ever since the winds had picked up, she had been keeping an eye out for his return, pretending she was not a tad worried about her older brother. After all, aside from being blown over, not a great deal could happen to him, she told herself. Though the narrow miss with the roof tiles rather belied that thought.

Tommy almost fell through the front door, still clinging to his hat which had been threatening to take off on its own route home for the last half hour. The dogs, Bramble a small black poodle, and Pip, a considerably bigger black Labrador, bumbled into the house looking delighted at their excursion. Tommy shut the door behind him and leaned upon it dramatically.

"Bit rough out there!"

Tommy and Clara Fitzgerald were equal partners in the Fitzgerald Private Detective Agency, which Clara had begun just after the war to make ends meet. Despite being the younger sibling, Clara was the driving force behind the business and Tommy would never hesitate to inform anyone that she was, most definitely, his boss.

Tommy took off his hat at last, trying to rearrange his dark hair which had managed to splay out in all directions despite him holding his hat in place. He sighed with relief to be back indoors. Tall, handsome, and athletic, Tommy was rather a contrast to his sister, who was smaller, with natural curves. They shared the same dark hair, Clara's longer, of course – she had not yet adopted the fashion for bobbed hair, she was certain it would not suit her. Clara was perhaps not the waif-like girl that all the magazines were parading as the fashionable ideal, but that did not detract from her charms. She was pretty and charming, with none of the harsh lines and angles that seemed to be what a lot of girls were aspiring to. In a world of straight waists and fierce bobbed haircuts, Clara rather stood out, but not for the worst.

Her appearance of an innocent young lady rather masked her sharp mind and ability to face the toughest criminals and win. She was the sort of person who people underestimated all the time, usually to their detriment.

"The papers on Saturday did mention a spell of high winds was coming," Clara said, slipping the lead from Pip before she ploughed down the hallway with it still attached and tangled herself with the staircase banister.

"Yes, but it was so calm first thing," Tommy

remarked.

"The calm before the storm," Clara replied.

At that moment they heard another crashing noise, and a shriek came from the kitchen. They both hurried to see what had happened to Annie, Tommy's wife, who despite their best efforts to persuade her otherwise, insisted on continuing as their housekeeper, which was the way she had come into their lives in the first place. Suggesting Annie could employ help, considering her status as Tommy's wife, had almost made her froth at the mouth – Annie did not require help in her kitchen. It had been her kitchen long before she married Tommy, in fact, it had become hers the first day she stepped in it all those years ago and declared that Clara was banned from touching the pots and pans, after she had witnessed the latter's attempt at making porridge.

"What is the matter?" Tommy asked his fair-haired wife who was hastily wiping wet hands on her apron and rushing towards the kitchen door.

"Something has fallen on the hen house!" she declared. "My poor girls!"

She was out the door before they could stop her, and so they hastened to follow. Bramble, always game for a bit of chicken chasing, tried to join them and was scooped back indoors at the last minute by a swift tackle from Tommy. He barked at the door that was shut in his face.

The chickens had escaped from their hen house and were fluttering about the garden, every now and again getting swept up by a sharp gust of wind and nearly taking off. Being chickens, they had a limited idea of flying, and this novel experience was sending them into a mild panic. Clara grabbed one that had made the mistake of flapping into the air to try to escape a sharp gust of wind, before it crashed into the kitchen window.

The hen house was ruined. A large, solid piece of wood had landed across its roof and caved the whole thing in. The door of the hen house had burst open under the force and the chickens had dived out in a panic. There was no point attempting to put them back into the ruined structure. Clara hurried down the garden to the shed where she remembered there was an old packing crate. She returned as quickly as she could with the large wooden box, which was not that quick at all since the wind kept catching it and threatening to take it out of her hands. She kept tight hold, putting herself at risk of being whipped up into the air along with the crate.

Tommy rushed over to aid her, while Annie tried to scoop up her chickens and prevent them from scattering across the garden. At last, they had the large crate by the back door and were able to gather the chickens up and into it. It was tall enough they could not flap out easily and they seemed rather happy to be in their new home, out of the wind.

"Is the hen house salvageable?" Annie asked Tommy in despair.

He took a closer look at the hen house, just avoiding an errant shirt that had blown off someone's linen line and nearly wrapped itself around his head in passing.

"If we can get that wooden board off, we can assess the damage," he said.

"Perhaps that can wait until the storm has passed?" Clara suggested.

"It could do more damage before then!" Annie said in horror.

She was already trying to wrestle with the board and there was plainly no dissuading her from the task. Tommy helped her and they managed to get the six-foot-long board into an upright position, only for the wind to catch hold of it and fling it back at the fence. It pivoted on the top of the fence panel, like a seesaw, and smashed soundly into the roof of the glass greenhouse next door. Tommy winced at the sound of tinkling glass scattering everywhere.

"Now there is glass in my hen house!" Annie said in alarm, ignoring the fact their efforts to remove the board had caused the damage.

She grabbed the board again and Tommy assisted her, because it was safer than leaving her to it alone. This time they managed to get the board down onto the ground without the wind snatching it away. Annie frowned at her destroyed hen house.

"Well, at a glance, the ridge beam for the roof is snapped in two and it may have wrenched the side walls inwards as a result," Tommy said, peering into the coop. "Fortunately, the way the beam snapped it completely missed all the roosts."

"Can it be repaired?" Annie asked him in despair.

Tommy examined the hen house further, leaning in to get a better look.

"I should say we can do something with it," he said. "It will need a new roof obviously and I think the hinges have been popped from the door, but it could have been a lot worse."

As he spoke there was a strange creaking noise. Tommy did not react, but his sister did. She grabbed his shirt and dragged him backwards just as the neighbour's damaged greenhouse took a stout gust of wind and toppled over on top of the hen house. Shards of glass and fragments of the metal framework were tossed everywhere and the fence panel between the two gardens sagged at an alarming angle towards them.

"Can we go inside now?" Clara asked, though the frustration and fear in her tone were unmistakeable.

"Fine!" Annie said, glaring at her now destroyed hen house in defiance. "But I am claiming this bit of wood that started the whole thing off as compensation for my hen house! It will make a new roof, at the least."

They did not try to dissuade her from grabbing the board and hauling it into the kitchen. There were some battles it was best to lose before they began. Between them, Clara and Tommy carried the crate of chickens indoors. Pip jumped up at the crate wanting to see inside, excited that the clucking, squawking things she was not allowed to chase had been brought indoors. The chickens were secured in the pantry, as this seemed the safest place for them. Annie had placed the board she had acquired against the base of the Welsh dresser, propped against it lengthways. Trying to recover after the shock of her hen house being smashed to smithereens, she set about making a pot of tea.

"I hope this storm blows out soon before we suffer more damage," Tommy frowned out the window, watching some distant trees tipping alarmingly against the force of the wind. His words were marked by the soft smash of someone else losing their roof tiles.

Clara had become distracted looking at the board they had brought indoors. They had only seen the reverse when it landed on the hen house, but Annie had spun it around when she brought it indoors and it was now plain to see neatly painted letters upon its surface. Clara was reading the words.

"'African Elephant, shot in 1922 and kindly donated to the Natural History Museum of Brighton by Mr C. F. Paget'," she read aloud.

Annie glanced over.

"What sort of a sign is that?" she asked, feeling aggrieved the board that had destroyed her hen house was so peculiar in nature.

"I would say it is a board for an exhibition item. In this case a stuffed elephant," Tommy replied. "And, clearly, it belongs to the Brighton Natural History Museum."

"At least we know who to claim compensation for my hen house from," Annie sniffed.

"How on earth did a sign from inside the museum end up flying across our garden?" Clara said, finding the whole thing curious.

Tommy paused for a moment.

"Wait, I remember something from the newspaper the other day."

He darted out of the kitchen. Annie gave a snort.

"All I care about is getting a new hen house," she declared. "How the thing arrived here doesn't matter."

"Are you not the least curious about the arrival of this board?" Clara asked. "Not to mention, where is the African Elephant that accompanies it."

"I am not curious at all," Annie said, in a bad mood because of the weather. "You know them next door will want us to pay for their greenhouse."

"It fell into our garden," Clara pointed out.

"They will find a way to claim it was still our fault," Annie puttered. "I know what they are like. They are snide about my chickens. They shall be hoping their horrid greenhouse squashed my poor girls."

Clara had not been aware of this rivalry until now but decided not to get involved right at that moment. Sometimes it was best to let Annie deal with these situations – quite often she caused them in the first place, anyway.

Tommy returned with the newspaper.

"There you go, I knew I read something about the museum."

It was the Saturday edition within which Clara had read the news of the impending storm, though like most of the residents of the town, she had not taken much heed. The newspaper was hopeless when it came to weather reporting. It would tell you sunshine was predicted, and you would have rain all week. It was novel that for once it had gotten something correct.

Clara looked at the tiny article Tommy was pointing out to her.

Brighton Museum acquires new exhibits. Due to a bequest by the late Mr Paget, long-time supporter of the Natural History Museum, two new exhibits will be on display within the next few days. These exhibits consist of an African Elephant and a giraffe, both shot by Mr Paget and latterly stuffed. These animals have been on display in his home but will now be relocated to the museum to form part of the Africa Room exhibit, which includes tribal artefacts and a vast display of taxidermy wildlife. The elephant and giraffe will be joining Leonard the African lion currently on display and the museum will be announcing a competition for the selection of names for the new animals next week. The animals will travel to their new home on Wednesday, an undertaking of considerable logistics as the giraffe is too big to pass under a bridge on the shortest route, so a new route has had to be considered. It is hoped the animals will arrive safely and will become new favourites for young and old at the museum.

Clara read the article with a mounting sense of horror.

"Today is Wednesday," she said and both her and Tommy found themselves looking at the wild weather outside their window. "Can you imagine what would happen to large objects being transported in this weather?"

"Well, if the wind whipped off that board and sent it flying all the way here, I don't fancy the chances of anything else," Tommy added.

Clara was growing more agitated by the minute.

"Whoever is transporting those animals could find themselves in serious trouble," she said. "They could end up badly hurt and no one would know."

"You think we should go take a look, just to be

sure?" Tommy asked. "In case they need help?"

"I think it is the only thing we can do," Clara agreed. "We know they have already encountered this weather."

She cast her hand at the long board in their kitchen.

"How will you find them?" Annie asked, listening intently.

"Well, we know where the Brighton Museum is, all we have to do is locate Mr Paget's home and we can then plot the most likely route between the two. Following it should lead us to the exhibits," Clara replied. "I shall get a directory so we can work out where Paget lived."

"I shall fetch a map," Tommy added.

They both hurried to their tasks. Annie sighed to herself.

"Honestly, it is not as if it is a live elephant and giraffe," she muttered to herself.

Chapter Two

The home of the late Mr Paget proved to be a considerable distance outside of town. With the winds howling still, Clara did not fancy trying to bus hop or to walk there. She therefore made a call to Captain O'Harris, her very good friend and the proud owner of several cars. She had had dinner with the captain only the previous day, discussing plans for a potential future holiday – just the two of them – and debating whether there should be some sort of Easter fair held at the Convalescence Home O'Harris ran.

Captain O'Harris had served with the Royal Flying Corps in the war, and he knew all about the hidden scars a former serviceman carried, the ones regular doctors could not fix and often ignored. He wanted to help those men affected by these hidden wounds and had transformed his old family mansion into a place where servicemen could recuperate and learn to cope with normal life again. It was a noble, but difficult task and O'Harris often found himself fighting criticism, prejudice and misunderstanding among the general public, as well as those in local government. He needed a break from the home, Clara could see that, and making plans for a trip away together visibly lifted his spirits.

She rang him via the telephone while Tommy worked out potential routes from Paget's house to the museum.

"Have you still got a roof?" she asked as soon as he came on the line.

"I do," O'Harris chuckled. "The old gazebo has taken a battering, however. I fear it shall tumble down imminently and take with it all the lovely trailing roses that covered it."

"That's a shame," Clara said, thinking of the happy times they had spent in the gazebo, watching the sun set on a balmy summer day, the sweet perfume of the roses lightly scenting the air.

"I shall build another," O'Harris said cheerfully. "It will be a good project for my guests."

O'Harris refused to refer to the men he had at the home as patients. He felt that generated an idea of sickness and provoked memories of other times the men had spent in hospitals, their mental battles being disregarded. He always called them his guests.

"Annie has lost the hen house," Clara said.

"Oh dear," O'Harris said with genuine sympathy. "Are the hens all right?"

"They are tough old birds, and all made it out in one piece. Though I suspect they might go off laying for a while," Clara remarked.

"I am sure my fellows would take up the challenge of building a fine hen house for Annie's chickens," O'Harris added. "They think a lot of Annie."

Annie often visited the home to teach classes on things such as cooking and practical sewing. She maintained that a man ought to know these things and should not just leave it up to women. More than one reluctant guest who thought cooking a woman's job, had been won over by Annie's gentle belligerence.

"That would be appreciated," Clara added, dropping her voice to a whisper. "Tommy is not remarkable for his carpentry skills."

O'Harris lightly chuckled.

"I was ringing to be rather cheeky and ask to borrow your car," Clara added. "The item that caused the destruction of the hen house turns out to be a display board for the Brighton Natural History Museum."

"How curious. How did that escape the museum?"

"I think it was being transported along with two new exhibits this very day," Clara explained. "Somewhere out on the roads around Brighton are a stuffed elephant and giraffe who were meant to be arriving at the museum. I rather fancy they shall be in peril in this weather, and I am concerned an accident may have befallen whoever was transporting them, seeing as the sign that should be with them is now resting in our kitchen."

"I see your point. This is not the day to be transporting anything tall or wide," O'Harris concurred. "You want to see if you can find these exhibits and make sure no one has suffered a misfortune in these winds?"

"I do," Clara said. "Who knows what might have occurred in this weather?"

"I shall drive over at once," O'Harris said, all seriousness now. "Someone may be hurt."

"I hope that is not the case and that merely the giraffe and elephant have perhaps been blown off the vehicle that was carrying them, but someone needs to find out."

"I will be with you soon," O'Harris promised her.

Concluding their telephone conversation, Clara went to find Tommy and see how he was managing with plotting the likeliest route the museum transport would have taken. Clara gave him a questioning look as she entered the dining room.

"I have a good idea of the way they would have gone," Tommy said to her. "There is only one sensible route for a large vehicle from Paget's home, the others either have narrow lanes, or old bridges that might not be good for a heavy vehicle to cross. There is a railway bridge running over this road, which is the shortest route to Brighton, and I doubt anything particularly tall would go under it. Once past those obstacles, however, the number of potential routes expands immensely."

"It is still quite early. Let's hope the vehicle has not travelled very far as yet," Clara said. "O'Harris is on his way with the car."

A short while later, O'Harris pulled up outside. Clara and Tommy clambered into his car. Tommy took the front passenger seat as he had the map and the various routes marked out.

"I suggest we follow this road in the direction of Paget's home, and see if we come across anyone," he explained to O'Harris.

O'Harris examined the map and then set off. The gale was still in full force, and they felt it hitting the side of the car as they drove along. Despite the weather, many people were still attempting to go about their regular daily routine. They spotted the milkman valiantly making deliveries, his old horse fitted with mufflers over its ears and blinkers to try to keep it calm in the winds. The postman was making a similar effort, though on foot. He was ploughing headfirst into the wind, his head down and back bent as he marched onward.

The odd determined housewife was sweeping or scrubbing her front doorstep, ignoring the wind making her efforts quite in vain. Other people were heading to work or to the shops, trying to keep hats on heads or bags and briefcases in their hands.

"I would say they are all fools, except we are also out in this," O'Harris observed.

Tommy spotted a fellow dog walker braving the weather with four eager hounds pulling on their leads. He made no comment about their foolishness, well aware he had read the newspaper weather prediction and had gone out with his own dogs, nonetheless.

They drifted out into the countryside, becoming aware of the damage the storm was causing as it whisked through the town. A display board advertising Hovis bread had been battered from its fixings and was partly blocking the road. A bookshop had lost all the tiles from its front bay window and the owner was desperately trying to make temporary repairs, while the books on display in the window flapped in the wind like trapped birds.

Signs that usually stood outside shops were tumbling about the streets, along with lost umbrellas, newspapers and, in one amusing moment, a large ginger wig.

"I honestly thought that was a cat being blown through the air," Tommy remarked, pointing at the unexpected sight.

"How unlucky for the wig's owner," Clara replied, watching the hairpiece come to rest next to a chimney.

Further into the countryside the damage of the storm was even more visible. At one point the road was swamped in loose straw that had blown from a nearby open-sided barn. Further on, trees were leaning perilously over the road, and they had to divert at one point due to a large oak lying across the lane and blocking it completely.

"I hope your museum fellows read the weather forecast and revised their travel plans," O'Harris said, watching a flock of birds attempting to fly against the wind and failing.

"The evidence of the lost display board says otherwise," Tommy reminded him.

They continued until they came to a bend in the road lined with trees, as they drove around it something rather odd came into sight.

"Look at that!" Tommy said, unable to stop himself from laughing.

There was a tall crate wedged into a roadside ditch, propped at a jaunty angle, and from its top poked a giraffe's head. The head had been wrapped in a blanket, which had now almost completely blown loose. The creature had a puzzled look on its glassy eyed face. Next to it, still on the road was a long-bed lorry and a man stood beside it, looking fraught as he tried to keep his cap on his head. He flagged them down as they drew closer.

Behind his lorry was a second, and this had suffered the calamity of being struck by a falling tree. The tree had narrowly missed the driver's cab, instead crashing into another large crate that had been on the back of the lorry and which was now also in the ditch, the tree resting across it and the bed of the lorry.

"Thank goodness someone else has come along!" the first driver said as he reached the car and O'Harris rolled down the window. "We are struggling to sort this out on our own."

"Is anyone hurt?" O'Harris asked.

"No," the driver said with relief. "Thank God. He must have been looking out for us today. Though Terry is rather shaken up and I told him to sit in my cab until he feels more himself."

The driver pointed to a man who was sitting in the cab of the front lorry, a strange expression of horror and shock on his face as he clenched his teeth together.

"I'm Stan," the first driver introduced himself. "We are meant to be taking these crates to the museum, but I'll be damned if I can see how we are going to get them out of this ditch."

O'Harris, Clara and Tommy left the car to come over and see the situation for themselves. The first lorry was unharmed. Ropes that had been holding the giraffe crate in place had torn loose when it fell, leaving the lorry untouched. The second lorry had taken a harder impact, but again the elephant crate had taken much of the force of the descending tree. The main issue was getting the tree off the lorry and pulling the crates out of the ditch.

"We shall never do this alone," Tommy said, looking at the hefty crates. "What we need is a farmer with a tractor, or a team of horses to help pull those crates out."

"We need a saw for the tree," O'Harris nodded. "Where is the nearest farm?"

Tommy and O'Harris headed back to the car to examine the map again, while Clara took the opportunity to check on Terry. The poor man was trembling as he sat in Stan's cab, and he jumped when she opened the door.

"Sorry," she said. "I wanted to see how you were?"

"Nearly… died," Terry said through chattering teeth.

"But you didn't," Clara reminded him. "That is what matters."

Terry wasn't really listening to her.

"Nearly… died."

Clara realised she was not helping. Terry needed to be away from the scene of the calamity and sitting by a warm fire with a cup of sweet tea. She headed over to her brother and O'Harris.

"Have you found a farm nearby?"

"Medlar Farm is just up the road," Tommy told her. "With any luck, they will be able to offer us some assistance."

"I think you should take Terry with you," Clara told

them. "He has had quite a fright and needs to be indoors, somewhere quiet."

O'Harris looked up and spied Terry through the window of the lorry.

"You are right," he agreed. "He needs to be taken away from here."

They regrouped with Stan and explained their plan. O'Harris would take Terry to the nearest farm and request help. Tommy and Clara would stay with Stan.

"Do you think we could do something about the giraffe's head?" Stan asked, anxiously looking over at the stuffed animal which was being blasted by the storm directly in its face.

Clara frowned at the creature. The way the giraffe was tilted, its head leaned away from the road, but not quite close enough to the opposite side of the ditch for someone to reach it from there.

"The museum will be so upset if it gets damaged," Stan continued, looking aghast at the notion.

Clara headed to the giraffe's crate as O'Harris drove off with Terry safely in his car. She pushed on the crate to see how solidly wedged into the ditch it was. The crate did not budge.

"All right," she said, and placed a foot on the crate.

"Clara, you are not seriously considering climbing up there?" Tommy asked her, dashing forward to try to stop her.

"It is just like a ramp," Clara informed him, now fully on the side of the crate and standing up with her arms outstretched to balance her.

"Clara!"

Clara ignored her brother and carefully walked up the crate until she was at the top, or at least what was considered the top when the crate was correctly upright. The giraffe's head poked out before her. She leaned forward to try to grab the blanket which had been swaddling the head.

"Get down Clara!" Tommy insisted.

Clara snatched hold of the edge of the blanket and managed to pull it towards her. With a deft flick she whipped it under the giraffe's head so now when the wind blew it was holding the blanket in place rather than trying to carry it off.

"There!" she said, pleased with herself.

At that moment a sharp gust of wind caught her off guard and she lost her balance. She slipped forwards and rolled off the side of the crate into the soft, damp mud of the ditch below.

"Clara!"

"I am fine," Clara informed her brother.

She lifted up her left hand which was coated in mud and cringed at the sight. As she lifted her eyes, she saw another hand and froze. She blinked and looked harder, but there it was, plain as day, a hand beneath the fallen elephant crate.

"Oh dear," Clara whispered to herself.

Tommy was jumping down into the ditch to her aid.

"Clara, are you hurt?"

"Not an inch," Clara informed her brother. "Which is more than can be said for the fellow beside me."

Tommy followed her pointing finger.

"Oh dear," he said.

Chapter Three

O'Harris did his best at the farm. A rather disgruntled farmer's wife accepted the shivering Terry into her kitchen, while O'Harris explained the urgent need for a tractor or team of horses down the road. The farmer was summoned, though he too was annoyed at the interruption. He had been standing in his feed store watching the roof rattle and unhappily anticipating it blowing off at any moment. Though watching the roof was neither helpful to the situation, nor terribly safe, he had been quite intent on doing just that for the duration of the storm.

Discovering a man trembling from shock in his kitchen and being told that two lorries had deposited their loads on the road did not impress him.

"What fool was out in this weather?" he asked, ignoring the fact he had been wandering around his farm all day in the gale and that, if it had been his pig market day, he would have thought nothing of braving the weather to take his stock to market.

"They are from the museum," O'Harris said, knowing that what he was going to say next was unlikely to inspire much sympathy. "They are transporting a giraffe and an elephant to Brighton."

"Poor beasts," the farmer's wife said. "They must be terrified in this weather and with their crates in ditches."

O'Harris cleared his throat sheepishly.

"They happen to be stuffed," he said. "They are a gift from the late Mr Paget. He shot them in Africa, apparently."

"Wait, you want me to leave my farm with this storm howling to rescue a stuffed giraffe and a stuffed elephant from a ditch?" the farmer said in astonishment.

"There is a tree as well," Terry offered, trying to be helpful. "It came down on my lorry. I nearly died."

"Serve you right being out in this weather," the farmer's wife berated him.

Terry huddled up into himself, looking miserable and unconvinced it was better in the kitchen than sitting in the cab of Stan's lorry.

"Look, the road is blocked," O'Harris said, trying another tactic. "It has to be cleared to allow others through and as you are the nearest farm the task is naturally going to fall to you. Sooner or later, you will be asked to remove the tree and clear the road. You might as well get it over with now."

It was a logical statement, and the farmer knew it. At times like these, people never appreciated how much damage his farm had taken and always assumed they had priority over his own troubles. At least if he helped now, that would be one less thing he had to think about later.

"All right," he sighed. "I'll bring over the tractor."

O'Harris was relieved to hear that, and doubly relieved the farmer was one of those with enough income to afford a tractor. Using horses in a gale to drag out the crates had never seemed like a sensible idea.

"I think the storm is blowing itself out," the farmer's wife said with undue optimism.

O'Harris glanced out of the kitchen window in time to see a metal bucket whip past, defying the laws of physics and developing the ability to fly. He rather fancied that belied the woman's comment.

A short while later, O'Harris was leading the way back towards the stranded lorries, unaware that the crisis had just become a lot more sinister. He arrived and pulled up onto the verge to give the tractor plenty of room to get past. It was a compact, pale blue vehicle, with an iron seat and no suspension that meant anyone who drove it for any length of time developed an agonising backache. This somewhat explained the farmer's demeanour, seeing as he was on it quite often.

Stan started to rush over to the farmer, intent on blurting out that there was someone in the ditch beneath the elephant and they had to rescue them at once. Clara intercepted him, feeling the situation required a little more tact than Stan could offer. The farmer was descending from the tractor to take a closer look at the situation as she spoke to him.

"We need to remove the elephant crate first. There looks to be a person trapped beneath it," she said, knowing there was no easy way to explain the matter.

The farmer looked less shocked than might have been expected – but then all sorts of odd things ended up in ditches on farms and he took the news with a similar acceptance to how he would have reacted to the news a heifer or sheep was in the ditch. Actually, he would have been more upset about a heifer or sheep.

O'Harris had just joined them and heard the tail end of Clara's words.

"A person?" he said in alarm.

Clara nodded.

"We spotted a hand sticking out from beneath the

crate. We are not sure if they are simply trapped, or..." she let them fill in the blank.

"Probably a tramp sleeping in the ditch," the farmer said matter-of-factly. "They do it all the time. Expect the fellow went down there to get shelter from the wind."

Unperturbed by this news, the farmer walked over to inspect the second lorry which was still wedged beneath the tree, and then observed the crate lodged in the ditch. O'Harris moved closer to Clara and whispered.

"You hardly think the person beneath that crate is alive, do you? Why haven't they called out for help?"

"They may have been knocked unconscious," Clara replied. "The farmer is right that a tramp might have picked that ditch to take shelter from the storm. It is nice and deep and would have provided a good wind break. It is just bad luck the crate dropped in that spot."

"Crushed to death by a stuffed elephant," Tommy said, testing out the idea. "That is not something you hear of every day."

"Until we know otherwise, let us assume the fellow is just unconscious," Clara told him.

The farmer was returning to his tractor.

"I'll have to cut away the tree first," he said. "I have a two-man saw to do the job. Who is volunteering to be the second man?"

Clara, under other circumstances, would have pointed out that a woman was perfectly capable of doing a man's work, but in this instance, she was rather relieved to be overlooked.

"I'll help," Stan said. "This is my responsibility. We can't let that tree damage the elephant."

The farmer could care less about the stuffed elephant. He just wanted the job done so he could get back to his farm.

"We can take turns," Tommy said. "Between us we shall have this done in a jiffy."

The farmer had produced the long saw with its two handles, one either end.

"Ever used one of these before?" he asked them.

Everyone was silent.

"Great," the farmer muttered to himself, heading for the lorry.

It took an hour to saw the tree into manageable pieces and drag each section away with the tractor. The wind howled around them as they worked, occasionally throwing objects in their direction to make things interesting. All through that time, not a sound came from the ditch and Clara became increasingly certain they would find a corpse beneath the crate. Every now and then she glanced down at the hand, willing it to move and prove her wrong. It never did.

The last piece of the tree was sitting on the elephant crate. There were a lot of branches as this was the topmost part of the tree. The farmer clambered on the crate and hitched sturdy ropes around the trunk, then returned to his tractor and pulled the section of tree into the ditch, where it wedged and would not budge an inch. After making a few efforts, the farmer decided the tree would have to be cut into even smaller pieces and that could wait until the storm had blown itself out.

Stan clambered into the cab of the second lorry and tried to start it. The engine made a choking sound, which did not appear promising. O'Harris was a keen mechanic, and he popped the bonnet of the lorry to take a look at the engine. While he was helping to get the vehicle going again, Clara and Tommy stood at the side of the ditch and took a long look at the forlorn hand. The farmer joined them, taking the opportunity to have a break and a cigarette.

"Doesn't look good for the fellow," he said casually, echoing the thoughts Clara and Tommy were having.

Tommy pulled a face. It was grim thinking how the man had perished.

"Once saw a man crushed by a haystack," the farmer continued. "Though, I suppose, technically he was suffocated. It all came off the back of a wagon and buried him. We went to dig him out but could not reach him in time. Strange things happen on farms. I have seen the same thing happen to other fellows and they have been dug out fine, just embarrassed they let it happen. And then this fellow was killed."

The farmer mulled on this a while.

"How much does an elephant weigh?"

"A lot," Clara said. "Over a ton, I think. Though I am not sure if this elephant was fully grown."

"It will do," the farmer said, with a sage nod. "Fate can be cruel."

"You can say that again," Tommy said, frowning into the ditch and thinking how unlucky could you get to be stuck out in a gale, find shelter, and then be crushed by an elephant – in England. It sounded preposterous when you thought about it.

Behind them an engine turned over and began to purr. The lorry was at last able to be moved out of the way.

"I'll attached my ropes to those handles on the top of the crate," the farmer said.

He was referring to metal rails that ran along the top of the wooden box and presumably had been fitted so it could be lifted by a crane. Straps had gone through those same rails to hold the crate on the back of the lorry but had been too insubstantial to prevent it falling into the ditch.

"How do we stop the crate from slipping and falling

further onto the person in the ditch?" Tommy asked.

"That will not be easy," the farmer admitted. "But I do have an idea."

He headed over to where they had stacked some of the smaller sections of tree trunk.

"If we wedge these underneath, we can stop the crate falling back on itself as I pull it out," he said.

This seemed a reasonable plan and so Tommy and O'Harris descended into the ditch and were handed the large chunks of tree by Clara and Stan. The crate had fallen partly on its side in the ditch, so it tipped at an angle. There was a gap at one end where the wedges of wood could be pushed underneath to stop the crate slipping in further.

Meanwhile, the farmer secured chains to the rails on the crate and prepared to drag it out of the ditch. When they had prepared things as best they could, he climbed back onto the tractor and started forward slowly.

The crate began to tip back towards the road and then began to slip off the wood wedges. O'Harris cried for a halt, as he and Tommy worked to better position the wood. With things seeming more secure, they called for the farmer to try again. The chains went tight, and the crate leaned towards the road without slipping this time. As the tractor edged forward, the crate continued to be pulled towards the road and the wood wedges held in place.

It was not long before the person in the ditch came into view. This moment had been one of uneasy anticipation. Stan decided he did not want to see and moved away. Clara peered down from the bank of the ditch, ready to shout for the tractor to stop if needs be.

The person in the ditch was a young man with fair hair, though this was mottled with mud and entwined with leaves and dead twigs. He lay in a spread-eagle position in the ditch, his arms spread out either side of him, while his legs were partly resting up the side of the ditch. His head was turned to the right and he was so pale, he could have passed for a ghost.

Once the crate was pulled onto the road and in no danger of falling back into the ditch, Tommy leaned down to the man and felt his neck for a pulse. He then attempted to lift up an arm. The body was stiff and rigid. He had been dead a while.

"Is he all right?" Stan asked from the far side of the road.

Clara turned to him, her expression saying everything. The farmer had descended from his tractor and was wandering over too.

"Dead?" he said.

"Yes," Clara nodded. "We really need to summon an ambulance and the police."

"But it was just an accident!" Stan said.

"We still need to summon the police," Clara explained. "We don't know who the man is, for a start, and it is our duty to inform the authorities."

"Probably just a tramp," the farmer shrugged.

"I doubt that," Tommy said from the ditch. "Not many tramps wander around in formal evening dress and with a fancy new wristwatch dangling off their arm."

Everyone paused at this news. Clara, who had also been thinking the poor fellow was a tramp seeking shelter, now turned to her brother and took a closer look. Though he was covered in leaves and had been pressed into the mud by the weight of the crate (which had, unfortunately, landed heavily on him) if you looked hard enough you could see the clothes were new and of good quality and the appearance of the fellow was far from that of a tramp living out in all weathers.

"We've killed a posh fellow!" Stan said in horror, the situation going from worse to worse.

O'Harris climbed out of the ditch.

"I shall drive back to town and inform the police," he said.

Clara agreed that was the only option they had. In the meantime, they would continue to clear the road, getting the elephant crate out of the way and preferably back on the lorry, if they could.

"I won't be long," O'Harris promised.

The farmer scratched at his head and surveyed the man in the ditch with disinterest. Stan looked fit to join Terry in a state of extreme shock.

"It was not your fault," Clara told him firmly.

"But we killed a man," Terry sniffed. "How can we live with ourselves?"

Clara patted his shoulder, there was not really much else she could do or say.

Chapter Four

Inspector Park-Coombs arrived at the scene in the early afternoon, having been delayed by a number of crises within Brighton, including the roof coming off the outside toilet at the police station. Clara, Tommy, Stan, and the farmer had cleared the roadway and managed to get the giraffe crate out of the ditch. Both the elephant and the giraffe were now sitting in their boxes on the verge, as it would require a crane to lift them back onto the lorries, or at least a lot burlier men than were currently present.

The farmer's wife had brought over some dinner for them all, having mellowed from her earlier irritation. Terry had been telling her all about the giraffe and elephant and this had aroused her interest in the recovery operation. Fortunately, Terry had remained at the farmhouse, otherwise he might have suffered a further shock had he seen what was lying in the ditch.

The storm was abating a fraction when the police car drew up with Park-Coombs inside. He emerged onto the road and immediately lost his hat to a stray gust of wind. He glared behind him as it spun across a

hedge and into a field, not stopping until it had come
to rest some distance away.

"Inspector," Clara came over to greet him.
"O'Harris has explained the situation?"

"He has," Park-Coombs said, still glaring at his
absconding hat. "Sounds to me like a curious accident.
Dr Death is on his way. I spoke to him before I left.
Where is the body?"

Clara showed him over to the ditch. They had
covered the dead man with an old blanket they had
found in the cab of Stan's lorry. It had seemed the
respectful thing to do. Park-Coombs clambered down
into the ditch with as much care as he could. His feet
slipped beneath him and there was a perilous moment
when it seemed he would fall flat on his face. He
arrived by the body unharmed however and lifted the
corner of the blanket to take a peek at the man.

"Doesn't look like a tramp," he said. "How did he
end up in a ditch?"

"I supposed he was walking home from a party and
the storm overtook him and he decided to find shelter
in the ditch?" Tommy suggested, having had time to
consider such possibilities.

"A party? Around here?" the farmer chuckled. "Oh,
certainly a shindig on a farm or two, maybe a barn
dance, but nothing you would wear clothes like that
for."

"How else do you account for it?" Tommy asked
him, a tad annoyed his idea had been laughed at.

"I don't say I do. I just know people don't have
swanky parties around these parts. The biggest house
for miles is that hall owned by Mr Paget, the one where
these animals came from. And he is dead," the farmer
stated this bluntly.

"Well, how ever the fellow came to be here, this is
where it all ended for him," Park-Coombs stood up and
brushed leaves from his trousers. "Has anyone checked

his pockets?"

"We have not touched him, Inspector, other than to check for a pulse," Clara replied.

Park-Coombs started to search through the man's pockets. He found a cigarette case, with an enamelled decoration. When he opened it, there was a picture of a semi-naked woman inside and three cigarettes. Park-Coombs raised his eyebrows at the picture, flicked it over to see if there was anything written on the back and noticed there was an engraving inside the front of the case.

"To Wills, my one and only, love Fran," he read out loud.

"Wills is a shortening of William," Tommy said. "So, assuming that fellow is the one the engraving refers to, we can surmise his first name is William."

Inspector Park-Coombs was still searching through the dead man's pockets, though he was coming up with very little. He finally searched an inner jacket pocket and produced a folded piece of card. It had been smudged by rainwater at some point, but when he unfolded it, he found it was an invitation to a party.

"This must be where William was last night," Park-Coombs passed the invitation to Clara so she could take a look.

"Royal Gala party for the Friends of the Brighton Performing Arts," Clara read. "This gala was held last night at the Maxwell Music Hall. That is down by the seafront."

"And a very long way from this ditch," Park-Coombs frowned. "For this young man to have walked from there to here in a space of a few hours is impossible."

"And ridiculous," Tommy added. "Why would he come out here?"

The matter was certainly curious. However, for the moment it seemed that no matter how William had made it to this ditch, his death was the consequence of being in the wrong place at the wrong time.

"I can see where that crate was resting on him," Park-Coombs pointed to the man's chest, where there was a mark across his jacket in a straight line. A deep impression left by the weight of the stuffed elephant. "Would have constricted his breathing."

"Don't say that!" Stan said in horror. "Please don't say that! We killed the fellow! Sent an elephant down upon him!"

"You did not know he was there," Clara tried to calm him. "And you did not intend for this to happen. It was just the culmination of a series of misfortunes."

Stan looked far from convinced. O'Harris offered him a cigarette to try to ease his nerves.

They were all distracted by the arrival of another vehicle. This was the coroner's van, which was rather like an ambulance in its construction, but painted black and with room in the rear only for the dead. Dr Deáth might have had an unfortunate name for his line of work, but it was certainly appropriate. He descended from a long line of coroners, stemming back to the medieval era and he often speculated that his name came from this time and had been first used as a descriptive term for what one of his ancestors did in his line of work. Whether it was a nickname, an insult, or a morbid job description, the name had stuck.

"Hello!" said the sprightly coroner, who was one of the most jovial men Clara knew. He headed over to the ditch with his bundle of medical tools, a broad smile on his face. "How are we all faring?"

It was a strange thing to ask, under the circumstances, and it might have made you suppose Dr Deáth did not take his work altogether seriously. Nothing could be farther from the truth. Dr Deáth was an advocate for the dead, he helped the unfairly deceased tell their stories. He just also happened to believe that life carried on and moping about a corpse was going to help no one.

"It has been a long day," Tommy informed him. "A curious day too."

Dr Deáth had become distracted by the sight of the giraffe poking out of its crate.

"Ah, these are the new displays for the museum!" he declared. "I have been wanting to take a look at them. I have never seen a giraffe before."

"Dr Deáth, in your own time," Park-Coombs muttered sarcastically from the ditch.

The coroner glanced down.

"I did not notice you there, Inspector. Is that my corpse?"

Dr Deáth entered the ditch with remarkable elegance for a man who was somewhat stout and small, and did not inspire confidence in his nimbleness. He seemed to just walk down the side with not a hint of a slip. Park-Coombs endeavoured not to be annoyed at the man's ease compared to his own ungainly entrance to the ditch.

"We think the young man might be named William," the inspector said.

Dr Deáth knelt by the body and pulled back the blanket.

"Poor fellow," he said. "This mark on his chest?"

"Made by the edge of the elephant crate landing on him," Park-Coombs replied.

Dr Deáth took out a notebook and tape, and carefully measured the mark.

"Bad place for a lot of pressure to fall on you," he said, then he tried to turn the man's head, so he faced upright. He was still too rigid to move without damaging the body. "He is in full rigour. When did the accident occur?"

"About four hours ago," Clara replied.

Dr Deáth tapped the pencil he had produced from

his bag against his lip.

"That does not make sense," he said. "To be in this state of rigour, considering the temperature and the fact he was outdoors, means he has been dead much longer than four hours."

"I swear we did not lose our crates more than four hours ago!" Stan said, thinking this was an accusation against him.

"We know that," Clara assured him. "What the coroner is saying is that this man was probably dead before your crates landed on him."

Stan had a grimace on his face, but as Clara explained the matter it lifted, and he looked much happier.

"Then, our crates did not kill him?"

"I shall need to run a few tests to be sure," Dr Deáth said from the ditch. "But I fancy this young man was dead long before you came along."

The relief on Stan's face was apparent. Then he remembered they were still discussing a young man who had died in a ditch all alone.

"Poor fellow," he said, trying not to smile as he thought about how he was off the hook.

"How did he die?" Park-Coombs asked the coroner.

"A little too soon to say," Dr Deáth replied. "He is so covered in mud that any wounds are hidden. But, from this angle at least, I can see no bullet or stab wounds. My initial thinking is that he died of exposure, but I will know more when I can get him back to my mortuary."

"Exposure," Park-Coombs said thoughtfully. "He comes out here drunk, wanders off the road and falls into the ditch. Lies there dazed and drifts off, only for the cold to get him."

"It happens a lot in winter," Dr Deáth said. "Though normally to tramps, at least out in the countryside like this."

He frowned and looked around him.

"Now, if this fellow was found in an alley in town, well, you could understand the circumstances better. We had a case like that a couple of years ago, do you recall, Inspector?"

"I do," Inspector Park-Coombs nodded. "The gentleman in question was a former soldier who had been at a banquet and overindulged. Walking home he must have slipped, or stumbled, and fell down in the passageway between two shops and knocked himself out. He was so drunk he never woke up and the cold took him."

Dr Deáth was nodding along.

"Terribly tragic. The family were most distraught and found it hard to believe, but the combination of large quantities of alcohol and severe cold can be quite deadly."

"Then, this is a natural death?" Tommy asked, because in general that was not the case when he and Clara came upon a corpse.

"It appears so at this moment," Dr Deáth replied. "I can say nothing for certain until I have examined him fully. That raises the question of how to get him out of this ditch and onto a stretcher when he is so rigid."

Dr Deáth paused for a moment.

"I wonder," he said to himself before scrambling out of the ditch and going to his van to measure the width of the interior. "Just a fraction too narrow."

He glanced over at the flat beds of the two lorries and a new idea came to him. He walked over and measured up those as well.

"He will just fit on this lorry bed," Dr Deáth said with delight. "We can cover him with blankets and transport him that way. If not, it could be hours before we can move him."

Stan's look of relief was gone, replaced by one of

mounting horror.

"A dead man, on the back of my lorry?"

"It is the only way," Dr Death told him gently.

Stan was struck dumb by the news. He tried to protest but all that tumbled from his mouth was a string of disparate sounds.

"Let's get on with this," the farmer said, unmoved by the distress of the driver. He was used to having dead pigs and cows on trailers behind his tractor.

Dr Death produced a stretcher from his van and hopped down into the ditch again. The farmer joined him and with Park-Coombs' assistance (though some might have argued it was more hindrance) they managed to get the body onto the stretcher. Getting the corpse out of the ditch had to be done with care, because his legs were bent up from where they had rested against the side and his arms stuck out either side of the stretcher.

Tommy, Clara and O'Harris reached down to help bring the body out of the ditch, between them able to manage the stretcher. Seeing the young man this close, Clara felt saddened that his end had come so suddenly. He looked so very youthful, even with the colour gone from his face.

Dr Death emerged from the ditch and shuffled them towards the nearest lorry. Stan was staying as far away as possible, bitterly regretting he had ever gotten out of bed that morning.

They placed the body on the bed of the lorry and Dr Death arranged further blankets over it, to cover it from view. Then he used straps from his van to secure the body in place.

Even covered up it was a strange sight, because of the raised legs. No one would likely guess there was a body beneath the blankets, but they would certainly wonder what curious object was being carried. Dr Death was satisfied with his arrangements and then went to talk to Stan, who was clearly unhappy about the whole situation. If Dr Deáth could not bring him around to the idea, no one could.

Park-Coombs examined the sleeves of his coat, staring at the mud coating them and knowing his wife was going to be furious. He went to adjust his hat on his head, which was the moment he remembered it was off on an adventure in a field by itself. He waggled his moustache, most unhappy.

"We shall be on our way, Inspector," Clara said to him. "I thought I might go past the Music Hall on my way home, to see if anyone can tell me who our victim was."

"You cannot let a mystery rest, can you, Clara?" Park-Coombs smiled at her.

"Someone out there is wondering where their loved one is," Clara shrugged. "So, no, I can't."

"If you learn anything, let me know," Park-Coombs nodded.

"As always Inspector. Take care and don't get blown away."

Park-Coombs was reminded of his hat yet again. He was going to miss that hat; he had just broken it in the way he liked.

Chapter Five

The Maxwell Music Hall had been built in the last century and named after a performer who had been famous in the 1870s but was largely forgotten by the 1920s. Such was the fickleness of fame, Clara reflected.

O'Harris was able to park right out front of the hall. It was quiet, except for some bunting hanging over the doorway which bobbed in the wind.

"No one is here," Tommy pointed out the obvious.

"No guests, no," Clara replied. "But there is more than likely a caretaker inside quietly cleaning up after the events of the night before, and he may have some insight into who organised the event last night."

Clara left the car, followed by Tommy and O'Harris and considered knocking on the main front doors, before changing her mind and walking around the side of the building and making her way to the back. Like all such places, the music hall had a backyard where the practical elements of its existence were housed – the bins, the storehouses, the coal shed. Clara made her way through the yard, being buffeted by the wind, and knocked on a door which was marked with the word – Private.

"What if no one is here?" Tommy said.

"Then we shall have to think of something else," Clara shrugged.

She knocked on the door again, harder. It seemed the music hall was empty, and they were about to leave, when a man came sauntering into the yard whistling to himself. He stopped at the sight of them. He was wearing a long, brown coat, the sort workmen donned when doing messy tasks. In one hand he had a mop, in the other he had a bundled stream of bunting, similar to that over the front door.

"Who are you and why are you here in this private yard?" he demanded crossly.

"Clara Fitzgerald," Clara introduced herself. "Are you the caretaker for the music hall?"

The caretaker eyed them suspiciously.

"If this is about more bunting wrapped around a washing line, I don't want to hear it. I just spent half an hour rescuing this lot. I told them putting bunting up outdoors in winter was a bad idea, but would they listen? No! And it is me who has to go rescue it!"

The caretaker wagged the bundle of bunting at them.

"This is not about bunting," Clara promised him. "This is about the event you held here last night."

The caretaker frowned.

"That?"

"Could we talk about this out of the wind?" Tommy asked. "I have spent long enough freezing in this weather and I really would like to get warm."

The caretaker did not move, still reluctant to allow them into his domain.

"We would very much appreciate it," Clara told him. "We need to discuss the event that happened here last night and who was organising it."

"Has there been trouble?" the caretaker asked, not

budging from his stubborn refusal to let them in. "I have nothing to do with bookings. That is beyond my responsibilities. I can deal with bunting, but complaints have to be made to the manager."

"If we could just come inside and explain?" Tommy begged, his teeth chattering.

The caretaker eyed them up, clearly wondering whether they were liable to cause him bother, or maybe even rob the music hall the second he turned his back. After a long time of consideration, he decided they looked an unlikely bunch of robbers.

He moved past them and opened the back door. Grumbling under his breath, he led them into a tiled hallway and through to a compact kitchen area. He dumped the bunting into a sink.

"I shall have to ask before I can throw it away," he said, shaking his head at this complication. "Can't throw away so much as a paper napkin around here without asking first. Costs they keep telling me. Can't be wasteful."

"You appear to be doing a fine job," Clara said, buttering him up. "Especially in this weather."

"The old place is built well, I shall say that for it," the caretaker nodded. "So far nothing has come loose. I am more concerned about the old tree in the next-door garden. It looks liable to fall at any moment."

He pointed out the window at a tree that was a considerable distance from the music hall and unlikely to cause any problem to them.

"What do you want to know about last night?" he asked.

"There was a royal gala party for the Friends of the Brighton Performing Arts?" Clara said.

"There was a party," the caretaker sniffed. "Couldn't tell you what it was all about. Lots of haughty people in evening attire making small talk and being careless with their wine. I found two spillages in the main hall, you know. Thank goodness it has linoleum on the floor, else I never would have got the marks up."

"Who arranged the event?" Clara asked.

The caretaker sighed in exasperation at her.

"I just prepare for things and clean up afterwards," he told her.

"We really need to know who was in charge of the event," Clara said, trying to impress on him the urgency of the matter without revealing too much.

The caretaker was not so gullible.

"Why?" he asked.

Clara cleared her throat, thinking fast.

"There was an incident during the storm, involving someone who had been at the event," she said. "However, the poor fellow has no identification on him, and we are trying to work out who he is, so we can inform his family."

The caretaker narrowed his eyes.

"Why can't he simply tell you?" he asked.

"He was crushed by a heavy object blown on him by the wind," Tommy said flatly. "It happened as he was walking home alone."

"Oh," the caretaker was a little taken aback. His eyes went to the window and the visual clues to the wild wind outside. He was thinking about his adventure retrieving the bunting and how he could have been crushed at any moment, should a stray object have blown his way. He winced. "That is rather unfortunate."

"Perhaps there is a record of the booking to tell us who arranged it?" Clara suggested.

"There will be," the caretaker agreed. "It will be in Mr Martin's office. I suppose I can let you in, under the circumstances."

"I am hopeful we can locate the man's family and at least let them know what has occurred. They must be most anxious," Clara pressed her point home, just in case the caretaker became twitchy again.

The caretaker took them back into the hallway and across to another door. He had to unlock it with a set of keys and then showed them into a neat, but rather small office.

"Mr Martin did not come in today," he said, a strange expression coming onto his face. "That was rather odd, but I supposed the storm had kept him at home."

"That would seem logical," Tommy concurred. "In this weather, the safest place is at home."

"Yes, well some of us don't have that option," the caretaker huffed. "Why are you out in this weather, anyway?"

"The incident that took the life of the poor fellow we are trying to identify, also took out my wife's hen house," Tommy explained. "She was rather upset and wanted me to find out who was responsible for the flying debris."

"Ah," the caretaker said, being fully aware of the complexities of the female condition, and what it was like to be married. "That would explain it. Safer out of the house than indoors, I imagine?"

"The chickens are in the pantry," Tommy pulled a face. "My wife is not happy at all."

"About this booking," Clara interrupted the male bonding.

"It will all be in that black book on top of the desk," the caretaker pointed out. "Mr Martin keeps things very organised."

Clara opened the black book and saw it was a diary with plenty of room for entries. She flipped to the previous evening and saw there was an extensive amount of writing concerning the gala, including who was responsible for arranging it, the catering, the music and also a series of sums to work out the cost.

Clara had to mask her surprise at the final figure. Royal galas did not come cheap.

"It says here the person in charge of the overall event was Mrs Peacock of Bloomington Drive," Clara was making notes. "Do you know what time the gala ran to?"

The caretaker shrugged.

"Late," he declared. "When I arrived at seven this morning, a couple of folks were only then leaving."

"That is quite the party," O'Harris noted.

"And against the rules. The booking stated they had the hall until three o'clock the next morning, and it was expected that they would lock up after themselves. I was not impressed."

"Mr Martin shall have to reconsider renting the place to Mrs Peacock another time," Clara suggested.

"Oh, but he won't," the caretaker shrugged. "Money talks and there are only so many people who can afford to rent this hall. Anyway, that is his business."

They headed back into the hallway.

"Thank you for your assistance," Clara told the caretaker.

"It's a shame about this poor fellow crushed to death," the caretaker murmured, thinking about how suddenly life could be snuffed out. "I shall let Mr Martin know when I see him."

They left through the yard again and came back to the car. They were near the seafront and could see the waves lashing at the promenade, whipped up into a frenzy by the wind.

"This storm does not seem to be abating," O'Harris said, noting that the waves seemed a lot higher than before.

"The tide is coming in," Tommy said. "It makes it worse."

"Of course," O'Harris nodded. "I should have realised. Do you want to head to Bloomington Drive?"

"I think we should," Clara said. "We cannot really leave people wondering what happened to a loved one longer than necessary."

The winds had finally brought rain with them as they made their way to Mrs Peacock's address. There was a tree blocking a road at one point, having fallen across some telephone lines, and taking them out as well. They had to double-back and find an alternative route.

Mrs Peacock had a villa-style property located on a hill with a good view of the sea. Her home was very exposed and was taking a battering from the weather. Attempts had been made to protect the palms she grew in her front garden by wrapping them in sacking, but this only seemed to make them bend and sway more in the wind.

They could smell the sea in the air as they left the car and headed to Mrs Peacock's front door. Clara was sure she could taste salt on her lips. She rang the doorbell and was relieved that it was not long before a woman in her late forties opened it.

"Mrs Peacock?" Clara asked, wanting to get out of the weather swiftly.

"Yes?" Mrs Peacock looked at the newcomers with a mixture of confusion and curiosity.

She was a handsome woman, with a tall, refined bearing, though she did rather lack in the chin department. She was dressed casually and looked to have been having a relaxing day, at least as much as one could when a storm was rattling the windows.

"Could we come in? One of your guests from the gala has been in a storm related accident," Clara said hastily.

Mrs Peacock looked appalled.

"Come in at once," she said and welcomed them through to a thoroughly modern sitting room. It was very stark, and very white, with a minimal amount of furniture and decorations. It also had enormous windows to give anyone sitting within a good view of the ocean. Right at that moment, with the surf churning and the waves leaping up against the seawall, Clara would have gladly closed the curtains on the view.

"What has occurred?" Mrs Peacock asked, motioning carelessly for them to be seated.

"One of the guests from the gala was found earlier today crushed by a heavy object that had been blown over in the storm," Clara explained, deciding this was the better explanation than saying he had died of exposure after falling into a ditch. Mrs Peacock looked like the sort of woman who would not appreciate such antics and would have more sympathy for the victim of an accident.

"How terrible!" she declared. "Is he badly hurt?"

"Sadly, he is dead," Clara elaborated. "The full details are being dealt with by the police, though they do not consider this anything but an awful accident."

"I had a near miss with a fence panel earlier today when I was checking on my garden furniture," Mrs Peacock said, thinking how easily she could have been struck down. "It can happen in an instant."

"It can," Clara agreed. "We are trying to discover the identity of the gentleman so we can inform his family of what has occurred. They must be terribly worried."

"You do not know the man's name?" Mrs Peacock was surprised.

"He had no identification on him," Tommy said. "Just a cigarette case with the name Wills in it and an invitation to your gala in his pocket."

"Wills," Mrs Peacock mused the name.

"We supposed it was short for William," Clara said.

"Probably, but it is not a nickname I have heard in relation to any of the Williams I know attended last night," Mrs Peacock shrugged.

"The gentleman was not very old, with fair hair," Tommy added.

"That does not really narrow things down," Mrs Peacock replied.

Clara decided to try a different route.

"Did you personally know all those invited, Mrs Peacock?"

"Most of them," the woman nodded. "I dealt with the invitations. If you wish, I can fetch the list I made of those I invited?"

Clara indicated she would like to see this list and Mrs Peacock departed for a short time to fetch it. She returned with two pieces of typed paper and handed them to Clara. The first thing Clara noticed was that a lot of the male guests were listed as either being called William, or having the initial W.

"William is a rather common name," O'Harris said, glancing at the list in Clara's hand. "For a certain generation."

"I am sorry I cannot be more helpful," Mrs Peacock said sadly. "If there were anything I could do…"

She left the words hanging, which was dangerous around Clara.

"There is one thing," Clara said. "You can come with us and identify the body."

Mrs Peacock looked aghast.

"But…"

"Consider it your civic duty," Tommy said before she could refuse.

Mrs Peacock glared at him.

Chapter Six

They drove Mrs Peacock towards the morgue where the body of the mysterious William would now have arrived. The woman was sour at being removed from her home to inspect a corpse. Her protests had failed to win Clara over. Some situations warranted being a little persistent, Clara believed. The dead man had to be identified and Mrs Peacock seemed their most likely option in the matter. Who else could they ask?

Clara kept imagining that somewhere out there, a family was worrying about what had become of their William after he had failed to return home. The news they would ultimately receive would not be the sort they wanted, but it would be better than wondering and worrying.

Mrs Peacock did not see things in the same light. She had merely organised the gala and written the invitations – what did that have to do with a dead body? The man was a guest, but what did that matter? He had not died at the gala. The only reason Mrs Peacock was in the car, (sulking dramatically) was because she had the impression Clara would not back down or take no for an answer. Clara was something of a force all of her own, and when her stubborn streak kicked in, there was nothing anyone could do.

They arrived at the morgue just ahead of a shop sign that narrowly missed the front of O'Harris' car.

"When will this storm end?" O'Harris said, thinking of how much damage to the gleaming paintwork and metal that sign could have caused.

"It will blow itself out," Clara said unhelpfully.

"There is one thing I have been wondering, Mrs Peacock," Tommy said to the woman in the back seat, aiming to be friendly. "What makes a gala royal?"

"A word," Mrs Peacock huffed. "We always call them royal galas because once upon a time one of Queen Victoria's granddaughters happened to attend an event. It was a misunderstanding, as she was meant to be at another engagement altogether, but she enjoyed herself and since then we have called them royal galas, in cause another member of the monarchy wishes to attend."

"Ah," said Tommy, disappointed.

"This will not take long," Clara told Mrs Peacock.

The woman remained in a sulk as she exited the car and followed the trio into the morgue. Aside from blocking out the wind, the walls of the morgue did little to warm them up. The place was naturally cold for a reason. Built partially underground and lined with white tiles, it was always frigid within. Today it was positively icy, and Mrs Peacock was alarmed to see her breath fog before her face.

"This way," Clara instructed, leading her down the stairs towards the main room.

They could hear music playing and found that Dr Deáth was clearing up glass from a broken window to Schubert. The morgue's windows were high up, close to the ceiling, and were not terribly useful for providing light. One of them had been smashed.

"What happened here?" Tommy said, looking up at the window.

"A clock hand took out the window," Dr Deáth said cheerfully.

"A what?" Tommy asked.

The coroner pointed over to one of his workbenches were a clock hand the length of his forearm was sitting propped against the wall.

"I suspect it came from the nearby church's clock," Dr Deáth added. "It is truly remarkable how the wind can get behind things and wrench them free."

O'Harris picked up the clock hand to examine it closer. It was made of cast iron and pretty heavy. It not only explained how it had smashed the window, but also made you realise just what strength the wind blowing outside had.

"This is Mrs Peacock," Clara introduced the woman who was looking around the morgue with anxious eyes. "She has come to try to identify our mystery man."

"I was bullied into it," Mrs Peacock said at once, hoping for some sympathy from the coroner.

"Most people would prefer not to come along and look at a corpse," Dr Deáth told her merrily. "I have William over on this table. I am trying to warm him up, so his muscles relax. He won't fit into storage, otherwise."

"You are storing bodies?" Mrs Peacock said in mild horror.

Dr Deáth did not appreciate she was upset by this notion and instead saw it as a chance to expand on his line of work. He liked talking about his morgue, because he felt it was very modern and up to date, not like a lot of morgues. Dr Deáth also had no real concept that most people preferred not to talk about corpses and death if they could avoid it.

"The wall over there, lined with all those doors, that is where I store my bodies. The narrow compartments are like deep cupboards or perhaps you could describe them as high-ceilinged drawers. Each person has their own…"

"Is there a body behind every one of those doors?" Mrs Peacock said with a gasp.

"Oh, no," Dr Deáth said. "In fact, it would be unusual for them to all be full. But, in the event of a major crisis, such as the bombardments we suffered in the war, things can begin to fill up. It is best to be prepared."

Mrs Peacock had gone very pale. Clara intervened.

"I think we should get on with the identification," she said. "Mrs Peacock does not want to be here longer than necessary."

Dr Deáth took the hint and headed to a table covered with a cloth.

"Our mystery man has started to relax a little," he was saying. "I have been able to lower his legs and pull in his arms to a degree."

The body beneath the cloth did look less angular than Clara recalled from earlier. Dr Deáth pulled the cloth back from the victim's face. He had been able to move the head so that now the poor fellow was looking directly up, except that his eyes were closed. Mrs Peacock edged forward and looked unhappily at the victim.

"I don't know his name," she said bluntly.

"That's a pity," Dr Deáth started to replace the cloth.

Mrs Peacock had a pang of conscience.

"But I do know who he attended the gala with. Some of those I invited asked if they could bring along a companion. I had no issue with this, as long as I knew they were bringing someone. This gentleman was the companion for Stacy Freeman, who is one of our primary supporters. The young lady has a talent for classical music and is an accomplished harpist."

"Then we need to speak to Miss Freeman at once," Clara said. "It appears her companion got himself into a spot of bother after the event."

Mrs Peacock was looking at the body, a frown on her forehead.

"I might not know his name, but I do remember this young man at the gala. I saw him on the dance floor, but not with Stacy. I thought at the time it was a little caddish to ditch one partner for another like that."

"Well, he won't be doing it again," Tommy said drily.

Clara cast him a look to indicate now was not the time.

"Thank you, Mrs Peacock," she told the woman. "We shall take you home now."

Mrs Peacock was starting to shiver, though whether it was from the cold or the horror of seeing a dead body, even she did not know.

"Come along," Clara said gently, taking her arm and escorting her across the morgue.

"To think someone so young and vibrant could suddenly be so… dead," Mrs Peacock murmured.

"It comes as a shock," Clara agreed.

"And last night went so well, too," Mrs Peacock continued. "Everyone was happy, and we raised a good sum from our raffle. All the profits are to go to a charitable fund set up for performers who have fallen on hard times through no fault of their own. Many of our finest actors are barely surviving on the income they make. Sickness or some accident that prevents them working could be their ticket to destitution."

"That is a terrible thing," Clara sympathised.

Mrs Peacock kept talking about the raffle because it kept her distracted from the thought of the body behind her. By the time they had her back in the car, she had described every raffle prize and listed who had won it.

They took her home and she looked relieved to get back into her house and to shut them out, though not before she had given them the address for Stacy Freeman.

"Next stop, and hopefully the last," Tommy said, looking up at the sky which was growing black and gloomy. Evening was drawing on with the promise of further gales and rain.

Yet again they drove off, this time to the opposite side of the town. Miss Freeman lived in a maisonette at the top of an old, Victoria house. Her flat was bigger than a lot of regular houses and included two bay windows, one at each end. The bottom floor flat belonged to an older gentleman who served as the caretaker for the property and kept an eye on who came and went. When they entered the hallway of the house, he heard the bell over the door rattle and came to take a look.

"We are hoping to speak to Miss Freeman," Clara said as she caught sight of him.

The heavens had opened, and she was trying to shake water from her hands and arms. She was finding herself questioning the waterproof nature of her coat.

"Top floor," the gentleman said, giving them a quick look over, before returning to his cosy flat.

It was not his responsibility to vet visitors, and he certainly did not intend to do so off his own initiative. Besides, Clara, Tommy and O'Harris looked very respectable and did not cause people concern – at least, not unless they were murderers or thieves, and Clara was trying to catch them.

They headed up the main staircase, noting how the wind howled against the walls still.

"I wonder if the gazebo has blown down yet?" O'Harris said with a sigh.

Clara shivered, the cold finally getting to her. She was thinking it would take more than an evening by a warm fire to get some heat back into her bones.

They reached the flat of Miss Freeman and knocked. The young lady answered swiftly and had clearly been expecting someone else.

"Oh," she said, at the sight of them.

She was a pretty young thing with bleached blonde hair and the kind of face people term elfin in an endearing way. She was smaller than Clara, which was novel, and dressed rather smartly for an evening at home.

"Sorry to bother you," Clara said. "Are you going out?"

"If my ride ever comes," Miss Freeman sighed. "I thought you were him."

"We won't disturb you for long. We just wanted to ask you about the gentleman you attended the gala with last night," Clara continued.

"Wills?" Miss Freeman said in surprise. "You hardly need to ask me about him. Wait here a little while and you shall meet him. He is due to pick me up this evening. Actually, he should have been here half an hour ago."

Miss Freeman glanced at a very elegant and expensive ladies' watch dripping off her wrist.

"You have not spoken to Wills since last night?" Tommy asked.

"No," Miss Freeman said. "He dropped me home early after I developed a headache, and we made arrangements to go out again tonight."

"Wait, Wills has a car?" O'Harris asked.

Miss Freeman nodded at him.

"That is… curious," O'Harris added.

"What is this about?" Miss Freeman asked, starting to become nervous.

"Could we come in, Miss Freeman? We have some bad news about Wills," Clara explained.

Miss Freeman did not seem to comprehend at first,

then she started to think about how late her gentleman friend was, and how unusual that was for him. She had a bad feeling in the pit of her stomach.

"This way," she said and showed them through to her sitting room. "I am not going to like what I hear, am I?"

"Your friend, Wills, appears to have suffered an accident in the storm," Clara said, seeing no point in beating around the bush. "Unfortunately, he has been killed."

Miss Freeman took the news bravely. She stood very still, and her eyes glazed over, but there was never any hint she might faint or go into hysterics. Finally, she spoke.

"I could see it in your eyes when you arrived. I remember that was the way my mother looked when she told me and my sisters that our brother had died at the Front. Eyes never lie."

"What is Wills full name?" Tommy asked.

"William Hershel," Miss Freeman answered. "Everyone just calls him Wills."

"Does he have family in Brighton?" Clara asked.

"Yes. He lives with his parents. He is studying for his degree in chemistry," Miss Freeman paused. "He was studying for his degree."

She sat down suddenly in an armchair.

"His parents will be devastated. What happened to him?"

It was not the easiest question to answer.

"He was found in a ditch," Clara explained. "A heavy crate was blown off a lorry on top of him."

She did not mention that Dr Death thought he might have been already dead. That just made things too confusing.

Miss Freeman closed her eyes and absorbed the

news.

"A ditch?" she said.

"Yes, at the time we thought he must have been walking home," Clara elaborated. "However, now you tell us he had a car, and it seems strange he would not use that to travel in. We saw no car anywhere nearby."

Miss Freeman was only half-listening to her.

"A ditch? Wills would never go in a ditch, not willingly at least. I don't understand."

"Neither do we, at the moment," Clara admitted. "After William dropped you here, did he say where he was going?"

Miss Freeman shook her head.

"I assumed he would go back to the gala and continue his evening, no reason he shouldn't, after all," she said. "We were friends, but it was nothing serious, if you see what I mean. I did not mind if he went back to the gala without me."

"And he had said nothing about going anywhere else? Or that he might leave his car somewhere?" Tommy asked.

"If he did, I do not remember it," Miss Freeman was morose. "How could this happen to poor Wills? And why was he in a ditch?"

Those were questions Clara would like to have answers to as well.

"I am sorry to have spoiled your evening," Clara said. "I am sorry to have to bring you this news."

Miss Freeman shook her head morosely.

"Poor Wills," she whispered. "Poor Wills."

Chapter Seven

They stayed with Miss Freeman for a while. She was obviously upset and once the shock faded, grief replaced it and she started to sob.

"We were just friends," she insisted over and over. "But he was such a dear friend, how can he be dead?"

"What sort of car did Wills drive?" Clara asked her.

"A Vauxhall Velox," Miss Freeman answered instantly. "Not all girls know about makes of cars, but I do. I went with Wills when he bought it. It is a 1921 model with burgundy paint work. He bought it second hand from a man in Hove."

"That's a nice car," O'Harris said approvingly. "I have a 1920 Velox in my car collection. They are great touring cars, with a quiet exhaust."

"It is a lovely car," Miss Freeman concurred, dabbing at her nose with a handkerchief. "Wills adored it. He took us everywhere in it, even on a short journey."

"Where did he park his car last night when you went to the music hall?" O'Harris asked.

"There was room to park it in the street when we

first got there," Miss Freeman explained. "I have no idea where he parked it when he left me and returned to the party. If he returned to the party."

"We need to look for that car," Clara nodded. "But first, Miss Freeman, could you suggest any reason why Wills would be out in the middle of the countryside last night? He was found in a ditch near a farm."

"I don't know," Miss Freeman said. "Wills had no reason to be out of town."

"Thank you, Miss Freeman," Clara said. "Will you be all right?"

Miss Freeman nodded her head.

"It is horrible, but what can I do other than be all right? I think I shall see if my neighbours on the floor below are in."

She rose from her seat and showed them out of her flat, following them down to the landing below and then veering off to knock on her neighbours' door. As they were descending the next flight of stairs, they glimpsed the door opening and heard Miss Freeman bursting into tears as she told her neighbours her sorry story.

"Next stop, William's parents?" O'Harris asked.

"They need to know what has happened," Clara said. "They must be worried."

Miss Freeman had provided them with the address, and they travelled across town to a smart property with rose bushes in the front garden. There was no sign of a car outside, though Clara had wondered if they might find the vehicle parked there. The missing Vauxhall remained a mystery.

They parked up and headed for the door, but before they were on the front step it burst open and an older woman wearing semi-circular glasses stood before them.

"Oh, I had hoped…" she looked over towards O'Harris' car and it was easy to guess what she had thought.

She had supposed the rumble of the engine was the sound of William at last coming home.

"Are you Mrs Hershel?" Clara asked.

"I am," the woman said uneasily, she had sensed something in Clara's voice.

"We are here about your son, William," Clara explained. "Might we come in?"

"Where is he?" Mrs Hershel asked, her voice cracking.

Clara did not want to tell the woman her son was dead on her doorstep, but she might have to if the woman would not let them into the house to explain.

"Could we speak inside?" she asked.

Mrs Hershel wouldn't budge from her position in the doorway.

"When will he be coming home? What have you done with him?"

She was angry now, assuming whatever had caused William to remain away from home was Clara's fault. Clara remained as calm and patient as possible.

"Mrs Hershel, your son has been involved in an accident…"

"It was with the car, wasn't it?" Mrs Hershel cried out. "I told him it was a death trap."

"Actually, the accident was the result of the storm we have been enduring and no one could have foreseen what would occur. Please could we come in and explain?" Clara pressed on.

Behind Mrs Hershel, a man now appeared. He was tall but walked with a stoop and had slightly unruly grey hair.

"Martha?" he said to Mrs Hershel. "Is there news?"

"They say William has been in an accident," Mrs Hershel said, close to tears.

The man, Mr Hershel, they assumed, nodded his head as if this was everything he had anticipated.

"Can we come in?" Clara asked again. "There is a lot to tell you and it would be better said indoors."

Mrs Hershel still did not move, so her husband gently took her by the shoulders and led her inside.

"This way," he said to them.

They entered a beautiful house, furnished in the style of the last century and with many antiques dotted around. The sitting room they were shown to was warm and welcoming, a large fireplace hosting a glowing fire. Mrs Hershel was shuffled to a sofa by her husband and persuaded to sit down. He took a place beside her and motioned for their guests to sit on a matching sofa opposite.

"I am sorry to be bringing you this news," Clara began. "Earlier today, we went to help a pair of lorries that were bringing new exhibits to the Brighton Natural History Museum, which had been caught up in the storm. When we arrived to assist them, we found their cargo had been blown off their lorries. One lorry had been struck by a fallen tree. In the process of helping them to retrieve the cargo, we realised that there was someone in the ditch alongside the road where this had all occurred.

"To our horror, beneath one of the fallen boxes was a young man. We thought at first, he had been knocked down by a crate and crushed, but it might be he died from the cold while he was in the ditch. We summoned the police, of course, who are currently treating this as an accident. Being somewhat overwhelmed by the events of this storm and the problems it has caused, the inspector was happy to accept when I offered to discover the identity of the young man and trace his family. That is how I come to be here."

Mrs Hershel was weeping into her hands. Her husband was stoic, though his head drooped forward, and he seemed to have the weight of the world on his shoulders.

"It is a terrible shock," O'Harris said with sympathy. "No one should have to hear such news."

"Where did this happen?" Mr Hershel asked.

"There is a lane that runs past an area of open land known as Three Hills. The lane, itself, has no name, but it is not far from the railway bridge," Tommy explained.

Mr Hershel was shaking his head.

"Why would my son be there?"

"In a ditch!" Mrs Hershel said sharply. "In a ditch!"

Her husband patted her arm gently.

"None of this makes sense," he added to their visitors. "Where was his car?"

"That is something we don't know," Tommy said. "We haven't found it."

"Then how did he get all the way out there?" Mr Hershel asked the obvious.

"We simply do not know," Clara explained. "We have spoken to the young lady who invited William to the royal gala last night. She had to leave early because she had a headache. Your son drove her home and then departed. It was still relatively early in the evening. We do not know what he did afterwards."

"William was not a lad to do wild things," Mr Hershel said firmly. "He was reliable. It was why we agreed to the car. He was doing so well at university and the car was a reward for his hard work. William is the last person to end up in a ditch in the middle of nowhere."

The situation was beginning to sound very peculiar.

"I should add that I am a private detective," Clara said. "My brother is my partner in the business. If there is anything you wish for us to do..."

Before she had a chance to finish, Mrs Hershel was pointing a finger at her.

"You will find out what happened to my son and who caused him to be in that ditch!"

"Martha, calm down," her husband tried to soothe her. "The police are investigating."

"The police believe it was an accident, she said so," Mrs Hershel protested once more jabbing a finger in Clara's direction. "They will say he was drunk or something, wandered off from the party. I know what the police will think! William would never do such a thing! He was a good boy, and no one can tell me this was simply an accident."

"Really Martha…"

"Do not 'really' me!" Martha snapped. "My boy died in a ditch! In a ditch!"

Mr Hershel fell silent, the gravity of it all hitting him. He did not have the fight in him to battle his wife further.

"I thought to myself I was so lucky my son was too young to serve in the war," Mrs Hershel had removed her glasses so she could wipe at her eyes, they hung around her neck on a delicate gold chain. "And now he dies like this. It is not right!"

"I do feel there is something curious about all this," Clara replied to her. "If I can help…"

"I am hiring you," Mrs Hershel once more interrupted her. "You must discover what happened to my son and who is responsible for all this. I do not care what the police think, my son would not end up in a ditch of his own accord. Someone caused him to be there, and I need you to discover who it was so that I can put my hands around their throat and throttle them!"

"Martha!" Mr Hershel berated his wife.

"They have stolen my son from me! They have destroyed me!"

Mrs Hershel sunk her head forward and wept into her lap. It was a pitiful sight.

"I need to get my wife to her bed," Mr Hershel told them. "Then I shall come back, and we shall discuss you investigating this case for us."

He helped his wife to her feet and almost physically carried her to the door. He left them alone in the sitting room, though they could hear their footsteps on the stairs.

"I hate having to break bad news," Tommy groaned. "I did enough of that in the war. Writing letters to parents or wives about the death of one of the privates under my command. Or having to tell a man in the trenches his brother was dead. You never get used to it."

"You feel guilty, as if it is your fault," O'Harris concurred. "And it never is, of course. You are following orders just like everyone else. But it still feels that way."

The two men had become sombre, thinking back to their war experiences. Clara did not know what to say to help them. They all sat in silence until Mr Hershel returned to the room.

"You must forgive my wife, she is overwrought."

"There is nothing to forgive, Mr Hershel," Clara replied. "She has every right to feel the way she does."

Mr Hershel gave a sad nod of his head. He also wanted to break down, but he had to hold himself together, for the sake of everyone.

"I promised my wife to make the arrangements for hiring you," he said. "She would not rest until I agreed. I will make it plain I am reluctant to hire an outsider, rather than rely on the police."

"If it helps, I am on very good terms with Inspector Park-Coombs of the Brighton Constabulary, and I am often asked to assist the police on cases," Clara said. "I never interfere with the police doing their work, I merely aim to provide a helping hand."

Mr Hershel did not seem entirely mollified, but he was a man who put a lot of stake in promises and so he would not go against his wife's wishes.

"I have never hired a private detective before, we are not the sort of people who have ever needed one," he added.

"I do not think there is a particular type of person who normally requires my services," Clara said. "However, if you would like me to supply references…"

Mr Hershel shook his head.

"That will not be necessary. My wife has made up her mind," he eased himself back onto the sofa. "What do we do now?"

"You can start by telling me about your son," Clara suggested.

"My wife might be better placed to do that," Mr Hershel frowned. "I have always been a busy man with my job, and I never had much time for my children. William especially, as he was the youngest. I knew about his achievements at school, that sort of thing, but knowing him as a person is another matter."

Mr Hershel became morose.

"I regret that deeply now. I always assumed there would be time."

"Mr Hershel, you were not a bad father, just a busy one and many are like that," Tommy reassured him.

Mr Hershel was not appeased.

"No, you are too kind. I was too absentminded when it came to my children. They existed, but it seemed little to do with me. These last few years, particularly after the war, I began to realise what I had. Having seen others lose so much, I reminded myself to be grateful. It was not enough to stop me from becoming absorbed in my work and forgetting," Mr Hershel was holding back tears determinedly. "The car was rather a token gesture to settle my guilt. It was so pathetic, when I think of it, but it seemed at the time a way to show I cared without actually having to do anything."

Mr Hershel stared at the carpet, his mind elsewhere. Clara decided it was time they left him alone, they could ask questions another day.

"We shall see ourselves out," she told him. "When we have news, we shall return."

"He was a good boy," Mr Hershel said. "His mother is right about that. He was never in any trouble. I never had that worry. I mean, compared to my older son, he was truly a saint."

Mr Hershel gasped.

"Oh heavens, I just thought to myself how it would be so different if my older son had been the one to suffer this misfortune. How it would be preferable. How awful a thing to think is that?" Mr Hershel dropped his head into his hands.

"It is natural to have those sorts of thoughts," Clara told him, but he did not seem to hear her.

Quietly, the trio left the family to their mourning.

Chapter Eight

They regrouped at Clara's house. Outside the storm was picking up again, the wind starting to race fiercely down the roads and across the rooftops. They were all glad to get indoors as rain came crashing down in waves to accompany the wind.

"I think it is worse than this morning out there," Tommy remarked, darting into the front room, and looking out at the road. He winced as someone's empty metal bin skipped past O'Harris' car, narrowly missing it as it danced on the wind.

"You were gone a long time," Annie appeared from the kitchen, worry lines etched into her face. "I was starting to be concerned."

"Things proved a lot more complicated than we first expected," Tommy explained to her. "We found the lorries from the museum. Both had lost their cargoes and one of the drivers was pretty shaken up as a tree had landed on his lorry."

Tommy was emphasising the problems the museum crew had had to garner Annie's sympathy, otherwise she would continue to be unduly furious about her hen house.

"We thought that was the worst of it and set out to help them," Tommy continued. "But, beneath one of the crates, we found a person."

Annie's eyes went wide in surprise.

"Was he badly hurt?" she asked.

"He was dead," Clara replied. "One of the crates had fallen across his chest, though Dr Deáth thinks he may have been already dead before that happened."

"Dr Deáth? Then the police are involved?" Annie

asked.

"We had to summon them, as it was an unexplained death," Tommy elaborated. "It looks accidental, however. Except, no one can quite explain how the young man ended up in that ditch in the first place."

Annie tilted her head as she considered what he was saying.

"He was not a tramp?"

"No, he was dressed in evening attire," Clara told her. "We spent the rest of the day trying to work out who he was and when we achieved that, we went to his parents' home to tell them. Needless to say, they are very upset."

"They want us to determine how he ended up in that ditch," Tommy added.

"I am not surprised. What a terrible thing to occur," Annie said. "Have you eaten?"

As usual, Annie's mind was firmly set on making sure her family had all enjoyed three sound meals that day.

"We have not eaten a thing," Tommy admitted. "We have rushed from here to there without stopping."

"We have really imposed upon you today, John," Clara turned to O'Harris and reached for his hand. "I am sorry about that."

Annie and Tommy exchanged a knowing look at the scene before them.

"Do not worry about it, Clara," O'Harris grinned at her and squeezed her hand. "I was happy to help, and we had an important matter to deal with. It was not as if we were doing something frivolous."

Overhead, there was a rattling sound as some of the roof tiles began to succumb to the wind. Bramble turned his head up and started to make a pitiful howl. This caused Pip to become excited, and she jumped up at Tommy, thinking some game was afoot.

"I don't like this weather," Annie said with a

shudder, heading to her kitchen where she felt safest.

They could hear a clucking noise from the pantry, as the chickens debated their new home. Annie was just reaching the range when she gave a cry and hurried to the kitchen window. They rushed to follow her in time to see the great elm tree that grew in the garden of the house behind theirs sway dramatically and then fall across the lane that divided the gardens and straight into theirs, taking out the fence in the process.

They all stood in silence looking on at the scene.

"John," Clara said. "I don't think you should try to drive home in this weather. It is too dangerous."

O'Harris stared at the fallen tree, which must have been over sixty feet in height.

"You may have a point," he said.

"You must stay here," Clara insisted.

O'Harris was not going to disagree, not having witnessed such destruction.

"I'll just ring the Home and let them know where I am," he said.

Clara nodded in agreement and relief.

Annie knew only one way to console herself after seeing such a thing as the tree falling. She began to cook dinner for them all. A short while later they were sitting in the dining room with the curtains firmly drawn, pretending they could not hear the wind wailing down the chimney.

"What was the young man in the ditch's name?" Annie asked when they were settled to fried sausages and buttery mash potato.

"William Hershel," Clara told her. "He was attending a gala at the Maxwell Music Hall last night. No one knows how he ended up in the middle of the countryside."

"His car is missing," O'Harris said. "Which is very odd. It was nowhere to be seen when we drove to the area where the crates had fallen."

"Maybe it is still at the music hall," Annie suggested logically

"We did not see it there," Tommy explained. "I must admit, the more we learn about this matter, the more it does seem somewhat suspicious."

"However, as yet Dr Deáth has not suggested there was any violence involved in William's death. He appears to have perished from the cold," Clara pointed out.

"I would not be happy to be told one of you had just 'perished in a ditch'," Annie huffed. "That would make no sense to me, and I imagine William's parents feel the same."

"They were certainly convinced William would never end up like that of his own volition," Clara nodded. "That leaves us with a lot of questions."

"Thinking about the cigarette case William had in his pocket," Tommy said. "I wonder who gave it to him? It was clearly by someone who thought a lot of him, but the name inside did not match with Miss Freeman."

"That does not necessarily mean it is significant," Clara said. "It could have been given to him years ago."

They were about to discuss the matter further when there was an ominous crash outside. It sounded like breaking glass, but there was also a tinny sound, like something metal falling and spinning on the ground. O'Harris' eyes filled with horror as he had a premonition of what had occurred. He jumped from the table and dashed outside before they could stop him. He returned a few moments later, clutching in one hand the smashed, detached headlamp from his car, and in the other, a metal boot scraper. His miserable look had them all feeling sorry for him.

"That is just awful, old man," Tommy said.

"You need a strong cup of tea," Annie hurried to the kitchen to make her personal remedy for a nasty shock.

"And after your car had managed to avoid all those other things that blew its way," Clara shook her head. "Wounded by a boot scraper."

"You need to sit down," Tommy patted his friend's shoulder and ushered him into a chair.

"The paintwork is scratched," O'Harris said solemnly.

"It is a tragedy," Tommy consoled him. "But we shall get her back to being as good as new."

O'Harris placed the broken headlamp on the table before him and stared at it as if his world had ended. Clara decided this was not the moment to mention it was just a car, and not a living thing. That was not a helpful comment.

"Well, at least it happened while it was parked and not while you were driving home," she said instead. "It could have been worse."

O'Harris did not feel better at this comment. Annie returned with his cup of tea.

"Drink that," she said. "It will cheer you up."

~~~*~~~

The following morning the storm had at last died down and O'Harris was up bright and early to inspect the damage to his car. Clara and Tommy were surveying the destruction of their garden fence, while debating where to go next with their case.

"We need to know where William went after he left Miss Freeman. Did he return to the gala as she thought?" Clara said, sipping at a cup of tea she had brought out with her.

Tommy was studying the destroyed fence, wondering how one went about getting an enormous elm tree removed from one's garden.

"Mrs Peacock has a full list of everyone she invited to the event. Someone must have seen William after

Miss Freeman went home. That is, if he returned to the gala as Stacy assumed."

"Mrs Peacock mentioned seeing William dancing with another young lady," Clara remembered. "She commented it was odd because he had come with Miss Freeman, but supposing that was actually after Miss Freeman had gone home? William would have been free to dance with whoever he wished."

"If we learn the name of the woman he was dancing with, then she might be able to tell us more about what William was doing last night," Tommy saw the way his sister was thinking.

"We shall make that our first port of call, after we have dealt with all this," Clara motioned to the tree.

It was then their neighbour appeared and peered through the gap in their fence made by the tree. He pulled an apologetic face at the Fitzgeralds. Clara gave him a smile and a wave, to make him understand she did not blame him. No one could have done anything about the tree.

It was drawing close to eleven by the time they had finished discussions with their neighbour about having the tree removed and had negotiated that he would pay for the tree, and they would take care of their fence. It seemed fair, as the poor man had not intended for his tree to damage their fence. It turned out he had also suffered the loss of his wash house, which had completely collapsed into itself. All that remained was a pile of bricks and tiles atop the big copper.

He was looking at quite the task to have it rebuilt and, in comparison, a couple of fence panels seemed a minor thing.

O'Harris had managed to reattach the headlamp to his car, but it would need a new bulb and glass frontage. The paintwork was going to need to be stripped and repainted. Fortunately, a sound night's sleep had made O'Harris practical about the damage.

When the siblings appeared from the garden, he was ready for action.

"Where are we off to now?" he asked them.

"Back to see Mrs Peacock and get the names of everyone who was at the gala last night. We need some witnesses to what William was doing," Clara told him.

O'Harris was happy to oblige and take them by car to the woman's home. They were sorry to see that one of the palm trees she had aimed to protect from the battering weather had not survived the high winds that had come that evening. It was fallen over, its roots pulled from the ground. It was a forlorn sight, but at least it had missed crashing through the woman's front window.

Mrs Peacock was not delighted to see them again. It seemed very likely she would not let them through her front door. They seemed like heralds of bad luck to her, as if their arrival yesterday had foreshadowed the loss of her palm tree.

"We know the name of the young man who perished yesterday," Clara told her, trying to instil a sense of duty in the woman. "He was the son of the Hershels, and his name was William."

"Hershel?" Mrs Peacock was surprised at the name. "William was a relation?"

She had said the last to herself, but Clara had caught the words.

"You know the Hershels?"

Mrs Peacock did not want to have to speak to the infuriating young lady further, but she also had a conscience. After battling with herself over what to do, she caved in to her better judgement.

"Annabelle Hershel is one of the 'friends'," she explained. "I do not know her relationship to this William, but it is not a terribly common surname. I would suppose there is a connection."

"Now can we come in and talk?" Clara pressed her.

Mrs Peacock tutted under her breath, really not wanting them in her home, but conceding it would have to be done for the greater good. She stepped back and showed them into the sitting room they had entered the day before.

"You must have had a good view of the storm last night," Tommy remarked, looking out the big windows at the sea which was looking considerably more tranquil today.

"It was certainly dramatic," Mrs Peacock replied. "The waves were enormous. I watched them until it was too dark to see."

"I think I would have felt uneasy perched up here amid that storm," Clara said.

Mrs Peacock gave her an insincere smile.

"Few things make me uneasy. I did not choose this house without knowing how exposed it was. I like it that way. Give me a good sea squall to watch and I shall be content for hours."

Clara took little heed of the woman's arrogance, she was quite happy to let her think she had something over Clara, if that kept her talking.

"We hoped you could provide us with that list of all the guests who attended your gala last night," Clara said. "We need to speak to them, to determine what William was doing in the hours before he ended up in a ditch outside town."

Mrs Peacock gave her a sideways look. She had not forgiven them for making her come to the morgue to try to identify a man she turned out to not know.

"What is this all about?" Mrs Peacock puttered.

"William's parents want to know how he ended up dying in a ditch," Clara said, not mincing her words now. She was tired of Mrs Peacock's lack of help, and lack of empathy for the Hershel family. "We have agreed to help them. His car is missing too, which makes things even more curious. I am sure you would

71

agree it would be very bad for the Brighton Friends of the Performing Arts if word got out that a guest at one of their events had died."

Mrs Peacock hesitated just a fraction. Clara had stung her were it hurt.

"It would be better if we could resolve this matter discreetly, do you not agree?" persisted Clara.

Mrs Peacock glowered at her, but she knew she was right.

"Perhaps it is best you have that list," she said, reluctantly.

"Thank you," Clara answered. "And then, perhaps you can tell us about Annabelle Hershel."

Chapter Nine

"Annabelle Hershel has been a member of the 'friends' since 1914," Mrs Peacock began. She had found the list of names she had used to send out invitations for the gala and had handed this to Clara. Now she was sitting stretched out on one of the sofas, talking to them as if they were not discussing a mysterious death. "Annabelle is something of an amateur performer herself. She has a relatively good voice, not enough to make her a professional, but suitable for the odd local show."

"You sound slightly dismissive of her," Clara observed.

Mrs Peacock shrugged her shoulders.

"I merely say things as I see them."

"Do you know much about Annabelle outside of the Friends?" Tommy asked.

"We have never been friends. I mean, not in the sense of real friends, outside of the organisation. Annabelle and I… we have a tendency to clash."

Clara had a suspicion that Mrs Peacock clashed

with a lot of people.

"Annabelle has never mentioned her family?" she asked.

"Annabelle and I do not discuss our personal lives. We are purely interested in the organisation."

"What exactly does the organisation do?" O'Harris asked, genuinely curious.

Mrs Peacock was distracted for a moment.

"The Friends were set up in 1910, due to a worrying slump in theatre attendance which placed some of our most famous and important theatres in danger of closing," Mrs Peacock explained. "The cause of the slump was not entirely obvious, though some blamed those new picture boxes that were appearing on piers and at fairs. You know the ones you look through a tiny eyepiece and see a short moving image of a football match. People supposed the novelty of those devices drew people away from the theatres. I did not agree. The sort of person who went to a theatre, would not be swayed by such low-grade entertainment."

"What did you put the cause of the slump down to?" O'Harris asked, interested now.

"Personally, I felt the theatre had become staid and dull. The same old acts, putting on the same old stunts, singing the same old songs, telling the same old jokes. We needed an organisation to support the theatres and encourage innovation. You see, the theatre managers were clinging to the same plays that had always served them well in the past. They were afraid to take a chance. However, through fundraising and benefactors, the Friends could offer to subsidise new plays, and this meant theatre managers were prepared to try something more modern."

Mrs Peacock smiled to herself, she was proud of the part she had played in the Friends and was firmly of the opinion that it was largely due to her that the theatres around Brighton were still functioning.

"I was one of the founders of the Friends," she said, preening. "Without me, well, this town would have no theatres. That is not too farfetched a notion, either. I am stating a fact."

"The Friends certainly seem popular," Clara said, ignoring the boasting.

"It is something that a lot of people can really get behind," Mrs Peacock said, becoming passionate. "The war taught us the benefits of entertainment as an escape from reality and as a means of understanding ourselves. We saw a lot of new female members during that time, and we continue to increase in number. Quite frankly, Miss Fitzgerald, it surprises me you are not a member."

This was a pointed remark. Clara smiled politely.

"I am already extremely busy as a committee member for the Brighton Pavilion. To divide my time further would be of benefit to no one."

Mrs Peacock raised an eyebrow at her.

"The Pavilion is a money drain. I was all behind it being demolished and the land used for houses," she declared.

Clara was unmoved.

"Fortunately, many people do not believe that a wise option. While you are keen on innovation and modernity, I see the value in remembering our heritage and preserving our past. In any case, we have rather gone off topic. We were discussing Annabelle."

"I think I have told you all I can about her," Mrs Peacock replied moodily. "I see her at meetings, that is all."

"What do you clash over?" Tommy asked.

Mrs Peacock fixed her eyes onto his, her stare impressive, though he was unmoved.

"Everything," she said. "I doubt there is a single matter that woman would not argue over with me, on principle alone. If I say I like tea, she will declare she likes coffee. If I comment about the weather being fair, she will declare it is either too cold or too hot. There is nothing that woman will agree upon with me."

Clara felt at that precise moment in time, she could quite understand why Annabelle behaved in such a way. Mrs Peacock was the sort of woman that put one's back up almost at once.

"You must have an address for her? You sent her an invitation," Clara was looking through the list of names and addresses on the invitation list.

"I do not need to invite her," Mrs Peacock said coldly. "She is on the committee. She helps organise these events and is expected to attend. But, if you really must have her address, I shall give you a copy of our quarterly magazine, which contains the full details, including address, for all our committee members."

Mrs Peacock rose from her seat and disappeared for a brief time. She returned with a black and white magazine in her hand. It had a hand drawn image of a French Pierrot clown on the front. She gave it to Clara, and she opened it to the inside cover where there was a complete list of names and addresses for the committee members. Mrs Peacock's name was at the top of the page, somewhat unsurprisingly. Several entries further down came the name Miss A. Hershel and a familiar address.

"She shares the same address as William," Clara said. "She must be his sister or aunt."

Mrs Peacock had lost interest in them. She had lost interest in the whole affair. If a person wandered off after their gala, what did it matter to her? She had started to inspect her fingernails, which still bore a slight hint of dirt from her attempts to save her fallen palm tree. She scowled at the brown stains.

"Mrs Peacock?"

Mrs Peacock glanced up at Clara's voice.

"I asked you about the young woman you saw William dancing with last night," Clara repeated. "The one who was not Miss Freeman."

Mrs Peacock blinked, coming back to the moment.

"Oh, that would be Miss Addison," she said at once. "A fairly new member. She is a dreadfully flighty thing, but she does have an eye for illustration. She drew the cover image for the magazine."

Clara flipped closed the cover and took another look at the drawing. She was not completely convinced by it as a work of art.

"Perhaps Miss Addison will know where William went after the gala," Clara said.

"Perhaps," Mrs Peacock replied. "Are we done now? I have a lot of correspondence to catch up with."

Clara was certainly done with her, though she was tempted to ask a few more random questions just to take up the woman's time. Mrs Peacock had not made a good impression on her, but she had better things to do than waste her energy tormenting the woman.

They departed with the usual thanks and farewells, heading for the car. O'Harris glanced at his battered headlamp as they approached and touched it solemnly.

"It will fix up good as new," Tommy consoled him.

"I just hate seeing a machine of any sort bearing such damage. It makes me cringe and want to get her in the garage," O'Harris sighed. "They are more than things to me, you understand."

"We do," Clara assured him. "Why don't you drop us at home and then you can head to your workshop and fix her up."

"Oh no, you do not get rid of me so easily. I am invested in this case now and intend to see it through," O'Harris grinned at her. "Like it or not, you are stuck with me as a chauffeur."

"Very well, then I suggest we go see Miss Addison first. Maybe she can give us insight into what became

77

of William after the gala."

They headed back into town and then north, finally arriving at a nice, detached house in the late Victoria style, sitting in a large garden with mature beech trees gracing the boundaries. The house appeared to have survived the storm untouched, though one of the trees had lost a sizeable branch which lay on the lawn before it.

"Miss Addison presumably lives with her parents," Clara remarked as she climbed the front steps and rang the doorbell.

Within a short time, it was opened by a woman wearing a smock apron, the sort one wore when doing messy tasks. By the stains on the apron, Clara guessed the woman had been painting.

"Sorry to disturb you," Clara began. "We were looking for Miss Addison?"

"I am Miss Addison," the woman said.

This took Clara aback as the woman was considerably older than her and she had envisioned the 'flighty' Miss Addison who had danced with William as someone quite young.

"We have come about the gala night you attended," Clara stated. "In particular, about William Hershel."

"Oh, you don't want me then," Miss Addison laughed. "You want my niece. I should have realised. We are always getting mixed up."

Miss Addison stepped back from the door to allow them in.

"My name is Bridget, by the way," she said in a friendly fashion. "I live here with my brother and sister-in-law, and my niece, Florence."

"You are a painter," Tommy said.

"Well, I dabble," Bridget said modestly. "I like playing with oils, but it really is just playing. It passes the time. I shall fetch Florence for you, would you go through to the sitting room? Mind the easel, the best light is at the front of the house in the mornings."

Bridget departed upstairs and Clara led the way into the sitting room. It had a nice bay window that was allowing in the grey light of the winter sky. Taking up a prime position in the light was a canvas ornamented with varying squares of colour. Clara stared at it a moment, trying to decipher the image, and then realised it was a stylised representation of a pot of flowers that was perched on a nearby table.

"I have no idea if I like it or not," Tommy said, frowning at the painting.

"I like it," O'Harris remarked. "It is taking everything back to the bare bones of form and colour. One of the psychiatrists at the Home is keen on art therapy and about representing not what one is actually seeing, but what one feels when seeing something."

Clara had no idea what to say to that. Thankfully, Florence Addison arrived swiftly and spared her having to think of something intelligent to say about abstract art.

"You wanted to see me?" Florence asked as she appeared in the room.

She was exactly what Clara had imagined from the description given by Mrs Peacock. She was small and slightly built, with wispy hair that stretched away from her head at all angles and no doubt caused her great grief when she tried to style it. She was a pale little thing that probably did not get out as much during the day as she should.

Bridget entered the room behind her and was clearly not going to leave her niece alone with these strangers. Clara did not blame her. She would have felt the same if she had a niece of such seeming fragility.

"Florence, my name is Clara Fitzgerald, this is my brother Tommy and our friend Captain O'Harris," Clara began. "We are here at the behest of Mr and Mrs

Hershel, because a misfortune has befallen their son William."

What little colour Florence had in her face was rapidly draining.

"What sort of misfortune?" she whispered.

"Somehow, William ended up in a ditch on the night of the storm and perished," Clara said, keeping things simple. "At first glance it appears to have been an accident, the mystery is how did he come to be in a ditch so far away from the music hall and with his car missing."

Florence glanced at her aunt, her eyes welling up with tears.

"He is dead?" she asked no one in particular.

"Yes," Clara said, knowing there was no way to soften this blow. "He might have died from the cold. That is still being investigated."

Florence started to sob.

"Oh, Flossie," Bridget came to the girl and draped her arm around her shoulder. "I am sorry. Was that the young man you mentioned to me the other day?"

Florence nodded her head, weeping too hard to speak.

"This is just terrible. What an awful thing to occur," Bridget drew Florence into her arms and tried to soothe her.

"I am sorry to have to bring you this news," Clara said softly. "We are trying to track William's movements during the last few hours of his life to discover how he ended up in a ditch. His parents are distressed and want to know exactly what happened."

"I do not blame them," Bridget spoke. "People do not just wander off and fall in ditches and die. At least, not people like us."

She heard her own words and reddened.

"That sounded crass," she added.

"But it does make sense," Tommy reassured her.

"You do not expect middle-class young men to fall into random countryside ditches and die. At least, not when they were meant to be in town attending a gala."

"And his car is missing?" Bridget mused on the information. "Someone could have stolen it, of course. Found it along the road and decided to take a chance."

"A car like that is going to be noticed," O'Harris shook his head. "Anyone stealing it would have trouble getting rid of it once it was known it was missing. It would be more bother than it was worth."

Bridget nodded to indicate she agreed with him, then she turned her attention to her niece who was almost hysterical.

"Flossie, dear, you need to calm down," she said. "It is a terrible, terrible shock, but you will make yourself sick."

"You don't understand," Florence sniffed through the tears.

"I do, my dear, I really do," Bridget said sadly. "I bore my share of bad news during the war. I remember how it was to hear someone you cared so deeply about had been simply snatched away from you."

"No!" Florence said, her voice angry now. She pushed away from her aunt. "You are not listening. You cannot understand."

Florence turned to Clara.

"It's my fault he is dead," she declared, then she sunk into fresh fits of tears.

Chapter Ten

The revelation stunned them all. Bridget did not know what to do, except to try to go to her niece's aid again. She was pushed away once more. Florence headed over to an armchair at the back of the room and slumped into it sobbing.

"Perhaps you can explain to us what you mean?" Clara said delicately, coming over to face the girl. "How is this your fault?"

Florence was taking control of herself again, she managed to take in a shaky deep breath.

"That night, I was angry with him. Because he would not stop talking about Stacy all the time we were dancing. He kept fretting whether she was all right. In the end I told him he should either shut up about Stacy or go throw himself in a ditch," Florence started to weep again. "I did not mean it literally, and I did not mean for him to die, but he must have done what I said!"

Bridget visibly relaxed at this news, having feared far worse.

"Florence, I don't think William ended up in that

ditch because of something you said in anger. I think it is just a coincidence."

Florence glanced up at her, eyes wide and wet with tears.

"You do?"

"Yes," Clara said. "An unfortunate coincidence."

Florence thought about this a moment.

"You mean he was not really upset that I was angry with him?" Florence deeply considered what she was saying. "You mean he didn't really care?"

Florence was furious now.

"I mean he did not take your words as a serious suggestion," Clara replied, beginning to see why Mrs Peacock had described Florence as flighty.

"He should have done," Florence sniffed, annoyed now that her angry retort had meant so little to William.

"Flossie, recall that he is dead," Bridget said softly.

Florence did recall and her anger abated.

"Tell us about the gala night in as much detail as you can remember," Clara said. "Possibly there is something that happened that night that explains how William ended up in the countryside without his car."

Florence was not convinced there was anything she could say that would explain the matter, but she was willing to give it a try for William's sake.

"William came that night with Stacy. She had invited him, which was how he came to be at the gala," she began.

"William Hershel is a nice boy," Bridget interjected. "Was a nice boy, I suppose I mean. He was well-mannered and responsible. Not like some of the young men that hover around Flossie and are clearly rogues."

"Auntie!" Florence scolded her aunt.

"You know precisely who I mean, Flossie. Some of them have only one thing on their mind."

She did not need to elaborate on what that one

thing was. Tommy wondered if it was worth mentioning that most young men only had one thing on their mind a great deal of the time, and it did not make them rogues, but he suspected he would receive a stony reception for this information.

"I was expecting to hear an announcement concerning Miss Freeman and William any day," Bridget continued. "They seemed such a perfect match."

"Miss Freeman told us they were just friends," Clara said.

Florence, who had looked sour at her aunt's words, brightened up at Clara's information, only to then recall William was dead and none of it mattered anymore. She almost burst into tears again at the misery of it all.

"That is the grief talking," Bridget said firmly. "Miss Freeman is trying not to think of what she has lost."

"What has she lost?" Tommy asked Florence, who was pulling a petulant face. "I am guessing you know better than anyone."

When Florence looked up at him, her face was like that of a young child who has lost its favourite toy and cannot suppose they will be able to go on without it. It was not the face of a grown woman in grief, there was something about the expression that said she was not appreciating things in quite the way you would expect an adult to.

"William was kind and he danced well," Florence sniffed. "He had a nice car too."

As Clara had suspected, Florence had a tendency to focus on superficial things rather than the man himself.

"What time did he arrive back at the gala after taking Miss Freeman home?" Clara asked.

"I could not really say," Florence shrugged. "It was after nine. I had been waiting all night to dance with him."

"Had you not been accompanied to the gala by someone?" Tommy asked, surprised that a girl such as Florence had not had a companion with her.

"No. I was supposed to be escorted by Jonathan, but he rang earlier to say he was sick and could not come."

"Jonathan Woods," Bridget elaborated. "He is one of the least roguish of the rogues who hang around Florence."

"Auntie!" Florence rebuked her again. "Anyway, he said he was too sick to come and so I went by myself."

"I dropped her there and picked her up," Bridget added. "I could not possibly have her walk all that way alone."

Florence dabbed at her eyes.

"The party was rather a dive for me at first. Everyone had a partner, and I was the odd one out. I told myself I could weather it out, being all on my own. But it did sting, until William found himself without a partner," Florence became wistful. "I didn't see him and Stacy leave, but I saw him alone in the music hall later that evening. I went over and asked where Stacy was, that was when he told me she had gone home with a headache. I said, it seemed we had both lost our partners and explained about Jonathan. William got a strange look on his face, then he suggested we dance together."

"You were with him the rest of the night?" Clara asked.

"Yes, until Auntie came to collect me a little while after midnight."

"It was quarter to one," Bridget elaborated. "I used the family car and there is a clock in the dashboard. My brother had it fitted as a novelty. I parked under one of the streetlamps and could see the time."

"What about William?" Clara asked Florence.

"When I said I had to go, he said he was going to go

85

home soon as well. The guests had thinned out by then, a lot of the older folks do not like to stay up so very late," Florence said this dismissively.

"What about William's car?" O'Harris asked. "Did you see it?"

"It was parked just outside the music hall," Florence said. "Not many people have cars, so you notice, and William's car is lovely. I have ridden in it once or twice. Afterwards, I thought I should have rung Auntie and told her William would bring me home, then I could have spent longer at the party and had a ride in his car."

"And I would have insisted on coming to collect you," Bridget said firmly. "We agreed on the arrangements, and they were not to change."

This was clearly a conversation they had had many a time before, and Florence looked embarrassed her aunt had brought it up before them.

"Well, at least we now know where William was up until one o'clock," Clara said thoughtfully. "The next few hours are where the mystery lies. While he was with you, Florence, did anything occur? Anything odd, or upsetting?"

"He talked about Stacy a lot," Florence sulked.

"Yes, but that was upsetting to you. I meant, did anything occur that might have upset or angered William?" Clara rephrased her question.

Florence paused, considering her answer for a moment.

"Do you mean something like an argument?" she said.

Clara almost groaned in exasperation.

"Yes, an argument. But not between the two of you."

Florence gave her a look to imply she was not stupid; she was just self-absorbed.

"William went to get us drinks and food when there was a pause in the music," Florence explained. "My feet were hurting in my new shoes, so I had to sit down for a bit and take them off."

"I told you those shoes were too small," Bridget interrupted again.

Florence ignored her.

"I was rubbing my heels and absently looked over to where the food tables were and I saw that William was talking with a man, or rather, it began as talking and then William was pointing a finger at the man, and it looked as though they were arguing."

"Who was the man?" Clara asked.

Florence frowned.

"I did not immediately recognise him, but I do think I know his name. He is one of the Friends, I believe, and I have seen him at other occasions," she paused and then shook her head. "No, his name will not come to me."

Clara produced the list of invitees from her coat pocket and handed it to Florence.

"Perhaps you recognise one of those names?"

Florence ran her finger down the list thoughtfully. Bridget leaned forward, trying to see the list. Florence paused at a name and tapped her finger against it. Then she closed her eyes and seemed deep in thought.

"I think it is this man," she said. "I was picturing him from the other night and trying the name on him and I am almost certain it is correct."

"What is the name?" Bridget said eagerly.

"Asher Lightman," Florence answered.

She handed the list back to Clara.

"What is his connection with William?" Clara asked.

Florence shrugged again.

"I don't know. When William came back with our drinks and food, he seemed as cheerful as before. If I had not happened to spot him arguing with the man, I should never have known anything had occurred."

"Can you tell me anything about Lightman?" Clara tried next.

Florence thought about this a while, her frown deepening.

"I think he is something to do with theatres, but I might be wrong. He is an older man and, honestly, I don't have a reason to speak to him, so I never have."

Which meant that as he was not young enough to interest Florence as a potential companion, he was of no value to her whatsoever.

"How come William was not a Friend?" Tommy asked.

"The performing arts did not interest him," Florence replied. "He liked to come to the parties, but he was not interested in becoming involved with the society. William was interested in the new media of moving pictures. He said there was quite a lot of chemistry involved in processing the film that is used in those. He was always talking like that. If something involved chemicals, he was interested."

"Which still leaves us with no answer as to why he went into the countryside last night and fell in a ditch," Tommy stated. "I suppose we shall need to speak to this Lightman."

"Do you know Annabelle Hershel?" Clara asked Florence.

"Of course," Florence said at once. "Annabelle is William's older sister. She keeps trying to involve him with the Friends, but he shall not have it."

"She was at the gala last night?" Clara asked.

"She was, but she is like a lot of the older folks and left before midnight," Florence was again dismissive of the lack of endurance of the older generation.

"The Hershels must be devastated," Bridget spoke, over the last half hour of talking the reality of the situation had sunk into her. "William had such a future ahead of him. They thought so highly of him and after…"

She cut herself off.

"After?" Clara asked, curious.

"I do not think it is proper to speak about it," Bridget said.

"Under normal circumstances, maybe not, but these are not regular circumstances," Clara prompted her.

Bridget shook her head.

"It has nothing to do with William's death. I was just thinking how the family were so glad to at last have an academic son."

"Auntie is referring to Micah, William's older brother, who is a scoundrel and always in trouble," Florence did not have the same reservations for talking about others as her aunt did. "Micah was meant to go to university, but instead he went to prison."

Clara was intrigued, it was not every day you heard that people like the Hershels had a son who had spent time in prison.

"It was not as simple as all that," Bridget said, trying to mitigate the damage done by the revelation. "He was not in prison, as such. He was being held prior to a court case in the police cells. As it happens, before everything came to court, he was found to be innocent and released. The family keep very quiet about the whole affair, and he was sent to Scotland to live with cousins for almost a year."

"What was the case about?" Clara asked, professional curiosity always liable to get the better of her.

"A girl went missing," Bridget explained. "She was last seen with Micah, and he became the main suspect, some would say he was the only suspect for a while. Micah denied everything. This was during the war."

"Was the girl ever found?" Clara asked.

"No," Bridget sighed. "And no one was ever tried for the crime. That incident is one reason I am always so careful about making sure Florence gets home safely from parties."

"You fuss too much," Florence huffed.

Bridget gave Clara a sad look.

"Maybe, or maybe not. After all, William is now dead after such a party. Such tragedy has stalked the Hershel family."

"They do seem to have suffered more than their fair share of bad luck," Clara concurred.

Chapter Eleven

"Where to next?" O'Harris asked as they returned to the car.

Clara was taking a good look at the list of people who had attended the gala. Something was niggling her about the name Asher Lightman. It was not a name to be easily forgotten and she was sure she had heard it somewhere before, but exactly where was eluding her.

"I think, before we do anything more, we need to visit Dr Deáth and see what he has discovered about William Hershel's demise. That might give us some greater insight into the direction we need to go in," she said. "The morgue is on the way to Mr Lightman's address, so it makes things simpler."

They headed off again, glad to have the car to take them to all these varying addresses in different parts of town.

"Mind if we take a slight detour?" O'Harris asked as they were heading into the urban sprawl of Brighton.

"It is your car," Clara reminded him with a smile.

They diverted down a side street, took a couple of

turnings and then emerged at the Maxwell Music Hall.

"I have been thinking about William's car," O'Harris explained. "Its disappearance is the most suspicious thing about all this if you ask me. I wondered if we might have just missed it, somehow?"

Clara knew what he meant. The missing car was one of the reasons she felt there was something more to William's disappearance than that he went out into the countryside and fell into a ditch. Cars did not vanish on their own, so either William took it somewhere and left it before heading out on the long, long walk to where they found him – an unlikely scenario, it seemed – or someone else had moved the car.

O'Harris had left his car and was walking along the pavement outside the music hall, dodging various pedestrians. People were making up for a day stuck indoors because of the storm and were out in force, or so it seemed. O'Harris paused.

"If this is where William parked, he would have needed to check his oil levels," he said, pointing. "He had a leak."

On the road was a shimmery film of oil, partly dispersed by the rain, but too heavy to completely vanish.

"That looks like a substantial leak," Tommy said, noticing how the oil had run into the gutter and continued down the road for some way. "How long before a leak like that would become a problem to the engine?"

"Depends how long it has been going on," O'Harris replied. "But that car will not be going far without being regularly topped up."

"If William moved his car, then it would logically be because he was heading home," Clara said thinking aloud. "Otherwise, why bother when he was parked perfectly outside the music hall?"

"You don't think he drove out to the countryside

where we found him?" O'Harris asked.

Clara considered for a moment.

"If he gone out there alone, for some reason, then why was his car not near where we found him?" she replied. "No, the more I think about it, the more I think someone else moved that car."

"To get to where the crates fell it would be a four, maybe five hour walk," Tommy added. "You wouldn't walk that distance if you had a car."

"We also need to take into account the time we found him, and the time he must have left the party," Clara continued. "Florence left the party at one. If, for some remarkable reason, William really did walk all the way from here to that ditch, then he would have arrived at the spot around six at the earliest. It was a little after nine we arrived at the scene, and the crates had been in the ditch only a short while. Say they were blown over around half past eight. William would have been in that ditch just over two hours, he would probably have been dead barely an hour."

"And Dr Deáth felt he had been dead a lot longer than that," O'Harris nodded, recalling what the doctor had said when he examined the body.

"The cold temperature would make the exact time harder to work out, but to suppose William walked out there and made it to the ditch in time to die before the crate fell on him, simply does not make sense," Clara concluded.

"He either drove himself there, or someone drove him there," Tommy tapped his lip. "Makes everything look more and more suspicious."

"Shall we take a look around the back streets to see if we can spot the car?" O'Harris suggested. "Maybe someone has hidden it there."

They headed behind the music hall, past the yard they had entered the day before and started exploring the roads behind the building. They split up to cover more ground, and Clara advised them to ask anyone who appeared a resident in the area if they had noticed a red car. After wandering around for half an hour, they regrouped by O'Harris' car to reveal their findings.

"Nothing," O'Harris shook his head.

"Same here," Tommy replied.

"The car has most certainly vanished," Clara concurred with them.

They were about to climb back in the car and head on to the morgue when the music hall caretaker bustled outside.

"I thought I saw you going past the yard," he said, looking over at them. "Could I borrow you for a moment?"

Unlike the day before, when he had been surly and unhappy about talking to them, today he was anxious and eager to take up a moment of their time. Clara was intrigued and wondered if this was relevant to William's fate. She led the way as they followed the caretaker indoors. He paused in the foyer of the music hall, his hands clasped together in a nervous fashion. From the wall, a stern portrait of a whiskered gentleman glared down at him, as if rebuking him for not continuing with his work.

"I am not sure if you are the right person to speak to," the caretaker began. "But my other option is to speak to the police, and I am not sure Mr Martin would like that."

"What has happened?" Clara asked him.

The caretaker took a deep breath.

"Well, it actually is about Mr Martin. You see, he has not come to the music hall again today. Yesterday, when he never showed up, I thought the storm had kept him at home. I tried to ignore his telephone ringing, it is not my place to answer it, after all, and I told myself he would catch up with things tomorrow, or rather, today. But he has not arrived today either."

Clara glanced at her watch, noting it was nearly noon.

"Has Mr Martin ever been late like this before?" she asked.

"Never," the caretaker said. "Mr Martin values punctuality. I have never known him to take a day off for sickness. If he ever had to be away for business, he always told me in advance. I am starting to become worried."

As he finished speaking, the shrill ring of a telephone echoed from Mr Martin's office.

"That thing keeps going too," the caretaker winced. "People hounding me. But I am not allowed to answer it. It is driving me crazy."

The caretaker was clearly beside himself and deeply concerned about his employer.

"Calm down," Clara told him gently. "We shall investigate what has happened to Mr Martin, if you wish."

The caretaker nodded his head vigorously.

"I definitely wish you to do that," he said. "Mr Martin's absence is troubling."

"We should start at his house," Tommy said. "Maybe he has had a lot of storm damage he needs to repair?"

"He would have come and told me," the caretaker said with certainty. "Besides, Mr Martin is not the sort to be fixing things himself. He is a clever man, but he does not know one end of a hammer from the other."

"If you give us his address, we shall call on him and see that he is all right," Clara added.

The caretaker relaxed.

"He lives at 100 Crescent Drive. There is a white trellis porch over the front door, you can't miss it."

With more assurances to the caretaker they would determine what had become of Mr Martin, they left the music hall and returned to the car. O'Harris took out a map from the glove box and started to work out where Crescent Drive was, while Clara wrapped herself up in a blanket from the back seat. Tommy was shivering next to her, and after a moment, she threw the blanket over his knees as well.

"A man could die from this cold," Tommy said, only realising what had come out of his mouth a moment later. "That was crass."

"You did not mean it that way," Clara told him. "I hope Mr Martin is not stuck outdoors in this temperature."

"Why would he be?" Tommy said.

Clara did not have an immediate answer.

"It is just odd that two people associated with the music hall have apparently suffered misfortunes. If the caretaker is correct, something quite significant must have happened to cause Mr Martin to not come to work today."

"Crescent Drive is beyond the morgue," O'Harris said from the front of the car. "Shall we go to Dr Deáth first."

"Yes," Clara replied. "No point doubling back on ourselves."

They drove the short distance to the morgue and found themselves once again in its stark, white-tiled interior. It was still bitterly cold, and Tommy watched as his breath fogged before his face. They headed down the stairs and found Dr Deáth humming to himself as he weighed out what looked suspiciously like a heart in a pair of scales. As always, Dr Deáth was cheerful in his work.

"Ah, what a pleasure to see you three!" he said at the sight of them. "What is the weather like outside? My little window only offers me a small glimpse and right now it is boarded up."

He motioned to the broken window which had been covered over with the lid of a packing crate to keep the worst of the winter rain out.

"Cold, but currently dry," Clara told him. "We wondered if you had had a chance to look over William Hershel."

Dr Deáth grinned at them.

"Our friend at last warmed up enough that I could arrange his body more suitably and I was able to properly examine him. Having washed the corpse and taken a good look at the body, there are a couple of things that caught my attention," Dr Deáth wiped his gloved hands on his work apron, leaving smears of blood from whatever organ he was weighing. "First, William had an injury to the back of his head. I could not see it until I had thoroughly washed him and removed all the mud caked to his hair. It was only small, but it appeared he banged his head. There was a very slight cut and I dare say some coroners would not have even noticed the injury because of how his hair fell. But I thought there seemed a lump at the back of his head and I was correct. I speculate he banged his head falling into the ditch and knocked himself out."

"Was it a big enough blow to do that?" Tommy asked.

"Just because the cut was small, does not mean the blow was not significant," Dr Deáth explained. "It just means whatever he hit was not sharp enough to cause much damage to his skin. It could have been a tree log, for instance. The blow most likely knocked him out sufficiently for the weather to work to finish him off."

"You think he died from exposure then?" Tommy said.

"The signs are subtle, but I cannot see any other cause. There was fluid in the lungs, which is an indication of extreme hypothermia. He was otherwise in good health."

"What about when he died?" Clara asked.

Dr Deáth became thoughtful.

The cold temperatures make it challenging to tell precisely, however, considering how he was stiff when we found him and determining how long it would have taken for him to perish from the freezing temperatures, I would suggest you are looking at some time in the early hours of the morning. Maybe four or five o'clock."

"How long would he have had been in the ditch before he died?" Clara asked next.

"It is subjective, it depends on a number of factors. If he had been drinking, then the onset would have been swifter. Alcohol increases the risk of hypothermia. Considering the temperature last night, and also that he was partly immersed in muddy water from the ditch, which would have speeded up the loss of body warmth, it would not be far-fetched to suppose it was only a couple of hours."

"Around three o'clock?" Clara said.

"At the earliest," Dr Deáth nodded. "Bearing in mind none of these calculations are exact and are based on measurements that can be highly variable."

"He had to have reached that ditch by car," O'Harris interjected. "It is the only way he could have been there so soon after he was last seen alive by Florence."

"Then where is his car? And how did he get that bump to the back of his head?" Clara said. "I know, Dr Deáth, you mentioned it might have occurred when he fell in the ditch, but I am always prone to seeing things as more sinister, and I cannot help but wonder if the head injury happened before."

"A car accident?" Tommy suggested. "Two cars collide. William hits his head and falls unconscious. The driver in the other car thinks he is dead and panics. He throws him into a nearby ditch to cover the crime."

"What about William's car?" O'Harris said.

"There are two people in the other car, and one

drives off in William's car and hides it somewhere," Tommy concluded. "Everyone is a little drunk, no one is thinking straight, and the hope is that when William is found people will just suppose he wandered off and fell into a ditch."

"Which does not explain why he was out in the middle of nowhere in the first place," Clara pointed out.

"People do sometimes just go for a drive," O'Harris said helpfully. "Maybe he was trying to clear his head. I have done that. Gone driving around the country lanes at night to put my mind at peace."

Dr Deáth was following their conversation with a placid smile on his face.

"It sounds as though you have a lot to consider," he said. "I am sorry I was not of more help, but if I do discover anything else, I shall inform you."

He went back to the heart he was weighing.

"Now I must get this heart back into Mr Martin before he misses it," he said with crypt humour.

Clara nearly jumped at the name.

"Did you say Mr Martin?"

Chapter Twelve

Dr Deáth showed them over to a body covered with a large sheet. He pulled the sheet back from the head and revealed an older man with a podgy face. His hair was thinning on top and there was a smattering of broken veins on his nose which had faded after death.

"Mr Martin," Dr Deáth repeated. "You recognise him?"

Since none of them had ever met Mr Martin, nor seen an image of him, it was impossible to say they recognised him.

"We know his name," Clara explained. "He is the manager of the Maxwell Music Hall. Assuming, that is, this is not some other Mr Martin who has happened to turn up here by coincidence. What happened?"

"The police summoned me to a property earlier today. From what I understand, the gentleman who owned the house lived alone, but was in regular contact with his sister. She had been trying to contact him since the day before, wanting to know he was all right after the storm we had. When she received no response from his work telephone, she went to his house and let herself in with her spare key. She found Mr Martin in his bed," Dr Deáth elaborated. "She summoned a doctor, who pronounced him dead and said the police ought to be called as it was clearly unexpected and unexplained. That is how I came to be there."

"Was it some sort of fit or seizure?" O'Harris asked.

"You might wonder that from his age and physical condition," Dr Deáth nodded. "Certainly, he was a man who would have benefited from a little more exercise. But the actual cause of death was this."

Dr Deáth lifted up the corpse, pulling it from right to left to reveal the dead man's back. Just beneath the shoulder blade was a knife wound.

"The knife pierced the lung, and he would have started to leak air into his chest cavity, which ultimately compromised his ability to breath," Dr Deáth explained. "He suffocated."

"He did not bleed to death?" O'Harris said, surprised.

"No, the wound had not hit any major blood vessels and he had taken care to clean and bandage it," Dr Deáth replied. "While he certainly must have lost a considerable amount of blood and, possibly, without stitches, that would have ultimately killed him. I am certain it was the punctured lung that dealt the killer blow."

"How does a music hall manager end up stabbed in the back?" Tommy shook his head, amazed. "And does this connect to the death of William Hershel?"

"There is something else," Dr Deáth continued. "Take a look at his hands."

Dr Deáth pulled back the blanket a little further and revealed Mr Martin's hands. There were marks on the fingertips, ugly wounds.

"Burns?" Clara said.

"Specifically, chemical burns," Dr Deáth answered.

"I am not sure the precise chemical that caused these, but it was something caustic. I have tried to take some samples to determine what exactly the chemical was, but I do not hold out a lot of hope. The burns had begun to heal, so these injuries happened at least a day or two before the knife wound."

"He had to have touched something that caused those burns," Tommy frowned. "It looks as though he picked something up."

"It is very curious," Dr Deáth agreed.

Clara's expression was troubled. The coroner turned to her.

"What is it?" he asked.

"William Hershel was studying chemistry and Mr Martin has chemical burns on his hands. That is not a coincidence."

Dr Deáth nodded at her.

"I think you are right, but at this point I cannot explain the connection or quite what that has to do with two men being dead."

"Mr Martin died in his bed?" Tommy recalled what the coroner had said previously. "Was he attacked in his home?"

"The police would be better able to answer that," Dr Deáth answered. "From my perspective, the only blood I saw was on the bed where it had leaked through the bandage."

"We need to speak to Park-Coombs," Clara spoke. "Things are becoming more complicated. When do you think Mr Martin died?"

"Probably around the same time as William," Dr Deáth conjectured. "I don't think he was alive to see the storm blow in."

"They both met their ends the night of the gala," Clara nodded. "Something happened at that event. Something sinister."

They thanked Dr Deáth for his time and then

headed to the car and for the police station. They found it was busy with people making complaints about problems caused by the storm. Someone was moaning that their gas supply had been cut off and seemed to think this was something the police could solve. Another woman was complaining the streetlamps outside her shop were no longer working. Others were moaning about neighbours who refused to pay for repairing fences or smashed windows that were clearly their responsibility. There was also a lot of debate about how a person went about reclaiming or replacing dustbins that had disappeared in the storm.

The desk sergeant looked harassed and tired. Clara felt bad she was having to add to his burden, but when he spied her, he looked relieved.

"Miss Fitzgerald, come to the desk at once. I have a message for you," the desk sergeant waved aside the people queuing up to complain about storm damage and made a passage to his desk.

Clara received angry glares for being jumped to the front of the queue. She ignored them.

"The Inspector left you a message. He thought you might drop by," the desk sergeant said. "He wants to have a chat with you about the museum crates business."

The desk sergeant was being surreptitious, acutely aware that there were many ears listening in.

"He said, if you called by, to tell you to come to this address," the desk sergeant handed her a slip of paper. "He said this was quite a humdinger."

Clara took the paper.

"Thank you. I think he is right," Clara said, then in a louder voice. "By the way, sergeant, have you informed these people that the Brighton Gazette is running a piece about the storm and the first dozen or so people they get stories from about damaged property they intend to help with getting it repaired?"

Her voice carried nicely, and almost at once people started to scurry for the door, leaving behind only those who were more inclined to rely on the police. The police station foyer cleared out considerably. The desk sergeant sighed happily.

"Thank you, Miss Fitzgerald. I did not know about the newspaper business," he said.

Clara returned to O'Harris and Tommy.

"The Brighton Gazette is running a piece about the storm?" Tommy asked her with a raised eyebrow.

"Bound to be," Clara told him. "It is the biggest news around, and they will want stories about the damage to give that personal angle."

"What about them helping people with repairs?" O'Harris said.

"Did I say that?" Clara said with mock astonishment. "Well, being able to relay your aggrievances to someone is a form of help and no doubt the newspaper has a comprehensive list of tradesmen who advertise with them and are fully capable of fixing things."

"Should I be worried about how you are able to bend the truth so neatly?" O'Harris said, feigning serious concern.

Clara smirked at him.

"I only use my powers for good, and you know that."

"Of course," O'Harris chuckled.

They drove to the address they had been given and found a number of police present outside the property. There seemed a lot more constables about than Clara had supposed necessary for the mysterious death of Mr Martin, and when she saw a couple of men in military uniform, a chill ran down her spine.

"This is taking a new turn," Tommy said, upon spying the army men. "The insignia on their uniforms reminds me of the fellows who were responsible for making safe live shells that had not exploded."

"What?" Clara said in alarm.

"Shells did not always explode when they landed. Same with grenades. Some fault within them prevented them from going off in that instant, but they could go off at any moment. Someone had to deal with them. Usually, the fellows moved the explosives far away from the troops and caused them to detonate."

"That sounds a dangerous business," O'Harris winced at the thought.

"It was. Sometimes the bomb went off as they were handling it. They were learning all the time how best to handle these things. It was better than one of the regular lads trying his luck, however."

"That does not explain why they are here," Clara said, getting out of the car.

She hastened over to the house and was just going through the front gate when Park-Coombs emerged from the door. He looked more harassed than usual and the grey cast to his face did not inspire confidence.

"Inspector?" Clara said, turning one word into a string of questions about what was occurring.

"Glad you are here," Park-Coombs said to her. "You best come inside. There is a lot to explain, and it isn't nice."

Park-Coombs escorted them into the front room of the house. It was quiet in here, most of the activity occurring further down the hallway in the kitchen.

"How much do you know?" Park-Coombs asked them.

"We know Mr Martin, the manager of the music hall, died the same night as William Hershel and that he was clearly murdered. Dr Deáth also showed us the chemical burns on his fingers," Clara answered swiftly.

Park-Coombs breathed deeply.

"When I first arrived here, we thought maybe someone had entered Mr Martin's house and murdered him in his bed," he explained. "We started searching the house to find where it had occurred and any clues to the killer. All the doors were locked, which was odd, and the windows appeared secure. After finding no signs of blood outside of the bedroom, we began to think Mr Martin was attacked elsewhere and managed to make his way home. Where he changed into his pyjamas and went to bed, presumably hoping he was not badly hurt and could recover without help."

"What man fails to find help for a stab wound?" O'Harris shook his head. "Mr Martin could have afforded to go to the hospital, after all."

"That did seem curious," Park-Coombs nodded. "People who avoid hospitals when severely injured, tend to be those who have something to hide. I had this unhappy feeling about the whole affair and so I had my men search the house thoroughly. That was when we discovered a secret panel in the pantry. Someone had created a false wall at the end and behind it was a gap sufficient to hide several items. These items appeared to be bombs."

Clara heard the others behind her gasp, she remained silent, the horror of the matter creeping over her.

"How many bombs?" she asked quietly.

"We discovered two devices that looked suspicious. I pulled my men out and made a call to the nearest army base for someone to come take a look," Park-Coombs looked grim at the memory. "While waiting for them to arrive, we cleared the neighbouring homes, telling people there was a suspected gas leak. The army men arrived about an hour ago and they have determined that what we found in the pantry were just bomb casings. They do not have anything inside them."

"That is a relief," Tommy pressed a hand to his chest where he could feel his heart pounding.

"However," Park-Coombs continued, "the army

men found traces of certain substances that cause them to believe there was an actual bomb here. Someone made it on the kitchen table, and now it is missing."

Clara felt icy cold as the impact of the news took full hold.

"The army fellows are still investigating," Park-Coombs nodded his head in the direction of the kitchen. "They are trying to figure out what was used to make the bomb, how big it might be and any other clues as to what it might be intended for."

"This is… unbelievable," Tommy groaned, finding it necessary to lean against the mantelpiece in the room. "I thought I left all that horror behind at the Front."

"Chemicals are necessary for making certain explosives," Clara was thinking aloud. "Experimenting with them to get a mixture just right to suit the bomber's purposes could have resulted in the chemical burns to Mr Martin's fingers, and we also have a student of chemistry who is dead."

"It looks to me as if someone is covering their tracks," Park-Coombs added. "Someone wanted a bomb and for whatever reason asked Mr Martin to make it, with the advice of young William Hershel. Then, when the bomb was ready, the person who asked for it got rid of the two people who could point the finger at him."

"Or her," Clara said. "Never underestimate a woman, even in such nefarious matters. I agree that looks to be the way things were."

"We need to find that bomb," Tommy hissed through his teeth.

"Agreed. I have spoken with the army chaps, and they suggest a two-pronged approach to the matter. First, we try to figure out a likely target for the bomb, possibly a building or person. I can check out the usual political rabble-rousers and see if any of them know anything," Park-Coombs said. "Second, we find out everything we can about Mr Martin's and William Hershel's associates and try to find someone among them who could be a bomber."

"You missed a third avenue," Clara pointed out. "We solve the murders of William Hershel and Mr Martin, and by finding their killer, we find the bomber."

"You are right," Park-Coombs nodded. "Not that I have much sympathy for the fellows anymore. Dead bomb makers are better than live ones."

"We have promised the Hershel family we shall discover what happened to William," Clara did not react to his comment. "I shall continue in that direction, and any information either of us learns, we must share and hope we can prevent a tragedy from occurring."

"Agreed," Park-Coombs was nodding his head firmly. "Once the army fellows have cleared out of here, feel free to take a look around if you think it will help. Also, Mr Martin's sister is waiting in a neighbour's house down the road. You might want to talk to her."

"Thank you, Inspector," Clara paused. "What began as a seeming accident, has become something far more sinister."

"You can say that again, Clara," Park-Coombs looked shattered. "I never thought I would be chasing a bomb in my own town. I just hope we can find it before someone innocent gets hurt."

Chapter Thirteen

Mr Martin's sister was several years older than him. She had been married twice and widowed twice. She was dressed all in black when they found her in a neighbour's house. She was a grey-haired older woman, who could have passed for someone from the middle of the nineteenth century, her choice of attire seeming so formal and old-fashioned. She was even wearing a black lace shawl over her head.

When Clara and the others arrived to see her, she looked up at them with red-rimmed eyes, a white handkerchief tastefully embroidered with a delicate pink rose was pressed to her lips. She had suffered quite the shock that morning. Having previously found two husbands dead (one in his armchair, one in their bed) she had still been unprepared for the scene she had come upon that day.

She had been plied with sugary tea by the lady of the house she was currently sitting in, but it was not making a dent on the shock she felt. She was contemplating the fact she was now truly all alone in the world. Her brother had been her last relative and she had been comfortable in the knowledge she would outlive him, until that very moment.

"You must be Mr Martin's sister," Clara said upon entering the front room of the house and finding the woman perched on the edge of a sofa like a nervous blackbird. "I am Clara Fitzgerald. This is my brother Tommy and our friend Captain O'Harris. We are very sorry for your loss."

"I am Mrs Silverwood," the older lady introduced herself. "What is happening at my brother's house? The police said something about a gas leak? Was it that, that killed him?"

The next portion of the conversation was going to be difficult.

"Mr Martin, I am saddened to say, was murdered," Clara said, knowing there was no good way to explain all this. "Someone stabbed him in the back. He managed to make his way home, only to pass away in his bed."

The colour slowly drained from Mrs Silverwood's face, considering the dense face powder she was wearing which gave her an already pale countenance, the sight of her growing almost translucent with horror was impressive.

"Who are you again?" she asked, because it was easier than facing the news her brother was murdered.

"Clara Fitzgerald," Clara explained. "I am a private detective, and I was asked by the caretaker at the Maxwell Music Hall to discover why Mr Martin had not been to work in two days."

Mrs Silverwood listened intently.

"A caretaker hires a private detective?" she said in astonishment.

"It is a little more complicated than that," Clara answered. "We were working on another case that involved the music hall, and the caretaker asked us for help. He was deeply worried about the absence of Mr

Martin but was not in a position to be able to leave the music hall unattended. Seeing as we had already intended to speak to Mr Martin at some point, it was not out of our way to undertake the caretaker's request."

"Has something bad happened at the music hall, too?" Mrs Silverwood frowned. "That place was my brother's passion. He did everything he could for that hall."

"As I said, it is all rather complicated," Clara continued. "Mrs Silverwood, your brother appears to have been attacked the same night another young man disappeared and suffered an accident. Had he ever mentioned to you that he was in any trouble."

Mrs Silverwood shook her head.

"Everyone thought a lot of my brother. He was kind and generous with his time. He also lived a quiet life. He never married, his full attention being on the Maxwell Music Hall. It was on the cusp of closing for good before he took over as its manager. The pay was poor, but he was more interested in restoring the place and making it thrive. That he achieved."

Mrs Silverwood was overcome again, her voice shaking with tears. She pressed the handkerchief hard to her lips to stifle a sob.

"Mrs Silverwood, was your brother involved in any political movements?" Tommy asked cautiously.

"My brother had no interest in politics," Mrs Silverwood said firmly. "He was a man of the arts and, dare I say, he rather had his head in the clouds much of the time. He used to make our parents despair. They had hoped he would do so much more with his life."

"He had no interests outside the music hall?" Tommy persisted. "Nothing political?"

"No," Mrs Silverwood snapped. "Why are you going on about this? My poor brother was stabbed, I suppose while he was locking up the hall. He used to be there so very late. I told him it was dangerous."

Tommy glanced at his sister, not sure how to broach the next matter. Clara took a deep breath.

"Mrs Silverwood, the police have found the trappings of bomb making in your brother's kitchen," she said quietly, not wanting to be overheard by anyone else in the house. They were alone with the woman in the sitting room, but sound could travel and particularly words such as 'bomb'.

Mrs Silverwood stared at her, stunned. She might as well have been told her brother had turned out to be an elephant disguised as a man, that was how bizarre and incomprehensible to her the news was.

"There was a secret wall in his pantry," Clara continued, because it was better than saying nothing. "Behind it were two bomb casings. They were empty. There were traces on the kitchen table of chemicals for producing explosives and it is believed there was another bomb, a finished one, that is now missing. Your brother had chemical burns on his fingertips, indicating he had recently handled caustic chemicals. The evidence points to him making bombs."

Mrs Silverwood was aghast.

"You would not say such nonsense if you knew my brother at all!" she declared.

"Madam, the police had to call in the army as soon as they realised they were dealing with bombs," Tommy added. "The army sent bomb disposal experts who have confirmed the kitchen was the site of explosives manufacture. The reason everyone was evacuated was not because of a gas leak, but because it was feared there were live bombs in your brother's house."

"Now the house is safe, we could show you," Clara said gently, sensing that her brother was angry at the woman's continued denial. "This is not something anyone would care to hear about their loved one."

"It is a lie," Mrs Silverwood said firmly. "My brother had not a violent bone in his body!"

Mrs Silverwood stood suddenly and walked across the room.

"Someone must have put those things there," she insisted. "My brother was always letting people take advantage of him. He allowed someone to use his kitchen without being aware of what they were doing, that is it!"

Clara thought that highly unlikely, but decided it was best not to steal this fragile hope from the woman. Sometimes people needed such notions to cling to, to help them cope.

"We need to discuss what happened to your brother," Clara said carefully. "Someone hurt him, and I do not think it was some random attack at the music hall while he was locking up. I think someone deliberately wanted to take your brother out of the picture. You may be the only one who can give us an insight into who would have done such a thing."

"My brother made friends, not enemies," Mrs Silverwood was turned away from them, hiding that she was weeping again.

"Even the nicest of people have enemies," Tommy told her. "They don't intend to make enemies, but people take against them for some reason. You know that, Mrs Silverwood."

Mrs Silverwood's shoulders shook as she cried silently, but it was only for a moment or two, until she regained her composure and looked back at them.

"My brother did not mention anyone who was troubling him," she said, her voice fragile.

"How did he seem lately?" Clara asked. "Perhaps he was agitated or seemed uneasy?"

Mrs Silverwood pursed her lips together.

"He seemed tired, but then he was always very busy," she said. "To keep the music hall thriving he had to constantly work to draw in new people and to host new events. It was time consuming."

They seemed to have reached a point where nothing further could be said. Mrs Silverwood fell silent, her head tipped down a little, her hands clasped around her handkerchief like it was a lifeline. Clara felt they had tormented her long enough and saw no reason to pester her further. The woman had a lot to get her head around, juggling her grief with the knowledge her brother was building bombs.

"Thank you, Mrs Silverwood, for speaking to us. I shall leave you my card in case you think of anything further."

Clara took a business card from her pocket and set it on the arm of the sofa, where Mrs Silverwood could not miss it. She was about to go when the woman spoke.

"There is just one thing…" Mrs Silverwood coughed, seeming to choke on the words.

Clara turned back towards her.

"I must press upon you that I do not, in any way, think my brother is behind these bombs," Mrs Silverwood said hastily. "I am sure he has been used by someone else. But you mentioned politics and thinking about why people make bombs, well, it sparked a thought."

"What is it?" Tommy asked when the woman stopped.

Mrs Silverwood drew in a deep breath before going on.

"My brother was working on organising a very special event at the music hall. It had not been publicly announced just yet because the arrangements were meant to be as secret as possible, for security."

"You make it sound sinister," Tommy said.

"No, just… sensitive," Mrs Silverwood explained. "The King is coming to Brighton in a fortnight's time.

My understanding is that he is looking for some water therapy for his health and hopes Brighton will provide him with the cure for his ailments. He is coming to the town under an assumed name, because he does not want to be recognised, or for the public to know he is unwell."

"Royalty heading to Brighton in secret," O'Harris said. "It would not be the first time in the town's history. How did Mr Martin know about it?"

"Well, the King is still the King," Mrs Silverwood remarked, as if it was obvious. "He might not be making public appearances, but certain arrangements were being made to welcome him, including a banquet at the music hall. My brother was charged with organising the food, selecting appropriate guests, and doing all of this with great discretion."

"The police are not aware of this royal visit," Clara mentioned, wondering if Mr Martin had made up the story for his sister, perhaps to cover his other activities.

"The King has his own security, and it was felt best to keep the police out of things. They are very loud-mouthed, and once they knew, the whole town would," Mrs Silverwood pulled a face, expressing her opinion on the police and their ability to keep a secret. "But all I say is true."

"If someone wished harm to the King, and they learned that he was to be dining at the music hall, they might consider it a prime opportunity, especially with such secrecy surrounding the event and the police out of the loop," O'Harris suggested. "It would be ideal for someone wanting to blow up the King."

"My brother would never, ever dream of such a thing!" Mrs Silverwood said quickly, horrified at the implications. "But perhaps someone he had spoken to in confidence about the arrangements was less patriotic?"

Mrs Silverwood was clutching at straws, Clara feared. All the evidence pointed to her brother being directly involved, but if his intention was to blow up the King, then at least they had thwarted the effort. They would have a message sent through the correct channels and the palace would call off the visit. Meanwhile, they could hunt out associates of Mr Martin and determine who he was working with on the bomb.

"My brother was so pleased to be asked to arrange that dinner," Mrs Silverwood had become introspective. She sat again. "He told me about it with strict instructions to say nothing to anyone. I asked if I could attend, as I would love to meet the King, but he told me the palace had final say on the guest list and he had already submitted it."

Mrs Silverwood had clearly been disappointed by this, and a little hurt her brother had not thought to include her. Clara decided it was prudent not to mention that if her brother was planning on blowing up the King, it would be best if his sister were not present to be put in harm's way. There were still many questions to consider with the matter, not least what had caused Mr Martin, a seemingly harmless individual, to become involved in a scheme to blow up the king. And how precisely was William Hershel involved? Had he come up with the bomb recipe for Martin?

"I must prove my brother's innocence," Mrs Silverwood said suddenly. "I am the only one he has left in this life, and I cannot fail him. I shall not rest until I prove he would never do something as terrible as blow up our king!"

Clara did not have the heart to suggest to her she might be battling a thankless endeavour.

"If you think of anything else," Clara tapped the

card on the sofa arm.

Mrs Silverwood glanced at it, but it was rather a fierce look. Clara doubted the woman would confide anything further to her.

Clara led the way outside and they paused in the front garden to consider their next move.

"We need to talk to Park-Coombs first," Tommy said. "Explain the matter and have this visit cancelled."

"Agreed," Clara nodded.

"Why are you frowning?" O'Harris asked her. "Something is bothering you."

Clara could not deny he was correct.

"It is just that everyone we have so far spoken to seems to agree that Mr Martin was dedicated to the music hall. His sister says he was restoring it out of passion, rather than duty. The caretaker tells us he was dedicated to the place and never missed a day of work. Yet, he was apparently contemplating blowing up the King within the building, causing a serious amount of damage and potential catastrophic destruction," Clara shook her head. "It does not seem to make sense."

"Perhaps the bomb was not intended to go off at the dinner?" O'Harris suggested.

"Maybe," Clara said, but she was not convinced.

They were missing something to explain all this.

Chapter Fourteen

Park-Coombs was still roaming about the home of Mr Martin. The army men had departed, taking with them the bomb casings so they could investigate them further. It seemed a slim hope that an examination would lead to some clue as to who was part of the bomb plot.

"They might find fingerprints," Tommy suggested after he had heard about the removal of the bomb casings.

"Mr Martin was the bomb maker," O'Harris reminded him. "And his fingerprints were erased when he burned his fingertips with something caustic."

"Maybe that was not an accident," Park-Coombs said darkly.

They all had to take a moment to consider such a possibility. Park-Coombs broke the silence.

"And Mrs Silverwood is in denial, I suppose?" he asked.

"She cannot believe her beloved brother would do such a thing," Clara answered him. "Her alternative theory is that he allowed someone to use his kitchen without knowing what they were up to."

Park-Coombs gave an amused snort.

"That is not just far-fetched, it is… it is…" he struggled to end his sentence. "It is extraordinary!"

"Well, that is how people try to avoid thinking too hard about a loved one being a madman," Clara shrugged. "In any case, we now have a likely target."

Clara explained about the King's private trip to Brighton and the dinner at the music hall. Park-Coombs became displeased.

"Didn't tell us a thing!" he grumbled. "That is how tragedies occur, you know. They think they are better than us, just because we police civilians and the like. As if they know best. I would like to see them having to deal with some of the day-to-day stuff we get!"

He was huffing, working himself up into righteous indignation.

"At least we can cancel the trip and prevent these bombers causing any mischief," Clara reminded him. "You now have one over the royal security. You know of a bombing plot against the king which they do not."

This astute flattery warmed Park-Coombs and he smiled to himself.

"That is a very good point," he said, stroking his moustache and starting to preen with delight. "What a grand idea."

"Just think, if someone had not decided to be rid of Martin, we never would have known about all this," Tommy said.

"Just think if I had not ordered a thorough search of this house and had the good sense to recruit such intelligent constables who went above and beyond when they found that secret panel, we might still not know," Park-Coombs added, his self-importance increasing further.

"I think we can avert the worst," Clara said, trying to bring him back down to the ground. "We still need to find out who else was involved, because this will not be the end. They may have failed in this attempt on the king's life, but men who plot to blow people up, will not simply stop when they are facing a hurdle."

"Good point," Park-Coombs had come back to the ground with a bang as she said this. "Clara, keep working on your end of things and I will keep working on mine. Martin and William Hershel's deaths have to be connected, maybe that connection will reveal everything."

Clara concurred. She left the inspector wrapping up things at the house.

"Back to our original plan of speaking to Mr Longman," she said as they returned to the car.

She glanced at her watch. It was now the middle of the afternoon, and she was beginning to feel the weariness of rushing all around chasing people, not to mention the toll the bomb scare had just had on all of them. They had all been running on nervous energy for the last couple of hours and it had drained them. They agreed that before seeing Mr Longman they would stop to get a cup of tea and a sandwich from a Lyons teashop. The short rest and refreshment restored them, and they headed off again on their investigation.

Asher Longman lived in a smart Georgian townhouse that had been split into two properties. He occupied all of the ground floor, including the basement area. He was luckily home that afternoon, having been busy making repairs to the garden of the property. These included some trimming of broken branches from the old fruit trees that grew in the grounds. He had come in for a break from chopping and sawing when Clara's trio arrived on his doorstep.

Asher Longman was not a man who minded answering his front door while still wearing his old gardening trousers and an ancient sweater that was unravelling in several places. He was aged in his forties, still ruggedly handsome, though starting to lose the taut skin around his jowls, which would eventually leave him with a saggy-looking jaw. His expression was not friendly.

"I thought you were the coalman," he said. "Who are you?"

His tone implied he was not open to any form of selling and would quite gladly close the door in their face at the slightest provocation. Clara hastened into an explanation.

"I am Clara Fitzgerald, and these are my associates. I am a private detective working on behalf of the Hershel family…"

Despite speaking at speed, trying to get everything out before Longman could say anything, he interrupted her almost at once.

"A private detective? But you are a woman!"

Asher Longman had just sunk considerably in Clara's opinion of him. It had been a long time since someone had last used those words towards her, she had almost come to think people were finally accepting that a woman could do any job a man could. She felt a knot of anger tense in her stomach.

"Mr Longman, William Hershel is dead, and his parents want to know what happened to him. I am making enquiries on their behalf and those enquiries have led me here," she said, her tone fierce.

Tommy glanced a warning look at O'Harris, who pulled a face back. They knew that tone, and it was not one you wanted to hear.

"William? Dead?" Longman frowned. "That is preposterous. I saw him only the other night."

"You argued with him," Clara said sternly. "We have a witness who saw you two."

Longman narrowed his eyes.

"I don't know what you want with me, but I have

stuff to do…" he was on the cusp of closing his door.

Clara threw in her killer blow.

"If you will not speak to me, I shall have to report to the Hershels that you refuse to explain why you were arguing with their son the night he died, and I shall advise them to inform the police. I do not suppose you get many police inspector's knocking on doors around here. It will give your neighbours something to consider."

Asher Longman knew when he was beaten. He winced at the notion of police knocking on his door, attracting the attention of everyone, and having them ask questions about him. It would tarnish his reputation, have people wondering about him. He might lose his seat as chairman of the town's Community Safe and Sound committee – which was all about making the town a pleasant and secure place to reside. How could a chairman who had been under police suspicion be allowed to remain?

Longman groaned to himself and then opened the door fully

"As usual, you win, Miss Fitzgerald," he sniffed, before walking off towards his front room. He expected them to follow him, which they did.

"As usual?" Clara asked.

"You do not even remember me!" Longman laughed. "That just makes it all the worse"

"I am sorry, but I meet a lot of people…"

Longman spun around and faced her.

"You protested my appointment to the Brighton Pavilion Committee. You had the casting vote and you voted against me!"

Clara suddenly recalled where she had heard his name before. As they say, the penny dropped, and she now looked at him with fresh eyes.

"Ah," she said, "I believe it was a complex decision,

based on a lot of different factors."

"The deciding one being you did not like me," Longman declared. "Or was it the fact you wanted another woman on the committee? The appointment I was denied was taken up by a woman, I believe?"

"Clara is nothing if not fair," O'Harris said firmly from behind Clara, making sure Longman remembered he was present.

Clara was not troubled, she nodded at Longman.

"I made my decision because I felt you would not be the right fit. Your ideas for the future of the pavilion were not consistent with its conservation as an historic site," she explained.

"I would have made it profitable," Longman retorted. "I would have made it a viable commercial concern. Then you would have no money worries."

"You proposed selling off some of the grounds for building projects and instead of restoring parts of the pavilion, knocking them down and rebuilding them in concrete," Clara said.

"We would have made them look just like the rest," Longman snorted. "Nothing would be different on the outside."

"Your plans would destroy the old brickwork and the wallpaper and decoration within the rooms that were demolished. You were not intending to preserve an historic monument, but to make a fake version, a replica."

"What would be the difference!" Longman snapped.

"I think I see precisely why you are not on the committee," Tommy said wryly.

Longman glowered at him.

"We are not here about the pavilion," Clara said, aiming to defuse the situation. "We are here about the untimely death of William Hershel."

Longman folded his arms across his chest and glared at her.

"What happened to him?"

"The night of the royal gala, William ended up in a ditch in the countryside with a head injury. He died from the cold before he was found," Clara elaborated. "He could not have reached that ditch on foot. He must have either driven himself or been driven there. Which brings us to the matter of his car being missing."

"I know nothing about his car," Longman said quickly. "I don't care to drive."

"But you did know William?" Clara pressed him.

"As an acquaintance," Longman shrugged. "William attended the Friends of the Performing Arts events frequently and I talked to him here and there."

"You were not friends?" Tommy checked.

"No," Longman snorted. "We had nothing in common. He didn't attend the functions because he was interested in the performing arts. He was there because Stacy Freeman asked him."

"What were you arguing about that night?" Clara asked.

Longman shrugged.

"I don't think I remember."

"Everyone remembers arguments they have had, old man," Tommy said in a warning rumble.

Longman was not easily intimidated.

"It was probably about his behaviour," he said diffidently.

"His behaviour?" Clara asked in surprise.

"Why yes. He came with Miss Freeman, then the next thing he was dancing with another girl. Miss Addison. I remember thinking how uncouth such behaviour was."

"Miss Freeman went home with a headache and was quite happy for William to return to the gala," Clara commented.

"That doesn't mean he should have done it. Stacy is too generous of heart if you ask me. He should not have returned to the party alone," Longman was unmoved.

"You like Miss Freeman," Tommy observed.

Longman almost did not reply at first.

"My feelings for Miss Freeman are private," he said. "She is a decent girl. Got a sensible head on her shoulders. I value that, as any right-thinking man would."

"And William casting her aside, seemingly without a thought, made you angry," Clara remarked, beginning to understand. "It was bad enough to be jealous of him, but then to see how little he cared about Stacy, it made you angry."

"I said I will not discuss my feelings concerning Miss Freeman. I merely was reminding a young man that he ought to have a little more respect for his regular dancing partner," Longman gave the impression that this was his last word on the matter.

Clara did not doubt his statement. It was a logical reaction to William being with another woman, seeing as it seemed Longman had feelings for Miss Freeman.

"What did William say in response?" Clara asked him.

"Some nonsense about doing nothing wrong," Longman shrugged. "The sort of thing young men with limited morals always say."

"Did you see Mr Martin, that night?" Clara asked next.

Her change of subject caused Longman to momentarily be thrown. He had been expecting more questions about William Hershel. He hesitated. Maybe it was because he had been thrown off his train of thought, or maybe it was something else.

"Now you mention it, I think I saw Mr Martin wandering towards his office about midnight. I know him quite well, as we are both members of the Maxwell Music Hall Preservation Board. I called out to him, but he barely acknowledged me. That was Martin for you."

"Mr Martin was also attacked that night and sadly has passed away," Clara continued. "I do not suppose you noticed anything odd that night? Or maybe witnessed any trouble?"

"No!" Longman said, looking appalled. "Dead? That cannot be. Martin did not have an enemy in the world!"

"What time did you leave the party?" Tommy asked. "It went on quite late I understand."

"I left shortly after I saw Martin," Longman stated. "Actually, I was going to fetch my coat when I saw him, I believe. I was home before one in the morning and warm in my bed."

"You knew Mr Martin, what were his political leanings?" Clara asked.

"That is a peculiar question," Longman snapped.

She had hoped he would not pick up on the odd change of direction, though it was a slim chance.

"It is one I must ask," Clara said.

"Well, I have no answer for you," Longman replied. "As far as I could tell, he did not care for politics."

"Was he friendly with William Hershel?" Clara asked next.

"They knew of each other, but what would that matter?" Longman was becoming agitated.

"It would seem probable that both men were killed by the same assailant," Clara explained. "That they both were attacked around the same time does not seem a likely coincidence."

"I already told you everything I know," Longman puttered. "If you want to know more about them, talk to William's parents or Miss Freeman. I really only knew them both in passing."

Mr Longman was trying to hustle them towards the door. They had outstayed their tentative welcome as it was, and they consented to leaving.

The front door was snapped shut behind them as they stood in the front garden.

"I think I see why you did not want him on the committee," O'Harris said.

"I did not realise I had offended him so by my decision," Clara was amused. "Still, some people are very sensitive about these things."

"Where next?" Tommy asked.

"I think we need to go back to the Hershels," Clara said sadly.

Chapter Fifteen

Clara repeatedly ran over in her head how to explain to Mr and Mrs Hershel that their son appeared to have been involved in a bomb plot without finding an answer that satisfied her. There was no good way to explain this affair to them, and the reaction she had received from Mrs Silverwood would likely seem nothing compared to the reaction she would get from the grieving parents. She was not looking forward to the meeting.

As they arrived back at the Hershel house, a woman was walking up the garden path. She stopped at the sound of a car pulling up and turned to look in their direction. She was older than Clara by at least a decade but there was something remarkably striking about her features. She was nearly a mirror of William Hershel and she had to be his sister Annabelle.

Clara left the car as quickly as she could without appearing to be in haste. She would like to have a moment to speak to Annabelle without her parents overhearing. Annabelle had not moved and was watching her with curiosity as she came towards her.

"Would you be Miss Fitzgerald?" Annabelle asked before Clara could speak.

"I am," Clara said. "Might you be Miss Annabelle Hershel?"

Annabelle smiled and presented her hand to Clara.

"Delighted to meet you, though the circumstances are not all that pleasant. I have read about your endeavours in the newspaper from time to time. I admire a woman getting out there and making her mark."

Clara was rather invigorated by the praise. After a trying day, it was just the sort of thing she needed to hear to spur her on and rejuvenate her energy.

"This is my brother, Tommy Fitzgerald and our friend Captain O'Harris," Clara added as the two men appeared behind her.

"I am the chauffeur," O'Harris grinned. "It is easier than the detective business."

"O'Harris is too modest," Clara corrected. "I am glad you know who I am and why I am here, Annabelle. I wanted to talk to you about your brother if you have a moment?"

"Of course, come inside," Annabelle said, then she noticed Clara's hesitation. "My parents are not currently at home, if that is your concern."

"I would like to speak to you on a delicate matter and it would be easier without fear of being overheard," Clara admitted. "I need to talk to your parents as well, but the matter needs to be broached… sensitively."

Annabelle was astute enough to know exactly what she was saying.

"My mother may react badly to what it is you have to say," she nodded. "I know what she is like, especially when it comes to William. He was the youngest and therefore the baby of the family. She doted on him. My older brother Micah has always been a disappointment to my parents. William was the complete opposite, and they placed such hopes in him for the future."

Annabelle paused, a cold wind briskly whipping around them and reminding them the weather was still game for a few larks before the Spring finally arrived. She shivered.

"Please, come inside. It is appalling talking out here. No one is home, we shall have the house to ourselves," Annabelle pointed to the house and then wandered up the path towards it.

They followed, the cold getting too much even for Clara's usually iron resolve. They were soon in the sitting room waiting for the fire in the hearth to become hot enough to heat them through. Annabelle insisted on making them tea, departing for the kitchen, and preparing it herself and then returning with everything on a tray.

"I told you the house was empty," she said to them. "Our housekeeper only works in the mornings."

She placed down the tray and began to pour for them.

"Now, what is this delicate matter you have to ask me about in private?"

Clara braced herself. Annabelle seemed open and sensible, the sort of person who would not shoot the messenger, but you never knew how people would react to the suggestion their brother might have been making bombs.

"William was studying chemistry?" Clara began, the question an opening line because she knew the answer.

"Yes," Annabelle answered.

"Did he ever mention being friendly with Mr Martin of the Maxwell Music Hall? Perhaps that they shared an interest in chemistry?"

"No," Annabelle replied, frowning. "I don't think

they even knew each other. I know Mr Martin quite well, as the Friends have a number of events at his music hall every year. He is most accommodating."

"Mr Martin was attacked and killed the same night as your brother died," Clara said bluntly.

Annabelle's hand shook as she started at the news, and she nearly spilled tea from her cup.

"Attacked?" she said in a whisper.

"Stabbed, to be precise," Clara explained. "He managed to make it home and he died in his bed from the injuries. I do not believe that it was a coincidence both men died that night after being at the music hall."

Annabelle was too shaky to keep her cup steady now and she put it down in the saucer speedily.

"Am I correct in saying you are suggesting both Mr Martin and my brother were murdered that night by the same person?"

"I think that a strong possibility," Clara said. "The complication is how the two deaths are connected and why the men had to die. We do have some insight into the possible reason behind Mr Martin's death. Within Mr Martin's home were found the paraphernalia for making bombs."

She had stilled herself, not knowing the reaction she would receive and expecting the worst. Annabelle was too bemused by the words to know how to respond at first. It was one of those times when bad news seemed so absurd it was difficult to take it in and process it. Annabelle had to consider for a long time before she could speak.

"Mr Martin made bombs?"

"It would seem so," Clara said. "He had chemical burns to his fingertips from the process. Your brother was studying chemistry."

Clara did not have to go further. Annabelle smiled strangely; her eyes darkened.

"My brother would never hurt anyone."

"Mrs Silverwood said the same thing about her brother, Mr Martin," Tommy pointed out.

"I don't care what she said," Annabelle's face was fierce. "I know my brother. He would never do something like build a bomb. It would be anathema to him. He loved peace. He loved goodness and kindness. He was a generous, gentle soul. I vouch my life upon that!"

"We do not want to argue over the matter with you," Clara said, aiming to calm her. "We just want to discover how these two things are connected, and we also want to know who else was involved."

"Who else?" Annabelle asked sharply.

"The bomb Mr Martin built was not at his house. Someone took it, perhaps the same person who put a knife in his back," Clara said.

"Maybe the same person who left your brother to die in a ditch," Tommy added. "We are just trying to work out how this all occurred and who is ultimately responsible."

Annabelle was breathing in short, staggered breaths, hyperventilating a little. This was all too bizarre and horrible.

"I don't know anything," she said. "Not about bombs. Not about why William was in that ditch."

"You said you knew Mr Martin?" Tommy recalled. "Tell us about him. Did he ever say or do anything that suggested he was angry about something going on in our country?"

Annabelle frowned.

"Mr Martin talked about the music hall. It was all that obsessed him," she said.

"What were his political views?" Clara asked.

"I didn't think he had any," Annabelle shrugged. "He was not someone who talked about politics, and he probably would not have mentioned the subject to a woman, in any case."

"Did you see him the night of the gala?" Clara continued.

"Briefly," Annabelle nodded. "He was there when we arrived to prepare for the guests. Mr Martin always worked long hours. I saw him wandering around in the back corridors when I was going past at one point."

"What was he doing?" Clara asked.

"He was walking to his office, I think," Annabelle said, confused as to why such a thing mattered.

"Did you see him with anyone?" Clara persisted.

Annabelle shook her head.

"I don't remember seeing him with anyone."

"What about Asher Lightman?" Tommy asked.

"What about him?" Annabelle said, her tone changing.

"He had an argument with your brother that night," Tommy explained.

Annabelle narrowed her eyes.

"Asher Lightman is someone I prefer to keep my distance from. He is arrogant and rude, to name just a couple of his finer qualities. His presence on the Friends' committee is a constant source of irritation for me and the main reason why William refused to join the Friends and only attended parties when he was invited by Miss Freeman."

"William and Asher did not get along?" Tommy wanted more.

"William despised Asher. He thought he was out only for himself and for money. Well, there was one other thing he is out for. He is desperate for a wife, and he joins all these societies and committees to meet eligible women."

"Really?" O'Harris said in bemused surprise. "I had not thought that something a person would do."

Annabelle nodded at him knowingly.

"That is exactly how Asher thinks," she said. "He wants someone to look after him and be a pretty thing on his arm. He was terribly jealous of William being with Miss Freeman."

"We gathered that impression," Clara confirmed. "Miss Freeman had to go home early because of a headache, but William returned to the party without her. Mr Lightman tells us he accosted William about dancing with another girl."

"Lightman, as I said, is uncouth," Annabelle sighed. "I suppose he is glad my brother is dead, and his path now clear to court Miss Freeman."

They seemed to have come no further forward. Lightman's story about arguing over Miss Freeman was confirmed by Annabelle's explanation and they had no seeming connection between William and Mr Martin, except for their shared knowledge of chemistry and the fact they had both died on the same night.

"You are still wondering if my brother was some sort of anarchist," Annabelle guessed. "Why don't I show you his room? Maybe something in there will give you a better idea of what sort of person he was."

Annabelle rose and escorted them upstairs and along a corridor. She showed them into a bedroom that was somewhat disorderly. It was stuffed with the jumble of boyhood belongings and adult trappings that often collide in the room of someone who is on the cusp of manhood. A shaving kit was awkwardly bundled onto a shelf next to a school certificate in a frame. Books on chemistry and advanced mathematics were piled next to adventure novels. The scene was a mishmash, a transformation from youth to manhood.

"William was meant to go back to university next week," Annabelle said sadly, she had picked up a chemistry book and was thumbing through it absently. "I still cannot get my head around all this."

She sat heavily on the bed as they took a look around the room. There was nothing that jumped out at them as being the hallmark of a bomber. There were a lot of old notebooks and letters from William's latter schooldays and his time at university. Clara paused to read several of the letters. They offered her an insight into a young man who liked his work, who was ambitious and engaging. There was nothing to suggest he had controversial politic leanings.

"Where did William stand on such things as socialism?" Tommy asked Annabelle.

"I don't suppose he gave it much thought," she replied. "My brother was interested in chemistry and that was it. Pretty much everything else passed him by."

There was a sound at that moment of the front door opening and closing with a sharp bang. Annabelle looked surprised and jumped off the bed to see who had arrived at the house.

"Oh, its Micah," she said, glancing down the stairs, then, louder, to her brother. "Micah, you are home early?"

"Nothing much of interest was happening," a male voice called back.

Clara was curious about Micah Hershel. She had heard a lot from his parents and sister about his wastrel nature, it was enough to paint a vague picture of him, but rather one-sided. She followed Annabelle to the landing to take a look at this man who had earned his family's disregard.

Micah spied her as she moved next to Annabelle.

"Hello," he said, his eyes noticeably lighting up.

"Micah, this is Miss Fitzgerald, the detective father hired," Annabelle said, annoyed by his sudden and clearly visceral interest in their guest.

"You are not what I expected from a detective," Micah said cheerfully. "In fact, you are nothing like Asher described."

Micah laughed.

"Asher Lightman?" Clara asked. "You know him."

"We end up in a lot of the same places," Micah nodded. "He really was not as flattering as he should have been when mentioning you."

"Micah, mind your manners," Annabelle scolded her brother. "Miss Fitzgerald is not here to be ogled by you. She is trying to find out what happened to William."

Micah snorted.

"William fell in a ditch and died of the cold," he said dismissively. "He was probably drunk. If I had done that, no one would have much cared."

"You seem a little drunk yourself, Mr Hershel," Clara observed.

Micah was unsteady on his feet and there was a slight slur to the edge of his words. He glared at her.

"People say stupid things," he snorted again. "Why would I be drunk this early, huh?"

Chuckling to himself at his own ironic logic, he stumbled off towards one of the front rooms, thudding occasionally into a wall along the way.

"And so, you have met my brother Micah," Annabelle shut her eyes and tried to pretend none of what had just occurred had really happened. "I am sorry about him. He has been a rotten egg for as long as I can remember. Sometimes I try to picture where it all started to go wrong, but I never succeed."

"I did not take offence," Clara smiled at her.

"It is terrible, but he is right, if he had been the one in the ditch, I am not sure I would have really cared," Annabelle ran a hand over her weary eyes. "I think I would have considered it inevitable."

"I think I should leave you in peace," Clara said. "You have helped us as much as you could, but if something springs to mind, or something occurs, you can contact me at any time."

Annabelle nodded, seeming heavy with the weight

of everything. Clara felt deeply sorry for her.

Chapter Sixteen

They regrouped at the Fitzgeralds' home. The situation had become darker than any of them had imagined it could and they were all a little shellshocked by the experience. Annie watched them enter the house with deep concern upon her face.

"What has happened?" she asked.

Clara began to give her an abbreviated version of the events of the day. Annie listened intently, her look of concern growing deeper with each passing moment. When Clara had finished, she was silent a while.

"Why would anyone think blowing up the King was a good idea?" she said at last. "What do they hope to achieve."

"Anarchy, mainly," O'Harris answered her. "That is all these people think about. Disrupting the law of the land, making waves to draw attention. Perhaps they think removing the King will bring a new order to the country, something more like a republic, such as France."

Annie shuddered at this notion.

"I would hate to be a republic," she declared,

though she only had a vague idea what a republic actually was. "I think you need a good dinner to console you all. You look exhausted. There is a mutton pie nearly ready, and I cooked a fruit cake earlier. I shall make custard and we shall have it as a proper dessert."

"Thank you, Annie," Clara smiled at her friend. "That sounds most agreeable."

They retreated to the dining room while Annie went about her chores in the kitchen.

"I am still thinking about William Hershel's car," O'Harris said once they were seated. "It has to have been taken somewhere."

"Nothing in William's room indicated he had dangerous politic inclinations," Tommy added. "I saw nothing to suggest he was interested in making bombs or blowing up monarchs. That is the part that is troubling me."

"He may have had somewhere else he kept those sorts of items," Clara told him. "I think it might be worth making contact with his university and see if they can tell us more about William. He may have joined some student organisations with political leanings."

"Universities are the sorts of places where young people debate notions they would otherwise not feel free to discuss. More than one revolution began among students," Tommy said, not expanding on precisely which revolutions he was referring to.

"I want to speak to William's friends and his tutors," Clara continued. "People he would have talked more freely to than his parents or sister. Maybe someone among them will give us an insight into what drove him to this."

They paused as Annie appeared with their dinner.

"Were you discussing something I should not know about?" she asked at the sudden silence.

"No," Clara shook her head. "We had just come to a point in our conversation where no one knew what more to say."

"I know what to say," Annie said, taking them by surprise. "Later tonight, we need to go out."

"Out, Annie, at night?" Tommy raised an eyebrow at her because Annie rarely left the house after dark, she saw no reason for it.

"There is a meeting we ought to attend," she added. "It will give you some insight into all this, maybe even present some suspects."

"What sort of meeting?" Clara asked. As far as she knew the sort of groups Annie might belong to involved baking cakes or knitting, not the sort of place you would expect potential bomb makers to lurk.

"The Brighton Anarchists' Society," Annie told them without a qualm. "Before you ask, I am not an anarchist and have no intention of becoming one. But my friend Mabel is."

"Mabel?" Tommy said. "The verger's wife?"

Annie nodded.

"Mabel is a first-class cake maker, but I suspect she spends too much time in her kitchen thinking. It is not good for her, and I tell her so, but I can attest that when you are in the rhythm of baking it is easy for the mind to start wandering. I think about all sorts of things while making my cakes. Fortunately, my thoughts are happily mundane. Mabel, on the other hand, has started to think about politics."

"Isn't anarchism all about rejecting authority including that of God?" O'Harris asked her.

"Well, Mabel says you don't have to take the whole thing seriously, anarchism, I mean. She says like all groups you join, there are bits you agree with and bits you don't," Annie shrugged.

"Does the verger know of his wife's interests?" Tommy asked.

"Mabel's husband really does not mind if it gets her out of the house making new friends. He worries she is lonely," Annie answered. "Honestly, how can a person be lonely when they are capable of making such fine cakes?"

"I couldn't begin to surmise," Clara said, feeling bemused. "Mabel told you all about these meetings?"

"She tried to recruit me," Annie explained casually. "I told her anything that involved disorder was like fingernails down a chalkboard to me. She likes to dabble in these radical things, it gives her an outlet. I think she gets very maudlin at times, especially in the winter."

"Quite," Tommy said, trying to picture the plump, homely Mabel he had seen chatting with Annie in the kitchen as a fiery anarchist keen to destroy the state and all the trappings that went with it.

"Last summer, one of the meetings was interrupted by the police," Annie went on. "There had been complaints from the neighbours about the noise and rabble-rousing. Mabel tried to get them to arrest her, practically begged them. She was very upset when they refused."

"Mabel perhaps needs a different hobby," O'Harris puckered his brow. "Maybe one that involves being outdoors in the fresh air, like hill walking, or beach combing."

"Give it another few months and Mabel will be bored with it all," Annie said dismissively. "However, in her efforts to recruit me she has supplied me with the dates and places for forthcoming meetings and tonight one is being held at a house not far from here. We should attend, because if anyone knows about plots to blow up a member of the royal family it will be the anarchists."

In that regard, Annie had a point.

"That is a brilliant idea, Annie," Clara said. "It may

just be the new lead we need."

Annie was delighted to have been useful

After consuming a hearty seam-busting meal, the company could easily have dozed off before the fire in the parlour. Instead, they set out for the meeting of the anarchists, Annie leading the way. She provided directions to O'Harris, and he drove them to a respectable-looking street lined with houses. They were nothing grand or remarkable, the sort of place shopkeepers and bank clerks resided, certainly not the kind of place you expected to find anarchists. Clara had been imagining a seedy backstreet where people with no work and a grudge against the world that had let them down hung out. She realised she had failed to appreciate just how widespread a movement such as anarchism could be.

They left the car a little way down the road and headed along to No.16, a house that looked no more like the hotbed of political rebellion than any other down this road. Annie knocked on the door and was swiftly greeted by an older man with a balding head and a paunch that was causing the buttons of his waistcoat to bulge.

He did not recognise her, and a question formed on his face. Quickly, Annie produced a slip of cardboard from her handbag.

"Mabel has been wanting me to attend for weeks," she said, showing the man the card. "I finally decided to come along."

The man nodded at the card, but then his eyes moved to the others behind her.

"There was nothing on the card to suggest I had to come alone," Annie said firmly. "You would not expect me to come out at this hour without company?"

Before the man could respond, Annie was moving past him and into a front room that was bright with gas lighting and noisy with the voices of a dozen or so people. Clara was impressed. The man at the door threshold did not know what to say. Clara smiled at him and moved to follow Annie, Tommy and O'Harris were hard on her heels. The man at the door, their host presumably, gave up the fight and closed the door, following them into the front room with a confused expression on his face.

Annie was being hugged by a short woman Clara vaguely recalled as her friend Mabel. Clara surveyed the room, taking in the people present. They mostly looked rather ordinary, rather mundane, not people you would suspect of harbouring malicious political thoughts. There were two fellows stood in the far corner of the room who caught her eye. One was scrawny and dressed shabbily, with a wild beard and eyes that bulged. The other was muttering to himself and scowling at the room. He constantly tapped his fingers across the back of one hand and if he happened to make eye contact with anyone he looked away at once. The two men stood out as much as anything because they did not seem to want to make this a social event. Everyone else was enjoying a drink and a natter as if this was just another gathering.

Clara wondered how the meeting would unfold, but soon discovered that anarchists – at least in this group – did not believe in being formal about their gatherings. No one stood at the front and called the supposed meeting to order or listed topics of discussion or even brought up news the group needed to hear. Instead, people milled and talked. Admittedly, the talk was largely of a pollical nature, but it still seemed more like a drinks party to Clara's way of thinking.

"This is anarchy," Tommy whispered to his sister with an ironic grin.

She gave him a wry smile.

"I suggest we split up and talk to people," she

replied, already with an idea in mind who she wanted to talk to.

They separated and did their best to insert themselves into the various conversations occurring in the room. Clara drifted across the floor, pausing here and there, but with every intention of ending up near the two men who stuck out like sore thumbs. Neither man seemed inclined to become involved in small talk with the others. She wondered why they even bothered to be there.

She moved around a woman who was speaking volubly about the price of onions and how this was a sign of the government's nefarious intentions. The woman suddenly thrust out her arm with her drink clutched in her hand and Clara had to stumble backwards or be punched in the face. She felt her foot catch on the rug and for a perilous moment she thought she would trip over, then a strong hand caught her arm and steadied her.

"Thanks," she said, looking around and discovering it was the young man with the beard and bulging eyes who had come to her aid.

"M... Mrs M... M... Mullen forgets h... h... herself sometimes," he said, revealing a significant stutter that was perhaps the reason he was avoiding conversation.

"People become highly charged when it comes to politics," Clara said lightly.

"The price of onions is not politics," the second young man, the one who could not meet your eyes, said in a deep voice.

"V... V... Victor gets upset a... a... about p... p... people not t... t... t... taking this seriously," the bearded young man explained torturously.

Clara was having to bite her tongue to avoid finishing his sentences for him. She doubted he would appreciate that.

"I'm Clara," she held out her hand.

This was the point where many a man quailed and became aghast at shaking a woman's hand. To his credit, the bearded man did not flinch. He took her hand and shook.

"Eric B... B... Barnes," he said.

"Nice to meet you," Clara replied. "This is my first meeting. I am still getting my head around it all. It is exciting."

"Not meant to be exciting," Victor muttered.

Eric gave him a nudge.

"B... be nice."

Victor sneered at him, then mellowed.

"This isn't really an anarchist meeting," he told Clara.

"Isn't it?" Clara pulled a disappointed face. "Are we not going to discuss tactics for bringing down the government? Or at least the local county council? They rejected plans to allow football on the green again, you know? How can anyone control an open piece of land like that and say what can and cannot be done upon it?"

Clara was hoping she was sounding like someone who might be an anarchist in the making. She sensed Victor and Eric were the real deal when it came to anarchy and that everyone else in this room was not going to be much use to her.

"They never discuss anything seriously," Victor sighed.

Clara did a good impression of looking forlorn.

"T... th... this is just a... a... a starting point," Eric explained to her. "W... w... we come alo... alo... along to s... sp... sp..."

Eric shut his eyes as his vocal chords failed him. Victor took pity on his friend.

"Me and Eric come along so that if anyone with a real desire for anarchy attends a meeting like this, we can point them in the right direction. That way we prevent the wrong sort of people from getting involved in the real business of anarchy."

Clara understood. This was a filtering pool, sorting out those just looking for something to pass the time from those who truly were interested in the serious aspects of anarchy.

"I can quite understand," Clara nodded. "Not everyone here would appreciate the true nature of anarchy or what it takes to make a stand."

Victor was nodding. Eric was curious.

"W... w... why are you h... h... here?"

"For a few reasons," Clara answered. "Wanting to know more about the movement. Feeling a need to do something about our society but not sure how. Frustrated by the limitations within politics for women. All that."

"W... what ab... about authority?"

"What about it?" Clara asked. "It is a means to keep us all in our little boxes. Trust me, I take no one in authority seriously."

That was quite true.

"I love this town. I want it to thrive. I am not sure how it can under the current system," she pretended to be troubled.

Her pretence was working. Eric and Victor were opening up.

"You will not find what you need at this meeting," Victor said. "It is all mindless talk. If you really want to know about anarchy, you need to come to our party meeting."

He fumbled in his pocket and produced a slip of paper.

"Tomorrow night. Come alone and tell no one. You can keep a secret, Clara?"

Clara smiled at him.

"Oh, I most certainly can."

Chapter Seventeen

It was a new day and Clara felt ready to face the challenges ahead. There was still a gaping hole in her knowledge about the deaths of Mr Martin and William Hershel, but she also had a way forward and that was what mattered. O'Harris arrived with his car just after nine and they set out first to comb the streets of Brighton looking for a red Vauxhall. There were only two garages in the town, most car owners endeavouring to do repairs and maintenance themselves – as O'Harris said, cars were fickle beasts and could break down on a whim, so it was best to know how to deal with them yourself. They called at both garages to ask if someone had brought in a car matching the description of William's motor. When that failed, they asked if any cars had been brought in with damage as if they had been in an accident, linking to one theory that William had been involved in a car accident out in the countryside and dumped in a ditch to mask the fact. Once again, the answer was no. One garage was working on a car with a smashed windscreen, but that had been caused by a flying branch whipped at the car during the storm. Parts of the branch had still been wedged into the metal frame of the windscreen when the car was brought in for repairs.

Clara was satisfied by the explanation for the car's misfortune and decided that the motoring accident theory was rapidly looking untenable. She suggested they next go back to Mr Martin's house, to see if further clues could be found there.

A constable had been left at the house, told to remain discreetly inside and to answer the door if anyone called. Park-Coombs was hopeful that someone connected to the bomb making would turn up at the house and give themselves away. Clara thought this was being overly optimistic, especially as Mr Martin had obviously been murdered by his cohorts, but at least it meant she could easily gain access to the house when she arrived.

"Anyone of interest been around?" Clara asked the constable who opened the door.

He had stripped off his tunic jacket and removed his helmet, clearly making himself at home and feeling this was a nice reprieve from walking the beat. A hint of toasted breadcrumbs on his lapel indicated he had made himself breakfast.

"No one has been around except for the milkman," the constable explained.

Clara nodded; she had expected as much.

"I wanted to take a look around?" she said.

The constable indicated that was fine and allowed them in, then he went back to the sitting room where he was drinking a cup of tea and reading a cheap novel. He seemed to be rather enjoying his job as doorman.

"Where do we begin?" Tommy asked.

Clara had to admit she was not sure. She imagined

that between the police and the army the house had been thoroughly searched. What they were looking for was anything that might have been missed as being inconsequential and to get a better feel for Mr Martin the man.

"We shall start in the kitchen," Clara said, as it was as good as anywhere to begin. "Maybe we can learn more about bomb making along the way."

The kitchen was clearly the home of a dedicated bachelor. It had an arrangement of pots and pans sitting on a small dresser, but the cobwebs and dust gathering upon them proved they were unused. A small saucepan and a frying pan were sitting on the draining board next to a deep sink and it appeared that these comprised Mr Martin's cooking equipment. The kitchen table had a pile of old newspapers upon it, Clara guessed these were used to line it when Martin was making up his bombs. The table had been wiped down at some point, but it was old and had a deep grain within which it was noticeable flecks of black powder had gathered.

Tommy was busy inspecting some cupboards and produced an intriguing toolbox that contained all manner of bespoke tools Mr Martin must have made for himself, such as the screwdriver with a right-angle head to enable it to reach difficult spaces, and a square of metal, with the centre removed, which seemed to be a template for something.

"Not quite the tools you expect to find in the possession of a music hall manager," Tommy remarked before he replaced the box.

"I wonder what the caretaker will make of all this?" O'Harris mused as they inspected the pantry with its false wall.

"I think he will be shocked and upset," Clara replied. "He may also refuse to believe it, just like Mrs Silverwood."

The pantry was singularly empty of food. Clara had never seen a place so bare before, at least not in the home of someone who could afford to feed themselves well. She was beginning to see why the pantry had drawn the attention of the police. Anyone with a sharp mind would notice there was something amiss about the place. However, the pantry had already revealed its secret and there was nothing more to be found.

Clara suggested they head upstairs and look for some personal papers Mr Martin might have left behind, and which could give them an insight into people they might speak to about him. Mr Martin's bedroom had a forlorn look to it. The bed still had rumpled sheets upon it and there was a rusty red patch on the mattress where Mr Martin's wound had bled. Tommy paused with a frown on his face. He was thinking how Mr Martin had somehow managed to make it all the way home, despite his injury. Had entered his house, hoping to be safe, locking the door behind him. Then limped up to his bedroom, tended to his wound as best he could and laid down on the bed exhausted. Slowly, the shortness of breath he had been putting down to the adrenaline rush and the exertion of getting home grew worse. He had started to struggle to breathe and could do nothing about it except lay there. There were few good ways to die, but Tommy was finding the way Martin had passed especially grim.

He felt a hand on his shoulder and looked around to see Clara was there. She had noticed his expression and was concerned.

"I was thinking too hard," Tommy told her. "About how he lay in that bed slowly finding it harder and harder to breathe."

"Your pity is admirable," O'Harris said from across the room. "But the man was making bombs and the type of death and suffering he intended to inflict on others rather limits my sympathy for him."

Clara squeezed her brother's arm.

"Try not to think on it," she said. "We have work to do. Mr Martin is now out of pain and suffering, that is what we must remember."

Tommy accepted her words and then started to look around the room. The police had taken anything they felt might be relevant to finding Martin's associates, but Clara knew how men thought and how it was possible they might overlook something. She started to remove the drawers of a dresser.

"What are you doing?" O'Harris asked.

"These drawers are full to bursting," Clara indicated one she had pulled out which was full of programmes from past events at the music hall. "When a drawer is like that and someone tries to put more stuff in, what often happens is things get shoved right to the back and fall behind the drawers, like this."

She had removed the last drawer and sitting in the space beneath was a slip of paper. She picked it up.

"What is it?" Tommy asked her.

"It is an address," Clara said, showing him as he came over.

"It could be anything," Tommy shrugged. "Mr Martin must have collected lots of addresses through his work."

"Yes," Clara agreed with a smile, "but this address happens to match the one I was given last night by those two friendly anarchists."

She took from her pocket a slip of paper with the identical address on it. It even appeared to have been written in the same hand as the one she had received from Victor.

"Those two looked shifty," O'Harris said, troubled.

He did not like the idea of Clara going to an anarchist meeting without them, but as she had pointed out, the invitation was for her and her alone.

If she brought them along people would become agitated, perhaps even refuse to talk to her. This was something she would have to do by herself.

"We have a connection between the anarchists and Mr Martin," Clara elaborated. "Whether that means anything I don't know."

"You mean the anarchists might not be plotting to blow up the King?" Tommy said with a precise amount of sarcasm.

"I don't think we can assume anything," Clara told him. "Just because you are drawn to anarchy does not mean you are also prepared to blow people up."

"I suppose that is a fair point," O'Harris admitted.

"Well, I have found no address book or anything else to give us a hint of who Martin might be working with," Tommy shrugged. "This is as much a lead as we have."

They could agree on that. However, it was only prudent to finish their search of the house and so they inspected the bathroom and the second upstairs bedroom.

"I am wondering where Mr Martin was attacked," Clara said when they regrouped once more on the landing. "There are no signs of it happening downstairs. The house was locked up when Mrs Silverwood arrived. The music hall is about fifteen minutes from here when walking."

"That is still a long way to go after being stabbed," O'Harris said. "Though not impossible. I knew of men in the war who walked miles with severe injuries looking for help."

"An animal instinct takes over," Tommy agreed. "You just focus on where you need to get to and everything else doesn't matter."

"No one saw him leaving the music hall," Clara continued mulling over the matter. "Asher Lightman said he saw Mr Martin around midnight. He was obviously not there to see that the Friends left as they had agreed they would at three in the morning, because as we know the caretaker turned up in the morning and found people still present. So, we can assume that something occurred between midnight and three, but where did it happen?"

"The music hall was busy with people," Tommy said thoughtfully. "Lots of potential witnesses, but no one saw or heard anything so perhaps it happened in the back yard?"

"We should go back to the music hall and see if we can find any traces of blood," Clara responded. "It is very odd no one saw or heard anything. It is not a place I would pick to murder a man."

"On the other hand, it was probably the fact the music hall was busy that enabled Mr Martin to escape to his home," O'Harris suggested. "His attacker rushed him and stabbed him but was too worried at being seen to hang around and see that he was really dead."

"Good point," Clara nodded. "Just think if Mr Martin had gone to the police or the hospital rather than come home, he might be still alive and able to tell us what happened."

"I don't know," Tommy said solemnly. "A punctured lung is a nasty business, and probably Martin was too concerned about being discovered as involved in a bomb plot to reach out to the authorities. If he had survived, he would have faced a lot of questions and found himself in a great deal of trouble."

"He chose to take a chance and come home instead," O'Harris agreed. "Not realising his lung was punctured."

"Well, it is a sorry business all told," Clara sighed, heading back down the stairs.

She was just reaching the hallway when Inspector Park-Coombs entered the house. He was talking to a man Clara did not recognise but looked like someone in authority. This man caught sight of her and glared in her direction. Park-Coombs cottoned on to her presence a moment later.

"Clara," he said with a hint of panic. "This is the Chief Inspector. Chief Inspector this is Miss Fitzgerald, an independent investigator who is assisting in the matter."

"You have a civilian helping you?" the Chief Inspector said in an angry tone.

Clara sallied forth.

"Chief Inspector," she held out her hand to him. "I am involved in the town's welfare and maintenance. I became aware of this matter by coincidence, and I have been tasked with ensuring that none of this affair becomes public or that anything occurs that would sully the town's reputation. Mr Martin, as you may be aware, was considered an upstanding member of the community and this incident could generate terrible shock and lead to distrust of authority. I shall not see the actions of this man ruin the town. You understand?"

Clara spoke with authority, and it was her tone, rather than anything she said that was powerful. When the Chief Inspector did not immediately shake her hand, she reached out for his and initiated a handshake.

"I am delighted you are here," she said, drawing him to one side. "We must talk. I am deeply concerned about the consequences of this mischief. Have you a moment?"

Clara ushered him towards the kitchen without giving the Chief Inspector a chance to respond. He would end up so hounded by her and on the back foot answering questions about the security of the town, that he would hopefully forget all about the fact she was a civilian interfering in a police crime scene. Park-Coombs breathed a sigh of relief and nodded at the others.

"Clara will have him so bamboozled he won't remember why he was even here," he said with a weak smile.

"Why are you here?" Tommy asked.

"I had to report this all to the Chief Inspector and he has come down to oversee matters," Park-Coombs explained. "He doesn't want to see Brighton become the place where an attempt was made on our monarch's life."

"Ah, but now the King's holiday has been cancelled…" Tommy began, but he was interrupted by the inspector.

"It is not cancelled," he sighed. "I am informed the King has no intention of delaying his trip here. I am charged with making sure he remains safe at all costs."

"He is placing his life in grave danger," O'Harris said in shocked surprise.

"I think the response from the palace was something along the lines that every other day the King receives death threats he ignores, why make an exception for this one?" Park-Coombs groaned miserably.

Chapter Eighteen

The news about the King's insistence on coming to Brighton had made the search for the bomb makers all the more urgent and yet also all the more desperate. They moved to the back parlour to continue talking out of earshot of the Chief Inspector.

"Did you find anything in this house that could assist us?" Tommy asked the inspector.

"Very little that indicated Mr Martin had such tendencies. One of my men found a school chemistry book from 1891 which contained an article on making gunpowder, but it was rather simplistic stuff designed for schoolboys to make miniature fireworks. It was not detailed enough to be the basis for a bomb."

"What about any political material?" O'Harris asked. "Something to indicate Mr Martin's leanings?"

"Nothing," Park-Coombs sighed. "No pamphlets or dubious books, even his newspaper selection was very middle of the road. Nothing that would suggest a person with strong views about the monarchy. We even checked Mr Martin's voting history to be thorough and determined he voted for the Labour party, which is currently in power."

"The election last year was not a clean win for anyone," O'Harris pointed out. "It produced a hung parliament with the liberals supporting Labour. Many people were not happy about the result."

"Yet, from Mr Martin's perspective he got the government he desired," Park-Coombs countered. "I really am at a loss to find a clear motivation for his actions."

"We haven't had much luck with William Hershel, either," Tommy said. "We have spoken to his sister who insists he would not be involved in making bombs. We searched his bedroom but nothing obvious sprang out. We plan to speak with his university tutors and any friends to see if they can shed light on things."

Outside in the hall, they could hear the Chief Inspector returning, Clara having distracted him as long as was possible. He made a huffing noise when he discovered Park-Coombs was not obediently waiting for him in the hallway. Park-Coombs grimaced and then called out where he was. The Chief Inspector appeared in the room with Clara just behind him. From the look on the man's face, a mixture of confusion, outrage, and humility, it seemed Clara had been successful in bringing him down a peg or two.

"Park-Coombs, we have a lot to do. We should get on," the Chief Inspector said. "I want to look over the arrangements you have made for the royal visit. The palace has sent over the King's itinerary, I suppose?"

"It had not arrived when we left the station," Park-Coombs mumbled.

"Then we need to chase it up. We need to know exactly where the King is going to be at all times when he is here. I have no intention of seeing him at all inconvenienced in my constabulary."

The Chief Inspector stormed out of the door, clearly expecting Park-Coombs to follow him. The inspector gave them all a morose smile as he departed. Clara wished she could do more to help him.

"Did the Chief Inspector say anything of use?" Tommy asked his sister.

"He has no more idea about this mess than the rest of us," she answered. "He has received no intelligence to indicate anyone was plotting to blow up the King, and nothing concerning Brighton. I think some of his ire is because this has caught him out of the blue and rather shaken him."

"That does not much help us," Tommy said, finding it hard to feel sorry for the surly Chief Inspector after seeing the way he had cowed Park-Coombs. "What shall we do next?"

"It seems to me," Clara said, "that if Mr Martin kept nothing concerning his political leanings in his own home, he might perhaps have kept such materials at the one other place he spent most of his time."

"The music hall," Tommy understood. "He probably spent more hours there than at home."

"Precisely," Clara nodded. "We need to explain all this to the caretaker, anyway. He is probably worried."

They drove away from the house and towards the music hall. The building had previously seemed a place of happiness and dancing to Clara. Now it seemed sinister and a place of secrets. Clara felt a shudder run down her spine as she thought of the deaths that might have been imagined within by Mr Martin and others. They left the car and went around to the yard to find the caretaker. He proved to be half-heartedly filling a coal scuttle from a small storehouse behind the hall. He jumped when Clara called out to him.

"I never heard you coming," he said, grabbing at the coal shovel which he had dropped in his surprise. "I have so much on my mind, what with Mr Martin still not appearing for work."

Clara knew this was going to be difficult.

"Mr Martin will not be coming back to the music hall," she told the caretaker. "He was attacked the night of the storm and perished in his bed."

The caretaker became very pale, and the coal shovel dropped from his hand yet again.

"You must be mistaken," he said. "Who would hurt Mr Martin?"

"We are trying to figure that out," Tommy added, stepping forward out of fear the man might suddenly collapse.

"I cannot believe it," the caretaker repeated. "Who would do such an evil thing."

He suddenly turned away from them, abandoned the coal scuttle and shovel, and headed for the music hall. They followed him into the kitchen area, where he sat down heavily in a chair at the kitchen table and pulled off his cap. He stared into space, aghast at the news.

Clara moved forward and took a chair on the opposite side of the table.

"Warm tea is good for shock," O'Harris said, channelling Annie in that moment.

He set about making up a pot of tea.

"I cannot fathom it at all," the caretaker said. "He was such a nice man."

"We haven't really had a chance to properly talk," Clara said to him, trying to sound friendly and sympathetic. She needed to distract him from his shock, just for a while, to get him to speak freely. "I don't actually know your name."

"Mr Mitchell," the caretaker replied automatically. "Mr Martin and I used to think that funny. Martin and Mitchell. Like we were a removals firm."

Clara smiled at him.

"You knew Mr Martin a long time?"

"As long as I worked here. Mr Martin took over in 1905 or 1906. The place was in a bad way then. No one had looked into maintaining it at all. The roof was leaking and some of the windows had been broken and never replaced. There was a major damp issue in the cellar."

"The music hall has a cellar?" Clara asked, intrigued.

"Yes," Mitchell replied. "Most people have no idea that this music hall was built on the site of a former house, one of the few that were built in Brighton during the Tudor period. The building had been in near ruins for years, but its cellar was solid brick and substantial. When they built the music hall, they incorporated the old cellar, thinking it could be used for storage. But it is not convenient for the purpose, what with the stairs down to it being so narrow. Mr Martin keeps old paperwork down there."

The caretaker paused.

"Kept," he corrected himself. "This music hall would be nothing without him. He saved it from being demolished. He put his heart and soul into this place."

Clara did not want the caretaker to lose himself in his shock and grief again, not when she had a lot to ask him.

"The night of the gala, what time did you leave Mr Mitchell?" she asked.

Mitchell rubbed at the bridge of his nose.

"It was about six," he said. "I usually leave then. I made sure the fires in the function rooms were lit and put the fireguards across them, that is my last task to make sure no sparks can fly out and start a fire. Then I checked the upstairs rooms to make sure they were secure, and the doors locked, so no guests could wander up there. People do odd things at times, and you can never tell what might occur. Then I said goodnight to Mr Martin and went home."

"Where was Mr Martin?" Clara asked.

"In his office, still working on some papers. I told him not to stay too late and that I would see him in the morning. He gave me this weary little smile and we both knew he was going to be staying longer than he ought to."

"He seemed tired?" Clara asked.

"He worked too hard," Mitchell shrugged. "This place needs a lot of income to keep it running. It was not built of the best materials, and it is a constant battle to keep the place sound and weatherproof."

"Sounds almost as if she should be replaced with something more substantial," O'Harris said as he brought the teapot to the table.

"Mr Martin would be appalled to hear such a thing said. This place is iconic, like the pavilion!"

Clara smiled at Mitchell's defence of the property and the decision not to replace it.

"I am on the Pavilion Committee," she told him. "I know what you mean."

Mr Mitchell relaxed at being around a kindred soul.

"Mr Martin loved this place. He said he would never leave, that he would die here," Mr Mitchell suddenly realised what he had said and frowned. "That cut rather close to the quick."

"Someone saw Mr Martin still here around midnight the night of the gala. Did he often work so late?" Clara said, moving him on before he could dwell too much on the thought.

"That would not be unheard of. I once had the police come knocking at my door, saying there was a light on at the music hall and did I know who was inside. They had checked the doors, but they were all locked. So, I came over with them, let them in and, of course, it was just Mr Martin working away in his office. That was around midnight."

"He was dedicated to this building," Tommy said. "He would hate to see harm come to it."

"Oh yes," Mitchell agreed wholeheartedly. "He told me he would not let anyone take this building away from him. He was very passionate about it all."

"Aside from being overworked, did Mr Martin mention any stresses in his life?" Clara asked. "Perhaps he had had a disagreement with someone?"

She was probing now to see if Mr Mitchell had accidentally picked up on any information relating to the bomb plot.

"Nothing that springs to mind," the caretaker said. "I mean, there were always little disagreements about fees for functions and such like, but nothing dramatic."

"He had not mentioned anyone lurking about the building?" Tommy queried. "Maybe someone who was always around when he was leaving at night."

"No," Mr Mitchell said bleakly. "If he had, I would have come back when he was locking up to make sure he was safe."

He sniffed to himself.

"What will this place do without him?"

Clara patted his hand sympathetically.

"Would you mind if I take a look in Mr Martin's office? There might be something there that would help explain what happened to him?"

The caretaker nodded his head to grant her permission.

"I should have done more," he said miserably.

"There was not more you could do," Clara replied gently.

She left him to drink his tea and get his head around the whole affair. She knew the way to Mr Martin's office and, with Tommy and O'Harris, she began to search through all the paperwork on the desk, in the drawers, and in the filing cabinet set in a corner. O'Harris even kindly poked about in the fire looking for potential scraps of burned paper. They found nothing concerning radical political views or bomb making. In fact, everything was firmly concerned with the running of the music hall and the continued struggle to find enough money to keep it open and to maintain it.

The more Clara looked, the more bills she found, and the majority were unpaid. There were also estimates for work the music hall desperately required, sometimes three or four for the same job, Mr Martin clearly trying to get the best deal. There was a ledger that contained all the income the music hall had made, and it was plain to see as Clara cross-referenced bills and estimates with the money coming in that the music hall was in desperate trouble. Despite Mr Martin's best efforts, the music hall was in chronic debt. She found several invoices sent to people who had hired the hall for events and had then failed to pay and these added to Mr Martin's woes.

Then she found a letter concerning the arrangements for the King's private banquet at the music hall. As she read through it, she realised that Mr Martin had been persuaded to host the event without charging the palace, being encouraged to consider it a patriotic duty. When she looked at the expensive supplies he would have to purchase for the meal, she wondered at where he would find the money. It was a depressing read. The King's banquet could have provided the music hall with desperately needed income, instead it was pushing the place further into the red.

"What I don't understand," Tommy said as he was going through the filing cabinet, "is why Mr Martin would agree to blowing up the King in the place he loved so much, effectively destroying it."

"Maybe he was not intending for the bomb to go off here," O'Harris suggested. "Maybe this was just the catalyst. He was in a position to know about the King's arrival and so he told his comrades about it, but he never intended for the bomb to be used within the music hall. It could be planted in the King's car or carriage, for instance."

Tommy nodded his understanding. Clara was only half listening. She had come across a letter from the trust who had taken over the music hall to save it and who employed Mr Martin. The letter stated bluntly that the trust was not happy about the mounting debt and felt Mr Martin was incompetent in his work. They were firing him, in short. In fact, his employment was due to end immediately after the King's visit, but apparently Mr Martin had told no one and was carrying on as if nothing had occurred.

"Anything?" Tommy asked her.

"Just a letter dismissing Mr Martin," Clara handed over the letter to him.

"He was so dedicated to this place he just couldn't leave," Tommy sighed as he read.

Clara was frowning.

"We should take a look down in this cellar where Martin kept his paperwork. Maybe he left us something there."

Chapter Nineteen

"No one ever comes down here," Mr Mitchell said as he fumbled about for a key to the door of the basement. "Except for the plumber."

"You have plumbing issues?" O'Harris sympathised, he knew the perils of maintaining an old property.

"Well, if you ask me there wasn't an issue," Mr Mitchell sniffed. "I am pretty good with pipes and valves. I can keep most things going. But Mr Martin was insistent there was a fault with the pipes somewhere and the pressure was not right. He said it needed to be investigated by a professional."

Mitchell sounded hurt that his skills had not been given the credit they deserved.

"If you ask me, it was one of Mr Martin's obsessions. He was prone to them, God rest his soul," Mitchell was growing morose again as he thought of the manager. "Sometimes he would get these notions, and nothing would please him. Like when he was convinced there was damp in the upstairs meeting room, and he had me rip up the floorboards seeking the cause. There was never any damp, but he would get these ideas into his head. It was the same with the plumbing. That poor plumber came back time after time looking for a problem that did not exist. He became frustrated in the end. I heard him arguing with Mr Martin down in the basement one day."

"Mr Martin sounds like a man who knew his own mind," Clara remarked. "For better or worse."

"He was certainly that," Mitchell nodded. "When he had a bee in his bonnet, nothing would shake it out."

He finally found the key he wanted and slotted it into the lock on the door. The door was situated in a corridor next to the kitchen and could easily have been mistaken for a cupboard. When it was opened, it revealed a dark rectangle of light that encouraged the view of it being just a storage space. Mr Mitchell reached in and grasped around until his hand fell on a light switch. He clicked it and a moment passed as the lightbulb flickered and then finally agreed to illuminate.

For a second, it still seemed that the space was just a cupboard, then Clara stuck her head inside and discovered that to the right of the door, where the lightbulb cast barely a glimmer, there was a darker space indicating a staircase leading down. It ran parallel with the corridor they stood in and looked to be most inconvenient if you wanted to move something larger than a chair down into the basement.

"Not really designed for ease of use," Clara said.

Mitchell shrugged.

"I suppose the staircase was left over from the previous house and they just built around it," he said. "It is the reason we only store boxes of papers down there. You will want a torch, there is no lighting down below."

He passed Clara a Bakelite torch. She flicked the button on its cylindrical body and a fuzzy beam of light revealed the stone steps of a very old staircase. She could see about two steps in front of her as she went down the stairs cautiously. They were narrow, not even the length of her small feet and she had to walk down sideways to keep her balance. Tommy and O'Harris kept close behind her, seeing as she was the only one with any light.

At the bottom of the staircase there was a sensation of a large space, even though Clara could still only see a few feet ahead of her. She swung the torch around and caught the edges of boxes stacked along the wall. There were a number of them, and Clara felt a little despondent at the thought of having to rummage through them all in the hopes of finding evidence of Mr Martin's anarchist activities.

"We should look for boxes that appear to have been recently disturbed," she suggested. "Unfortunately, we only have this torch."

Tommy was examining the wall near him. He had spied something briefly as the torchlight had drifted over it. He was groping along the wall when his hand landed on something large and with a bulbous body.

"I think there is a lamp here," he said.

Clara swung the torch back in his direction and saw he was correct. An oil lamp was hanging on a nail hammered into the wall. O'Harris had a pack of matches on him, being an occasional smoker, and he lit the lamp. At last, they had a decent light source, and the basement came into view.

"These boxes have finger marks in the dust on them," O'Harris pointed out as he moved the lamp around.

Clara opened the nearest box and found it contained various ledgers from the late 1800s. They were account books, along with a couple of scrapbooks filled with newspaper clippings about the performances held at the music hall.

"That is disappointing," O'Harris said as he glanced

inside. "Why would someone have recently been rummaging through these old books?"

"Maybe Mr Martin was thinking about doing a history of the music hall?" Tommy suggested. "To raise funds, he could publish a pamphlet."

"I think we are failing to look beyond the obvious," Clara smiled at them. "If I was an anarchist and I was keeping secrets down in the basement of the place I worked, I would not have them stored so obviously that a person happening to open a box would glance straight upon them."

She lifted out several ledgers and the scrapbooks. Beneath them there was a magazine, much newer and with a disturbing image of a fist crushing the Union Jack flag printed in black on the front. Clara lifted it out.

"The Anarchist's Journal," she read out the title. "Sounds rather formal for a publication promoting the downfall of the governance of this country as we know it. This issue is from last month."

O'Harris rooted in the box now and produced several further copies of the same magazine. Mr Martin had appeared to be collecting and storing these publications for some time.

"It tells us only he was politically inclined towards anarchism," Tommy said, aiming to be logical. "It does not indicate that he was making bombs."

Clara had reached the bottom of the box and she was back to old ledgers. The journals had been wedged between the account books for 1888 and 1889. A place no one would look.

"Maybe the other boxes contain something similar," she said, indicating further boxes with dusty tops that had been recently touched.

They began to widen their search and it was not long before Tommy made a discovery. In another box containing old ledgers and paperwork from the last century about various concerts, he located another paper that was far more disturbing. The paper was flimsy and thin enough that it could be used for tracing. When he unfolded it, it expanded to the width of this arm span. He laid it on the top of the box, his face drawing into a frown. He had not wanted to see something like this, but he supposed it had also been inevitable. It was what they were looking for, after all.

"It looks like a schematic for a bomb," he said, drawing the attention of the others.

O'Harris peered over his shoulder.

"It is very well drawn," he said. "By a skilled draughtsman."

The plans showed the bomb with a cut away section revealing its inner workings. There were notations and further diagrams dotted around the edges showing specific formulas for the chemical components or elaborating on the detonation system.

"I will confess I don't understand it all," Clara said, reading mathematical calculations that were meaningless to her. "I can see it is a bomb, but the technical details elude me."

"I think it is safe to say that these were built for someone with both mechanical and chemical skill," Tommy said. "Does that sound like Mr Martin?"

"It sounds like William Hershel," O'Harris pointed out. "Perhaps, after all, it was the case that Mr Martin was just offering his kitchen for the use of another. In this case, William who would make the bomb."

Clara had become distracted by another box that was suffering from being overloaded. It had become damp at some point, and this had caused its corners to weaken. It looked as though it had been moved recently and this had split the sides, revealing books within. One book was on the cusp of falling out and she assisted it to see what it was. She found she was holding a book on advanced mechanics. The sort people studied at university. She opened the box and started to dig inside. Beneath the usual cover of ledgers and old paperwork, she found a selection of academic books. They were either concerning engineering or chemistry. One was ominously titled A Student's Guide to the Use of Gunpowder. She had found the library of a bomb maker. There was everything here that Mr Martin needed to learn how to construct a bomb from scratch, as long as he had the capacity to understand it all.

"Mr Martin had secret interests," she revealed the books to the others. "This was how he learned his trade, and it was through the anarchists he had the motivation to build a bomb."

O'Harris looked at the collection, disheartened.

"I find myself asking, why? What drove Mr Martin to think blowing up the King was going to help our nation, but perhaps I am trying to be too sensible about the whole thing. Clearly, he was a man who had strong political leanings."

"We should inform Park Coombs about all this," Clara said. "It at least confirms Martin's intentions, even if it does not supply us with further leads concerning his co-conspirators."

"You know what is bothering me," Tommy said thoughtfully. "Mr Martin came down here often with this plumber fellow, but this room has barely any pipework in it."

"Mr Martin was obsessive about things," O'Harris pointed out. "He clearly thought there was something wrong with the pipes down here and wanted them fixed. Look at that box Clara found his books in. It has clearly been stood in water. He was probably worried this basement wasn't watertight and his journals and plans might be ruined."

"But this place is bone dry now," Tommy persisted. "It doesn't even feel damp and considering all the rain we had, if there was a leak would it not show up?"

"The pipework is an internal system, unaffected by the weather," O'Harris replied. "Mr Martin was not worried about rain; he was worried about the water from the internal plumbing system leaking out of the pipes."

Clara was listening to them both, weighing up their two arguments. She wandered over to a copper pipe and rapped on it. It sounded odd, hollow. Confused, she went back to the staircase and called up to the caretaker.

"Mr Mitchell, has the water been turned off in the basement?"

Mitchell appeared at the head of the stairs.

"Yes," he said. "I turned it off. I used the stopcock in the kitchen. You see, these pipes only supply a handful of taps in rooms that are not used by the public. Because of Mr Martin's concerns I turned them off."

"You told him that?" Clara asked.

"Naturally. Except, he did not believe me," Mitchell sounded hurt. "I told him no water was running through these pipes. I opened the taps and emptied them once the supply was cut off. He insisted there was still a leak down here which was affecting the water pressure throughout the building. No matter how much I insisted, he kept on about it."

"That was why he had the plumber in?"

"Yes," Mitchell huffed. "Nearly every week for six months that man would come here, go down into this basement with Mr Martin and try to explain to him that nothing was wrong with the pipes. I imagine the man was close to despair by the end. Not to mention the expense it must have cost!"

"Funny how when we were going through those papers in Mr Martin's office, we came across no bills from a plumber," Tommy said, beginning to catch

Clara's drift. "I am sure the trustees would have had something to say about such an unnecessary expense, but they did not seem aware."

"Who was the plumber?" Clara called up to Mr Martin.

"I don't know," the caretaker was sounding more and more maudlin that his efforts had been considered inadequate by his employer. "He was not the usual fellow we had in for such things. I rather fancied Mr Martin did not believe he was up to the job either and so went for this new, young fellow. I told you, when Mr Martin got a notion in his head, there was little to be done."

"Thank you, Mr Mitchell," Clara called up to the man, then she turned to her brother and O'Harris. "If you ask me, this plumber was not here because of faulty pipes, he was here because he was the man Martin was working with concerning the bomb."

"It was a perfect cover," O'Harris nodded. "This place was always needing repairs and the sight of a workman coming in would not have raised an eyebrow."

"And it meant that Martin could keep the majority of any incriminating evidence down here," Tommy added. "He could not make the bomb here. Too risky if Mr Mitchell came down into the basement, but he could keep all his papers and journals hidden."

"He was leading quite the double life," Clara agreed. "Supposing this young plumber was William Hershel, and his visits were to assist Martin with the bomb?"

"Why wouldn't he just make it himself?" O'Harris asked.

"Because his house was not secure. His siblings or parents may have discovered what he was up to," Clara postulated. "And, if he was seen regularly going to Mr Martin's home, that might have drawn attention as well. This was the best place for them to talk. Martin worked on the bomb at home, maybe William visited occasionally to see his progress."

"If your theory is correct, it would imply that William Hershel had the motive to take Mr Martin out of the picture and secure the bomb," Tommy spoke. "Except, as far as we can tell they were murdered at around the same time. There is a third man we have not located yet."

"Good point," Clara said. "We seem to have faltered once more. Maybe we can find someone else who saw this plumber coming and going and can point us in the right direction?"

"I hope so," Tommy sighed, looking around him and feeling discouraged. "We don't have long to save the King's life. Out there is a bomb and someone ready and willing to use it."

Chapter Twenty

They spent the next hour calling on the various homes
and businesses around the music hall to see if anyone
had noticed the unknown plumber. Several people
mentioned they had seen a workman regularly going
into the building but had taken no notice because the
music hall was old and always seemed to need work to
be done. At one property, where three accountants had
set up business together, Clara discovered that their
secretary had asked the mysterious plumber about
fixing a leaking sink in the building.

"He said he would take a look, but it seemed to me
all he really was interested in was staring at me," the
secretary huffed.

She was a pretty thing, but nobody's fool and had
no time for a workman who could not stop ogling her.

"He never fixed the sink, either," she added.

"What did he look like?" Clara asked.

"Tall, burly, wore the cleanest pair of blue overalls
I have ever seen on a workman," the secretary
answered.

"Fair hair or dark?"

"Fair, but not really light," the secretary replied, which eliminated William Hershel from the debate because he was distinctly dark haired.

"Was he young?"

"No, must have been in his forties, at least," the secretary sniffed. "He was an odd sort. Never known a plumber like him. He spoke very well, more like one of my employers than a workman."

This was all she could recall about the plumber, but it seemed to confirm Clara's notion that he was not there to fix anything, but rather to discuss bomb making with Mr Martin. It left them no closer to who the plumber was, however.

She regrouped with the others.

"We have come to a dead end once more," she said. "Though, it seems our plumber was not William Hershel, or really a plumber."

"I guess the next stop is this anarchist meeting you are attending tonight," O'Harris said, a hint of unease in his tone.

"I shall be perfectly fine," Clara reassured him. "I am only going to take a look around."

"What if someone we already have met in this case happens to be there?" Tommy pointed out. "They will know who you are."

"But they will not know why I am there," Clara said. "No one outside of the police and ourselves knows about the bomb plot or Mr Martin's links to the anarchists."

"Except for this mystery third man," O'Harris reminded her. "What if he is at the meeting? He would have to be pretty stupid not to realise why you are there too."

Clara smiled.

"If someone we already have spoken to is at that meeting, then we shall have a suspect. Whether they realise my intentions or not, I shall be fine. There will be plenty of people around and you are going to wait for me with the car just across the road, yes?"

O'Harris agreed he would be doing that. Tommy gave his arm a nudge.

"You won't win, you know," he said.

"I know," O'Harris sighed. "But I had to try."

They arrived back home and had lunch with Annie. She was delighted to have their company in the middle of the day, a novelty when Clara and Tommy were working a case. In the afternoon, Clara made telephone calls to William Hershel's university and left messages to speak with his various tutors. She was informed, as the college was currently on its holidays, it would likely be a couple of days before she heard back from someone. Clara was starting to feel the pressure of time, especially with the king's visit not far on the horizon, but there was nothing she could do about the delay.

After dinner that evening, she donned a dark coat and hat, deciding someone going to an anarchist meeting was likely to want to appear discreet. She made sure she had plenty of hatpins, not just because of the wind, but because hatpins were a handy weapon in a pinch. She secreted one in her right coat sleeve to be on the safe side.

O'Harris and Tommy accompanied her as far as they could, parking the car across the street from the venue. It was an old, wooden building that was close to the pier and Clara had a vague idea it had once been used for some sort of amusements. It looked as if it would not last many more winters. It seemed mildly miraculous it had survived the last storm.

"I shall be fine," Clara told the men as she left the car, feeling they needed the reassurance.

"Just… be careful," O'Harris said.

"If you hear a scream…" Clara began.

"We shall know you are all right, but that you have

jabbed a hatpin into someone," Tommy interrupted her with a grin.

"That was my line," Clara pretended to be annoyed with him, which made his grin grow broader. "I'll be back in a little while. I am not sure how long I can endure a meeting concerning anarchy unless I have a suspect or two to watch while I am there."

She crossed the road and opened the door to the building, entering into a room that was dense with smoke and the smell of human bodies packed close together. There was not a lot of room, and she was one of the last to arrive. It was necessary to jostle past people to find somewhere to stand that afforded her a good view of the room. She noticed the crowd largely consisting of working men, flat caps pulled down over their eyes and cigarettes or pipes wedged in their mouths. Anarchy and the promises it made about changing the balance of things was the sort of politics that called to the poor and downtrodden.

However, dotted among the crowd were several men who were better dressed. Their clothes were clean and in good repair and they stood out like sore thumbs among the workers with their filthy overalls and muddy boots. The only person who looked more out of place was Clara, for she was the only woman present in the room.

She sensed eyes upon her and a general quietening of noise in the area of the room she stood in. Her presence was neither welcome, nor expected. She was beginning to wonder if she might have to leave and send in Tommy instead, the looks on the faces of the men around her did not imply they would be keen to talk in her presence, when she spotted Eric.

"Good evening, Eric," she said very clearly and loudly.

Eric heard his name and glanced her way. He was delighted to see her and pushed his way through the crowd to meet her.

"Y...y...you are the f...f...first lady wh...wh...who has ever come to a m...m...meeting," he said, clearly happy he had at last convinced a member of the opposite sex to attend one of his gatherings.

"Are ladies not generally inclined towards anarchism?" Clara asked him.

Eric shrugged his shoulders.

"Wh...wh...who knows?"

Eric took her hand suddenly and guided her through the audience to a spot nearer to what could be loosely described as a stage. It was really just a couple of packing crates side-by-side with a chair on the top. From this podium, someone would be speaking. Clara suspected it would not be Eric, otherwise they could be here all night.

Eric let go of her hand and smiled as he climbed up onto the packing crates. Clara was impressed he was going to be the speaker, she did not think he would have the confidence, but then, just as he seemed about to talk, Victor jumped up beside him and Eric sat down in the chair.

"Brothers!" Victor called across the room, his voice bellowing.

It was a rough, raspy voice at the best of times and when he spoke loudly to the crowd it became even huskier.

"I want to thank you all for attending this meeting! The more we spread word of our cause, the more hope there is for real change!"

He pumped a fist into the air and was rewarded by rumbles of agreement and the clapping of hands. The people around Clara looked uneasy, and even slightly embarrassed. She guessed these were men who would normally stay clear of politics and were a little unsure of themselves in this new environment.

Victor began a long speech that rambled on about

the philosophical side of anarchism, the empowerment of the poorest and making the world a fairer place. Clara quickly stopped listening and instead started to pay closer heed to those in the room. She was trying to pick out anyone who she already knew and who could be connected to this case.

The faces around her were unfamiliar. Further back in the room, the orange light of the lamp became dimmer, and the shadows jumped forth, masking people's identities, but she was still confident that no one she had seen so far was anyone she knew.

She watched the crowd curiously, trying to judge their mood. Were these men the sort to want to blow up the King for a cause? She could not tell with a glance what was going through their minds.

Victor was getting to the best part of his speech. He was ramping up to telling the crowd how they were going to change the world starting with Brighton, when the door to the meeting room burst open and someone stumbled in.

"Sorry fellas," the newcomer chuckled. He had nearly fallen forward as he entered and as he now righted himself and swayed on his feet; it was obvious he was drunk.

Clara recognised Micah Hershel and for a second almost forgot to mask her surprise.

"Micah," Victor muttered to himself, then he nodded at Eric who hastened off the crates.

Eric pushed his way to Micah and grabbed his arm, bringing him further into the room while someone else went to secure the door which Micah had left swinging open.

"I...I...I didn't think you were coming," Eric said, looking fraught as he tried to find somewhere for Micah to stand where he would not cause any trouble to everyone else.

Micah was swaying back and forth on his feet.

"Actually, Victor said I ought never to come back, if I recall rightly," Micah laughed.

Victor was glowering at him from the makeshift stage. Eric signalled with his arm for Victor to carry on with his speech, but the flow had been broken and he could not quite get the same power into the words as before. They sounded stilted and foolish. He ended up skipping some of his speech and finishing early.

Micah Hershel applauded him when he finally stopped.

"Bravo! Bravo!"

He was the only one to react to the speech. Everyone else was looking uncomfortable. Clara was still trying to work out what had been accomplished by the meeting and what precisely its purpose had been when some of the men nearest the door departed. The arrival of Micah had caused friction among the crowd and the audience seemed keen to get out of the way. There was clearly something occurring between Micah and the anarchists that any sane person would prefer to avoid.

It was not long before the room had nearly emptied, though Eric and Victor did not seem to notice. Victor had jumped off the stage and was confronting Micah.

"I told you not to come back!"

"And anarchy means I am free to do as I will. No rules, Victor," Micah wagged a finger in Victor's face and looked close to having it bitten off.

Eric intervened.

"M...Mi...Micah, you always a...a...arrive late and c...cau...cause dis...dis...discord."

Micah turned on him, a nasty edge to his drunken playfulness now.

"D...d...do I, E...E...Eric?" he said, mocking the man's speech impediment.

Clara had been watching on with curiosity rather than concern, thinking she might learn something about the Hershel connection to the anarchists, but when Micah mocked Eric, something came over her. It was the way Eric's face fell and he dipped his head. It was the way Micah sneered and laughed. Clara detested bullies and in that instant her indignation got the better of her.

She marched smartly up to Micah and placed herself between him and Victor, giving Victor something of a shock.

"What a disgrace you are, Mr Hershel," she said to Micah, hands on her hips. "You turn up drunk and late determined to cause disruption and then you insult a man for something he cannot help. I have never seen such a despicable human being before. Do you not have better things to do?"

"You can't talk to me like that!" Micah snapped, prodding a finger at Clara, and hitting her shoulder. "No one talks to me like that!"

"Then perhaps you should consider your words and actions against these men?" Clara persisted, not reacting to his drunken swaying in her direction. She sensed he was on the cusp of turning nasty but backing down was not an option. "I think you should leave."

"You too?" Micah growled. "Kicking me out? I told you, against the rules of anarchy! First rule of anarchy, no rules!"

"That is an oversimplification!" Victor cried out. "You use our just cause and beliefs as an excuse to behave as you please and usually that is disgracefully!"

"No rules!" Micah repeated, this time at Victor.

"This is not about rules," Clara told him coldly. "It is about principals. You have to leave, now."

She was firm, using the voice that reminded her of an old schoolteacher. It reminded Micah of an old schoolteacher too; one he had despised.

"I'm not leaving!" he bellowed.

"You have to!" Eric said, his anger temporarily

overcoming his stutter.

"We are going to lock up!" Victor added. "The meeting is over!"

"Not for me!" Micah declared. "I think I shall just stay here all night! Haha!"

Micah had reached that irrational and belligerent stage of drunkenness that was the most dangerous. Victor was clenching his fists, not sure what to do. Clara put on her calm voice, the one that meant business.

"Mr Hershel, if you do not care for me to inform your parents of your behaviour tonight, I suggest you leave at once."

"My parents?" Micah scowled at her. "How dare you! Wait, how do you know my parents?"

"I know your sister Annabelle too," Clara pushed him. "Haven't you brought them all enough shame?"

"You are on their side!" Micah had lost interest in gate crashing the meeting, now he was back to old hurts concerning his parents and their shame over his behaviour. "They don't understand me!"

"You hardly improve things getting drunk," Clara declared. "Now is the time to leave!"

She was firm. Micah became quiet, he swayed back, then his eyes hardened. Clara had expected as much. As he drew his fist back to punch her, she dropped a hatpin into her hand and stabbed him with all her might.

Chapter Twenty-One

O'Harris and Tommy burst through the door of the building and charged into the room. They were not sure what to expect – they never were when screams occurred around Clara – but they were both relieved to see Clara apparently unharmed. She was standing with her arms folded as Micah Hershel lay on the floor scrabbling at his neck. There was a hatpin sticking out from just above his collar bone. Clara had aimed for somewhere the pin was not likely to be seriously harmful. Micah's shirt collar had been unbuttoned in his drunkenness and his collarbone had seemed to glare at Clara as a good target.

Micah was now trying to remove the pin, but every time he touched it there was a sting of pain and he whimpered and let go. Micah Hershel was not a man who coped well with pain.

Eric and Victor were looking somewhat dazed by the drama. Neither had expected Clara to stab a man. Both had reacted slowly to Micah throwing a punch and would have been unable to save Clara, had she not already been prepared to save herself.

Clara glanced up at her brother and O'Harris.

"Micah Hershel," she said, because they had not met the fellow when they were looking around the Hershel house. "Turns out he is as obnoxious as his sister informed us."

She waved a hand in Micah's direction.

"Could someone retrieve my hatpin?" she added. "I am not inclined to go near him."

O'Harris had a sneaky grin forming on his face. Tommy just rocked back on his heels and whistled to himself.

"Well, I suppose this is a meeting about anarchy," he declared.

"That is not what anarchy is about at all!" Victor blazed; his temper still frayed by recent events.

"I think we need to talk," Clara said to the two men and motioned for them to walk to one side with her, out of the hearing range of Micah.

O'Harris glanced at Tommy, who shrugged. Between them they starting to help the protesting and groaning Micah into a handy wooden chair.

"Wh…who are you?" Eric asked Clara as they found themselves back near the makeshift stage.

"Clara Fitzgerald," Clara told them. "I have never lied about my identity, nor my curiosity about anarchy. However, I was slightly surreptitious about my exact reasons for being here."

"W…what are th…they?" Eric asked. "Th…the real reasons?"

"I am here because of a man called Mr Martin," Clara said, waiting to see a response from the two men.

There was nothing, which surprised her. They were either extremely good at keeping a straight face, or neither had ever heard of Mr Martin.

"He was the manager of the music hall," she added. "He had a vast collection of anarchist journals in the basement of the building."

Still there was no recognition. Clara frowned.

"He built a bomb," she said, trying to spark something from the men. "To blow up the King."

This at least caused Eric to gasp and Victor's eyebrows to leap up to an alarming degree.

"You think he was linked to us?" Victor said.

"There cannot be many anarchist groups in Brighton," Clara pointed out logically.

"We do not agree with violence," Victor said sternly. "Certainly not bombs. We want our cause to be taken seriously. The second you descend to physical attacks on people you are labelled criminals and the people you need to listen to you simply stop."

"Ex...ex...exactly!" Eric agreed. "Wh...why do you th...think we kicked out M...Micah?"

"He comes here drunk and starts stirring up trouble. Talking about making a stand and hitting the government where it hurts," Victor concurred. "He wanted violence but did not want to get his hands dirty. He is just the sort of man we do not want in the anarchist movement."

Clara had to admit she was surprised by Victor's adamance. She had misjudged him, thinking he was the sort of man to believe actions speak louder than words. She felt abashed she had read him so wrong.

"Then you know nothing of Mr Martin's bomb plot?" she said, rather desperate for them to say that they had heard a whisper of it because she was running out of leads again.

"No," Eric said. "N...never been to the m...mu...music hall."

It was Clara's turn to frown.

"This Mr Martin made a bomb?" Victor said, the seriousness of things really sinking in.

"And it is missing," Clara sighed. "I had hoped to find someone here who might be involved in the plot. I am sorry. I misjudged your organisation."

Victor scowled, but Eric understood.

"It happens a...a...a lot," he said. "Wh...which is wh...why w...we can't allow violent ac...ac...actions from our m...members."

"It will just make things worse for us all," Victor nodded. "Mr Martin won't tell you where the bomb is?"

"He is dead," Clara said bluntly. "We presume stabbed by another of the people involved in the plot."

Victor and Eric exchanged looks.

"And you are certain about the anarchist links?" Victor asked.

"As I said we found numerous recent journals about the movement in the basement of the music hall. Mr Martin was the only one who went down there according to the caretaker. Also, he was having secret meetings with a man masquerading as a plumber," Clara looked over in the direction of Micah Hershel. He was refusing to let O'Harris touch the hatpin stuck in his neck. "It is curious Micah is here, because the same night Mr Martin died, so did his brother William. We have assumed William was involved in the bomb plot as well."

"We don't know anything about William Hershel," Victor said. "Micah is the only Hershel who comes here. You can see what he is like. Now, if you were wondering if someone was involved in a bomb plot I would certainly point in his direction."

"No," Eric shook his head. "M...Micah can't keep his m...mouth shut."

Victor paused to consider.

"Good point," he agreed. "Micah would be too unreliable."

Clara was disappointed. She was starting to wonder how they would find the third man in the bomb plot with so little to go on. What if there were also a fourth man and a fifth? They had to find the bomb and yet they had no idea where to look.

"W…we want to h…help," Eric said suddenly.

"You do?" Clara said.

They both nodded and Victor spoke.

"This bomb plot affects our cause too. If someone causes harm to the King in the name of anarchy, the police will shut down our meetings. It will cause lasting damage to our movement."

"W…we w…want change, but not through violence," Eric added.

Clara saw their point and perhaps they could help. They would be best placed to learn of anyone who might be a private anarchist, one who did not attend the meetings.

"I am happy to have your assistance," she said. "I am just not sure what to advise you to do."

"W…we can a…ask a…around," Eric said. "Someone m…may know something."

"Yes," Victor nodded. "Just because these fellows do not attend our meetings, does not mean they have not talked with some of our members."

They heard a yell and looked over to where Micah was shoving Tommy out of the way and trying to get up from the chair. O'Harris had pulled out the hatpin sharply when he was not expecting it, and this had not gone down well. Clara marched over to try to calm matters. Micah was bleeding from the wound the hatpin had left. It was not a great deal, but it was staining his shirt.

"I think you ought to sit down and compose yourself," Clara said loudly to the man, as he grappled with Tommy.

O'Harris had entered the fray and was trying to restrain him too, not with great success.

"You witch!" Micah yelled at Clara.

She was tired of him.

"Fine. Tommy, John, let him go. If he falls down in the street, what do we care?" she declared.

Tommy needed no further order to gladly release the man. O'Harris stepped back. Micah took a moment to get his balance as he was suddenly let go. He looked around him, expecting someone to grab his arms again. Then he grinned.

"You are all idiots!" he informed them with delight. "I could have you arrested for assault!"

"Go ahead," Clara told him. "I shall enjoy seeing you explain to the police how you happened to be at an anarchist meeting."

Even through his drunken haze, Micah realised how bad that would be. He lost his smile for a moment, then pulled himself together.

"I am going home. Good day to you all!"

Swaying and wobbling, he headed for the door, stumbling out into the dark, cold night.

"How is it William ended up in a ditch and not him?" O'Harris said, bemused.

"I think you will find that is exactly what his parents are wondering," Clara was tired of the matter. "We might as well go home ourselves. Thank you, Eric. Victor."

The two leaders of anarchy nodded at her somewhat miserably.

"We ran over our meeting time," Victor glanced at his watch. "The landlord will complain and want to charge us more."

They were all moving towards the door when they heard a faint rumble.

"That idiot has a car!" O'Harris said in horror. "We can't allow Micah to drive home in such a state. He could kill someone!"

They dashed outside, following the sound. The car was not parked at the front of the building. If it had been, O'Harris and Tommy would have seen it. Instead, the sound appeared to be coming from a side street a few houses down the road, on the opposite side to the meeting place. They hurried to the spot, relieved to hear that the engine was choking under Micah's heavy-handed attempts to start it. When they arrived at the side street, O'Harris was ahead and he tentatively looked around the corner, just in case the engine suddenly started, and the car shot forward.

"Micah, get out of the car," he said firmly.

The others were grouping either side of the street entrance.

"What?" Micah asked vaguely.

"Get out of the car," O'Harris repeated. He was about to say Micah was too drunk to drive, but then caught himself, realising the reaction he would get. Instead, he pretended to be helpful. "It sounds like the engine has flooded. It won't start."

Micah had one sole goal – to get home and get to bed. He was reaching the weary stage of drunkenness and his mind was having trouble focusing. He paused. He had his foot pressed down hard on the self-starter pedal. The engine was spluttering and failing to start.

"We need to tweak the fuel valve to get her moving," O'Harris lied, creeping closer. He was banking on Micah knowing very little about the inner workings of cars so that he could make up anything that sounded suitably technical and have him believe it.

Micah looked at him bleary-eyed.

"Really?"

He swore and stormed out of the car, falling against a wall in the process. He reached the front of the vehicle and attempted to open the lid of the bonnet, which went very badly and nearly cost him a finger.

"Let me look," O'Harris gently moved him aside and Victor sidled up to Micah, ready to grab his arm.

O'Harris opened the bonnet and began to fiddle around inside, doing nothing much but looking busy.

"Oh dear, yes, the V pin has gone. Just as I feared.

Common fault," he said.

"V pin?" Micah said, now sagging in his drunken weariness.

"Yes, can't start the engine without it," O'Harris insisted. "You will need a new one."

"But I want to go home!" Micah bleated.

"You will have to walk," O'Harris said.

Micah was becoming belligerent again. Clara stepped forward, her attention not on the man but on the car.

"That is a Vauxhall Tourer," she said to O'Harris.

"It is," O'Harris smiled. "Nice car too, when in the proper hands…"

As he finished it suddenly dawned on him what she was saying.

"A Vauxhall Velox Tourer! Is it red?"

In the darkness of the unlit side street, it was impossible to say what colour the car was. Micah proved helpful.

"Of course it is red!" he growled. "Only colour for a car!"

The information was sinking in. O'Harris froze. Clara turned and without a hint of accusation spoke to Micah.

"This is your brother William's car," she said.

"Yes," Micah grumbled, not sure what all this nonsense was about. "I smashed up my car weeks ago. William doesn't need his anymore."

He trailed off, becoming maudlin.

"You have William's Vauxhall," Clara repeated, clarifying to herself what she found hard to believe. "The car everyone thought was missing."

Micah was frowning at her, unable to appreciate what she was saying.

"I want to go home," he sulked. "I can't walk. It's too far."

"I think maybe we need to take Micah to the police

station," O'Harris suggested.

Clara was thinking the same, but she was not looking forward to the effort it would require getting him there.

"Micah, where did you get your brother's car?" she asked him.

Micah was in a sullen slump.

"Where do you think? The garage at home," he huffed. "He never let me drive his car."

Clara did not know if he was lying or really such a big fool.

"Micah, your brother was driven out to a ditch where he died. Driven out in this car, perhaps. We have been trying to locate this car ever since and it was in your garage?" she said.

Micah shrugged.

"Did you dump William in a ditch?" Tommy asked him, deciding a cautious approach was getting them nowhere.

"What?" Micah snapped.

"The question was plain enough," Tommy said.

Micah stared and stared at him.

"I have had enough of this," he declared. "I am going home!"

He shoved aside Victor and stormed away from them. O'Harris started to follow, but Clara stopped him.

"Let him go. He is too much trouble as he is. The car is the important thing. It is evidence."

They looked at the car, innocuous in the shadows.

"We should drive it to the police station and then we can let Inspector Park-Coombs handle Micah," Clara paused. "None of this makes sense. Micah was not at the gala and why would he hurt his brother."

"If he was involved in the bomb plot he might have argued with William?" Tommy suggested. "Micah, as we have all noted, is not reliable. Maybe William thought he would give them away?"

"And then he just drove the car home?" Clara said, then she shook her head. "In his drunken state how can we expect rationality? Come on, let's get this car to the police."

Chapter Twenty-Two

Inspector Park-Coombs was irritated to be dragged from his comfy chair by the fireplace for the sake of a car, even though he knew the discovery of the car was important. He had been working tirelessly to try to crack the case and discover the others involved in the bomb plot but felt as though he was banging his head against a brick wall. The Chief Inspector was not helping with his hourly telephone calls to ask about progress. To say Park-Coombs felt under pressure would be an understatement. He had been appreciating the chance to relax for a while in his own home, allowing the warmth of a gently crackling fire to ease some of the tension in his muscles. He had groaned when a constable came to the door and told him he was needed at once.

"Sorry to call you out so late," Clara said with sympathy when he arrived looking frazzled. "We have made an unexpected discovery."

She motioned to the car which was now parked in the yard behind the police station where the carriages and the single police car were also kept.

"Are you saying this is William Hershel's missing car?" Park-Coombs walked towards the vehicle and tried to get a good look at it in the darkness. "Can someone bring out a lamp?"

He bellowed the order in the general direction of a gaggle of constables who were loitering with interest as close as they dared near the car. It was not every day they saw a smart Vauxhall Velox, and each was itching to get his hands on it. When none of them immediately moved, Park-Coombs turned a stern gaze in their direction and that got the message across. They all scrambled to go find a lamp.

"Where did you find it?" Park-Coombs returned his attention to Clara.

"In the possession of Micah Hershel, William's older brother."

"I know Micah," Park-Coombs sighed. "Somewhat of a thorn in his parents' side. I have had the pleasure of arresting him more than once for public disorderliness, among other things."

"Has he ever been involved in something politically dangerous?" Clara asked.

"You mean a bomb plot," Park-Coombs snorted in amusement. "He has never demonstrated the intelligence for such a thing. He spends his days getting drunk as fast as he can. He will probably be dead before he is thirty-five."

"Yet, he was driving the car of his deceased brother," O'Harris pointed out. "That implies a lot."

"Did you get an explanation from Micah?" Park-Coombs asked. "And why is he not here?"

"Micah was so drunk he was barely able to stand up," Clara explained. "The reason we found the car was because we were preventing Micah from driving it home. He was not in a fit state to say much, and we did not fancy trying to drag him here. I doubt he will go far. He told us he found the car in the household garage."

"Which is preposterous," Park-Coombs agreed. "And yet, a very curious thing to say. Not to mention a curious thing to do, driving around in the car that belonged to your dead brother."

"If Micah killed his brother, it leaves us with a lot of questions," Tommy added. "He was not invited to the gala, and I doubt he would have been welcomed in if he just turned up, so where did he meet up with William? And why did he kill him?"

"Micah is a drunk who flails his fists around at the least of provocations," Park-Coombs reminded him. "I do not think we need delve deeply into motive."

A constable at last was returning with a lantern. It was an old one he had found in a storage cupboard, seeing as all the others were in the possession of a constable on the beat. The lantern was so old it did not have an oil reserve and it had been necessary to find a candle to fit inside it. The constable presented the lantern to his inspector cautiously.

"Now we have light, let's see if there is anything in this car that tells us about what happened to William," Park-Coombs took the lamp without acknowledging his constable. He lifted it up to cast a triangle of light over the bonnet of the car revealing it was indeed bright red.

Next, he walked along the car and allowed its light to shine into the rear, onto the leather bench seat where passengers could travel. There was a tartan blanket casually thrown across the seat. He picked it up carefully and examined it as best he could in the light of the lantern.

"Inspector, there is a dark patch upon it," Clara pointed to the edge of the blanket where there was indeed a dark area that appeared to be a stain of some sort. "It might be blood."

Park-Coombs put the blanket to one side and

continued to cast light into the car. There was not much to discover. Someone had lost a penny on the floor, and it glinted in the candlelight, and there were discarded cigarette butts which Clara would hazard a guess belonged to Micah rather than William, but otherwise the space was empty.

"Let's take this blanket inside and get a better look," Park-Coombs suggested.

They headed into the police station and found an unoccupied desk which they could spread the blanket out upon. They examined the corner with the suspicious stain. It was a deep brown in colour and difficult to determine what it was exactly, but it did have the ominous appearance of dried blood.

"If this is Micah's blood," Park-Coombs mused, "then it must have come from his head wound."

"Which means he suffered a blow to the head before he was placed in the ditch," Clara pointed out. "Dr Deáth postulated that in the fall into the ditch William had banged his head, this would indicate that was not the case."

Park-Coombs moved the blanket to get a better look at the stain.

"Transporting a man with a head injury and dumping him in a ditch is something you do to cover up a crime. Maybe the person who put him in that ditch thought he was already dead?"

"That would seem a strong possibility," Clara nodded. "Does that mean Micah knocked down his brother and in a drunken panic thought he had killed him?"

"It is certainly the sort of thing Micah is capable of doing," Park-Coombs said.

"How would that tie in with the death of Mr Martin?" Tommy asked. "We have been assuming the two deaths were related and that William was involved in the bomb plot because of his knowledge of chemistry. Could these two deaths really just be coincidence?"

"Stranger things have happened," Park-Coombs muttered. "I shall have this blanket sent to Dr Death at once and he should be able to tell us if the stain is blood. In the meantime, it looks like I shall have to pay a visit to the Hershel family and arrest Micah."

They made their farewells and Clara and her companions departed for home. It had been a long day and an even longer night. She was glad when O'Harris dropped her and her brother at her front door.

"By the way, what was the outcome of your original plan to use the anarchist meeting as an opportunity to spot one of our suspects and to link them with the bomb plot?" O'Harris asked as Clara and Tommy were heading up their garden path.

"Victor and Eric say their movement is non-violent and I believe them," Clara said. "They denied all knowledge of Mr Martin and were appalled at the idea of a bomb to blow up the King."

"Then, aside from Micah Hershel turning up with his brother's car, the meeting was a dead end," O'Harris sighed.

"So it would seem," Clara said. "Still, maybe something will come of Micah's discovery with the car."

"Until tomorrow," O'Harris said cheerfully.

He waved as he drove off.

"Ever feel O'Harris is becoming rather an honorary detective?" Tommy said to his sister.

She smiled.

"He would never admit such a thing, but I think he rather enjoys investigating crime. Come on, I feel like an early night."

~~~*~~~

The next morning, having still no leads as to the bombing plot, Clara and Tommy agreed they should head back to the Hershels and see if they could learn more about William and whether he was helping to build a bomb.

"What are the odds Micah and William were both anarchists?" Tommy said as they waited outside their house for O'Harris to appear with the car.

"I think it not so unreasonable, however, I doubt they would converse with each other about the matter. They seemed to me two brothers who avoided each other."

"It is curious, nonetheless," Tommy said thoughtfully. "Maybe Annabelle is involved too?"

"Let's not jump to conclusions," Clara reminded him.

O'Harris arrived and they headed to the Hershel residence. They proved to be not far behind the police, who had appeared at the house just a few minutes ahead of them. Park-Coombs had been driven there in the solitary police car to make an impression. Mr and Mrs Hershel had heard the car and had hastened to their front door, looking out with anxious yet eager faces.

"They think we have news about who murdered their son," Tommy whispered to the others.

"There was no way to avoid causing them to think that," Clara said sadly. "This will not be a good morning for them."

They let Park-Coombs go about his business first. He spoke to the Hershels on their doorstep and then ushered them inside so he could explain why he was there privately. Clara and the others hung back, feeling their presence was unwanted for the time being.

"Why don't we take a look in the garage?" O'Harris suggested suddenly.

His suggestion took Clara by surprise. It was not

like O'Harris to think about doing something so sneaky. She had to admit it was not a bad idea.

The garage abutted the house and had a pair of large white doors that swung outwards when opened. Little square windows dotted their upper portion and allowed in some light, along with adding a decorative feature to the otherwise plain doors. When O'Harris tried the doors, he discovered they were not locked.

They entered a spacious garage that could easily store a couple of cars. Work benches along one wall revealed that at least one of the Hershel sons was inclined to do his own car maintenance. The odds of that being Micah did not seem great. Tools had been left on the benches in a haphazard fashion as if someone had recently been using them and had abandoned them in the middle of a project. The space smelt of grease and petrol, and the concrete floor was stained with dots and splodges of oil.

"Out of interest, see if there is anything here that might have been used to make a bomb," Clara said, knowing it was a farfetched notion.

They were wandering around the room separately when Annabelle Hershel entered through the doors.

"I thought I saw you go in here," she said. "I fear you have news, and it is not good."

Clara had been looking through a box of spare parts idly, not really sure what she was hunting for. Now she stopped and approached Annabelle.

"We found your brother Micah driving around in William's car last night," she explained to the woman.

Annabelle's eyes widened.

"The missing car?" she said in astonishment. "Micah had it?"

"He claimed it was just sitting here, in the garage," Clara elaborated. "He decided to borrow it because his own car was out of action."

"He ran it into a tree the other week," Annabelle

said, rubbing her fingers across her forehead as she tried to accept the information they were giving her. "How did William's car end up back in the garage?"

"Well, the likelihood is that whoever dumped your brother in that ditch brought the car back here," Clara said delicately.

She allowed this information to sink into Annabelle. She startled as she realised what was being implied.

"You mean Micah killed William?"

A hand shot to Annabelle's mouth, and she paced across the garage, trying to adjust to this new information.

"That is preposterous," she turned back to Clara. "Micah is many things, but he is not a murderer."

"What was his relationship with William like?" Tommy asked.

"I am not sure you could term it a relationship," Annabelle said. "They recognised each other's existence. That was about it."

"It would have been natural for Micah to resent William," Tommy pointed out. "Seeing how he was constantly being compared to him in an unfavourable light."

"I suppose," Annabelle shrugged. "But Micah does not really listen to all that. If he did, he would behave better."

Clara thought this a naïve perspective. How could Micah not have felt resentful when his younger brother was being presented as the prodigy he was not?

"Did they argue?" she asked.

"They rarely came into each other's presence," Annabelle replied. "Micah rises late and skulks away from the house to do whatever it is he does. I believe he mainly goes to find drink and get drunk."

"We need to know if Micah was at the gala the night his brother died," Clara continued.

"The only person who can tell you that is Micah

himself, but I will say this plainly, if I had seen him around the music hall, I would have chased him away with a flea in his ear. I have no intention of Micah humiliating me," Annabelle sniffed, revealing her own feelings towards her brother.

"But you did not stay after midnight," Tommy pointed out. "Micah could have arrived later."

"He could have," Annabelle admitted reluctantly. "But Mrs Peacock was there all night, and she would have made sure he did not stay."

"The fact is, the police consider Micah a prime suspect for the death of your brother William and, unless he can offer us an explanation of where he was that night and prove he was too far away to have committed the crime, I think they will consider him guilty," Tommy told her.

Annabelle bit her lip, emotion coming over her again.

"Yet again, he brings ruin to this family," she whispered to herself. "I cannot believe he did this. Micah is not a killer, and I cannot abide thinking that to be the case. He would not have hurt William."

Annabelle was adamant. Clara felt her pain, she had seen it many times before when a family had discovered one of their own was a murderer. She did not have much to offer Annabelle, but she walked forward and placed a hand on her arm for comfort.

It was in that moment there was a crash from a nearby window, and the half-dressed figure of Micah Hershel was seen running across the lawn as fast as he could.

Chapter Twenty-Three

The events of the morning had taken a hard toll on Mr and Mrs Hershel. Mrs Hershel was in a state of near collapse when Clara was asked by Park-Coombs to come and speak to them.

"I don't have the talent for this," he informed Clara, looking fraught. "Besides, I need to work on catching a bomber."

He abandoned Clara and the others with the distressed Hershels, while he disappeared to try to locate Micah and finally bring this bomb plot to a conclusion.

"Does he really think Micah is ever sober enough to have orchestrated such a thing?" Tommy raised an eyebrow at his sister.

"In some regards, our inspector is a determined optimist," Clara sighed. "One might even say the blinkered sort of optimist. He is also thinking how to get the Chief Inspector off his back."

"That does not resolve this plot, though," Tommy pointed out. "Micah is involved somehow, but he is not behind all this. He can't be. Just look at him."

Tommy was somewhat alarmed to suppose that a man of such inadequacies could actually have formulated a plan to assassinate the King. Where did that leave a person when looking for such a suspect? It meant that nearly anyone could have the potential to be a bomb plotter, surely? And that was a disturbing thought.

"We best speak to Mr and Mrs Hershel," Clara said, not relishing the task. "I still need to explain to them I think William was involved in the bomb making."

"We will be right behind you," O'Harris placed a hand on her shoulder to seal the promise.

Clara smiled at him and responded with a squeeze of his hand. Then she braced herself and headed into the drawing room.

Mrs Hershel was semi-reclining on the sofa, unable to lay fully down because her husband was sitting at the end in a stiff upright position. Despite their proximity, the couple appeared to be making a determined effort not to touch one another. Mrs Hershel had a handkerchief fluttered over her face, clasped in one tight fist as she groaned to herself and repeated over and over – "Why me? Why me?"

Mr Hershel was solemn in his silence. His hands were in clawed balls resting on his knees. He could have been a statue, how still he sat. He was a little hunched forward and his gaze was down on the far edge of the rug. He didn't seem to be blinking.

Opposite them, sitting alone in an armchair, was Annabelle, trying to appear calm and in control of herself, while also wanting to break down into tears.

"Mr and Mrs Hershel," Clara began, "there is very little I can say to make this morning any easier for you."

Mr Hershel looked up at her and perhaps – just

perhaps – there was a glimmer of fury in his stare.

"You have brought us great woe Miss Fitzgerald," he said.

"That is hardly fair, father," Annabelle responded. "Miss Fitzgerald has done nothing but what you asked her to do. It is hardly her fault that it seems Micah was involved."

"Micah," Mrs Hershel whimpered beneath her handkerchief. "From the moment that boy was born it seemed he was destined to damn my life."

"My dear…" her husband began, but she would not let him finish.

"I was confined nearly twenty hours giving birth to him, and it took months for me to recover," she said, angered her husband would challenge her words. "You did not endure that ordeal, you cannot comment. He was always an irksome individual, even as a baby he was never pleased and it was difficult to show him to my friends for he always cried, all the time. He was truly an unpleasant baby and he never improved."

Mr Hershel did not have the strength to argue with her on the matter. Perhaps, he could not remember himself the good points of the child, who had grown into such a disappointment.

"I fear I did something terrible to deserve such a son," Mrs Hershel declared dramatically. "He is my punishment for some heinous sin I do not recall."

"Now, now, mother," Annabelle said, though with little energy.

"Mrs Hershel," Clara cut through the gloom and self-pity, "has Micah ever expressed anti-patriotic sentiments?"

It was not Mrs Hershel who responded, but her husband who now glared fiercely at her.

"Micah served in the war," he said. "He was decorated for bravery. He is a drunk and a scoundrel, but he is loyal to this country."

"We discovered him last night at an anarchist meeting," Clara continued carefully.

"Anarchist?" Mrs Hershel said the word with care. "What is an anarchist?"

"People who believe the way we are governed now is wrong. They do not agree with authority in any form," Clara explained. "They would overturn the government if they could."

"Micah would never be involved in such a thing!" Mr Hershel declared.

"In actual fact, Mr Hershel, your son was well known to the party and had been previously banished from their meetings for turning up drunk and stirring up agitation," Clara kept her voice calm as she spoke. "Even among the anarchists he has proven himself to be too disruptive."

Annabelle gave a dull snort.

"That sounds like Micah," she said.

Mr Hershel was trembling, unable to believe his ears.

"The police inspector only said Micah was suspected of being involved in the death of William," he spoke, clinging to this idea like a lifebelt. "That is why he was here, because Micah was in William's car which had been thought missing since our son…"

In his rant he had allowed himself to forget that his son was dead – murdered – now his words caught back up with him and it hit him all at once. His youngest son was gone, forever, and his oldest son was accused of killing him. He became very still.

"There is a lot more going on than the police have explained," Clara said, knowing the next part was going to be hard for them all. "We have become aware of a plot against His Majesty. It is a bomb plot, and the bomb is missing. We have reason to believe that William, and now Micah, were involved in this plot."

It was not Mr Hershel who responded with outrage to this statement; it was Mrs Hershel who sprang suddenly from the sofa remarkably recovered from her semi-faint.

"William would never do something like that!" she declared vehemently. "He was a good boy! Tireless in his studies!"

"The bomb makers needed a chemist to create their bomb," Clara told her gently. "William was a student of chemistry."

"That hardly warrants accusing him of something so fiendish!" Mrs Hershel declared, and she had a fair point.

"You are correct," Clara admitted. "I have yet to find any evidence that William was a radical in his political views. He was not known at the anarchist meetings. But, the night he died, the man who actually constructed the bomb was also killed. They were both attacked around the same time. The bomb was itself stolen away and we do not know where it is. Such a coincidence suggests William knew something about this plot."

"If William knew about a plot to blow up the King, he would have been the first to try to stop it!" Mr Hershel shouted.

Clara suddenly paused as his words hit her.

"He would have tried to stop it?" she repeated.

"Yes!" Mr Hershel said adamantly. "I remember, a year or so ago, there was a debate at his university about whether the country should become a republic, like France. It became heated and some of the students started a march through the streets calling for the King's head! Can you imagine? William was part of the group that calmed things down and stopped them. He helped lead another group of students to put a check on the march and to prevent the university being brought into terrible disrepute. He received a commendation from his tutors as a result."

Mrs Hershel was nodding her head vigorously.

"I have the letter his university sent me praising his cool-headed actions that brought the turmoil to a rapid conclusion. My boy was not one of these anarchy people."

"You said the same about Micah," Tommy pointed out quietly.

Mrs Hershel was thrown. Her husband opened his mouth, but words did not come out.

"Maybe Micah will be able to explain himself when the police catch him," Clara offered a smidge of hope. "It is a shame he ran."

Her words held an implication, and it was not missed by the Hershels. Their son had chosen to run rather than face the police – those were not the actions of a man wholly innocent of a crime.

"Could I take a look at Micah's room?" Clara asked now silence had fallen.

Neither parent responded to her.

"I will take you there," Annabelle said, rising and taking charge of the situation. "Perhaps there will be some explanation among my brother's things for all this."

She led them out of the drawing room and towards the staircase.

"You have broken my parents' hearts," she said softly. "Not that I blame you, after all, you are merely stating the truth. Perhaps we always knew it would end this way with Micah."

She paused.

"I do not mean murdering William. I never would have expected that. I just mean, perhaps we always knew Micah would get himself into some sort of trouble he could not be easily extracted from."

"He served in the war, then?" Tommy asked.

"Yes. Only as a private, but he was considered to be

a distinguished soldier," Annabelle said. "It was the one thing that made my parents proud of him."

"Did the war change him?" O'Harris asked.

It was the first time he had spoken, and his question sounded slightly sinister. Annabelle gave it due thought.

"I cannot say I noticed a change," she answered. "Though, I do know he was the most sober he had been since he was a boy during the war years. Since then, he seems to have been making up for lost time."

O'Harris said nothing, but the look he gave Clara and Tommy spoke his thoughts. Whatever Micah had been before the war, as with so many men, those years of bloodshed and battle had left him damaged. Perhaps the war had made him even question the governance of Britain. After all, it was the men in parliament who had sent thousands of young, innocent souls to die at the Front. That was the sort of thing that sparked resentment and resentment could grow into hate, and from hate it just took a small leap in some minds to start seeking revenge.

Annabelle showed them the door of Micah's room.

"I don't want to believe he could contemplate anything like this," she said, though it was not clear if she was referring to blowing up the King or the murder of her brother.

She opened the door to the room for them, but did not follow them in, lingering in the hallway instead contemplating the curious nature of life – her life in particular.

Micah's room was a mess, but Clara had expected that. Clothes were thrown about and the floor was almost invisible beneath the debris. There was a rancid smell in the air and Clara picked her way through the chaos with care. There were books and papers scattered about. It was not long before Clara found copies of the same anarchist periodicals she had seen in the basement of the music hall. She showed the others.

"Well, that is hardly a surprise," Tommy shrugged.

"It connects Micah to the same circles as Mr Martin. These are all the same magazines," Clara said. "This one, in particular, advocates rather violent action to promote the anarchist cause."

She showed them the publication she was referring to which had the dubious image on the front cover of a Union Jack being torn in two by a faceless man in a suit. O'Harris grimaced at the image.

"Who would want to read such stuff," he said, wondering how someone could fill their head with such vitriol.

Clara was flicking through the magazine and suddenly stopped. She turned it around to them to show the double page spread she had paused on. It was a detailed article debating whether the use of bombs to promote anarchy could ever be justified. From the brief elements she had read, it seemed the answer – according to the writer – was yes.

After O'Harris and Tommy had had time to digest the information before them, she took the magazine out into the hallway and showed it to Annabelle.

"I am sorry," she said, because she knew seeing the article and the things her brother was reading was going to cause Annabelle pain.

Annabelle was made of sterner stuff, and she read the article without a flicker of emotion.

"Well, that rather seals things," she said. "Micah has filled his head with this nonsense, and it has led to him believing in bombs and violence."

Clara wanted to say something that would ease this hard blow, but what was there to say? She remained quiet, instead.

"Clara!"

A shout from O'Harris drew her back into the

bedroom. He had been searching among a bundle of clothes that had been dumped on the floor in a heap. He had unravelled a dress shirt and an evening jacket, along with the crumpled length of a bowtie. In the process, he had noticed something heavy in one of the jacket pockets and had taken a look inside.

He had found a knife. It was a large pocketknife, the sort a hunter might use. When he flicked open the blade, he discovered that it was stained with blood.

"This could well be the murder weapon that finished off Mr Martin," O'Harris showed the knife to Clara as she returned.

Tommy came over to look as well.

"We need to get this to the Inspector straight away," Clara said.

In the police's haste to catch their potential bomber, they had not yet searched Micah's bedroom, thus leaving the evidence of his crimes for Clara to uncover.

Clara turned around to leave and saw that Annabelle was in the doorway of the room. She had overheard everything. She had seen the knife in O'Harris' hand. She stared at them with sad eyes.

"So, my brother is a murderer," she said. "I really hoped that not to be the case. I really hoped…"

She threw the anarchist magazine away from her as hard as she could, and then turned and ran to her own room.

Chapter Twenty-Four

Clara did not immediately leave the Hershels' home. She felt it was prudent to conduct a thorough search looking for the missing bomb, no matter how unlikely it seemed that Micah could be the mastermind behind all this business. Surely, he did not have the guile or common sense? At least, not in his perpetually drunken state. Yet, so far, he was the only other person they had found connected to the case and the fact he had run away was highly damning.

They searched the house as discreetly as they could, beginning with stripping out Micah's bedroom and looking for any concealed hiding places such as had been arranged in Mr Martin's pantry. They found nothing and decided to move their search downstairs, to rooms the family did not use often. Any area that was busy would not make a good hiding place; even if the family did not stumble upon the bomb by accident, it would seem likely the servants would at some point. Servants were always busy opening drawers and cupboards, poking around as they cleaned, and would be the first to notice something amiss.

Clara did have a quiet word with the cook and maid she found in the kitchen, enquiring if they had noticed Micah around more often, or if he had been acting strange. The servants shook their heads and denied everything, either out of family loyalty, or because they really did not know anything.

The trio had split up in their search and O'Harris was rummaging around in a cupboard built into the space beneath the main stairs when Mr Hershel came across him.

"What are you doing?"

O'Harris saw no point in lying.

"I am looking for the missing bomb," he told the older man. "We found magazines in your son's bedroom that prove he had a deep interest in anarchy. Some of them advocated the use of bombs as a form of protest."

O'Harris kept quiet about the pocketknife which was wrapped in a handkerchief in his pocket. He felt the information he had already given was terrible enough. Mr Hershel froze, appalled at the news, and also offended to hear it.

"That is the most preposterous…"

"Sir," O'Harris said, being as polite yet firm as he could, "your denials will not change the evidence. I could explain to you why men who served so valiantly in the war come home and begin to question the governance of this land, but it will not change a thing. I have no doubt your son served bravely and was a tribute to his country, just as I now have no doubt that he believes in anarchy."

"But… bombs?" Mr Hershel found himself flopped back against the banister of the stairs. "It is one thing to question the way our country is ruled and regulated, and another to consider blowing up the monarch."

"Not when you have spent four years watching the men around you being blown up and wondering if anyone in Whitehall cares," O'Harris explained. "You reach a point where it starts to seem that if the government can use such violence and justify it, well, perhaps the same can be true for the ordinary man."

"You speak as if you think the war was pointless. Are you a pacifist?"

Mr Hershel sounded horrified. O'Harris found himself smiling.

"No," he said. "I am not a pacifist. I served in the war too and I believe that, ultimately, we had no choice but to bear arms against Germany. However, I do believe ignorance and a disregard for the working man meant choices were made that saw thousands die needlessly. I also know well the damage such years of trauma do to a man's mind. Perhaps, I might add, I have understanding for your son. I do not think what he is doing is right, but I can appreciate why he is doing it."

Mr Hershel was too confused to know what else to say.

"He would not kill his brother," he said when he found his tongue.

"He might not have meant to," O'Harris replied. "William had a bang to the back of his head. It looks like he somehow fell and knocked himself out, then was placed in the car and transported to the ditch where he was left. He was not dead at that point, but someone might have supposed he was."

"An accident?" Mr Hershel tested out the notion. It calmed him. "Yes, that would make sense. He slipped, banged his head and Micah panicked."

It was not much compensation for the death of one son at the hands of another, but Mr Hershel was prepared to cling to anything he could.

O'Harris was finished with the cupboard. He stood

back and thought for a moment, before turning to Mr Hershel.

"It would help your son if we could find the bomb before anything occurred."

"You mean, before he has the chance to use it," Mr Hershel grimaced.

Mr Hershel seemed to slowly appreciate what he was being told.

"There are some buildings at the bottom of the garden we barely use. An old shed and a greenhouse. If Micah was looking to hide something, they would be a sensible location," he said.

O'Harris thanked him, then went to find Clara and Tommy.

The siblings had searched everywhere they could think of and had come up empty. When O'Harris walked into the kitchen and told them about the buildings at the bottom of the garden, it seemed the ray of hope they needed. They headed out across the large lawn, trees and shrubs blocking their view so that they did not spy the buildings until they were almost upon them. The shed was being slowly engulfed by ivy and a giant laurel bush, while the greenhouse had long ago lost its roof and was merely a frame.

At first glance the buildings might have seemed utterly abandoned, but around the door to the shed last year's fallen autumn leaves had been crushed down into the ground as if someone had walked across them regularly, and the grass that was otherwise long and dry around the base of the shed, had been caught in the shed door at some point, indicating the door had been opened and closed recently.

"Maybe this is it," Clara said when they were a few feet away.

In that moment, they heard a slight noise, like a flowerpot being knocked so that it made a ringing sound. They all froze instinctively and waited for another sound. Silence followed.

"Cat?" O'Harris suggested quietly.

"Must have been wearing boots," Tommy frowned.

They continued to approach the shed, more cautious now. The quiet that had descended was not reassuring, it was the sort of quiet that comes when someone is trying very hard not to make a sound. They were upon the shed, O'Harris closest to the door which was set into the left-hand side. Clara attempted to peer through the small window, but it was too dirty to let her see in.

There was no obvious lock on the door. O'Harris cast Clara a questioning look, pointing at the door. She answered with a nod. She wanted that door opened and to reveal what (or perhaps who) was inside.

O'Harris clasped the door latch and pulled.

The first thing that happened was a long-handled hoe that had been precariously balanced just inside the shed, fell outwards and nearly clobbered O'Harris on the head. As he jumped back to avoid the garden tool, a war cry came from within the shed and someone lunged forward, making a bid for freedom.

O'Harris was caught off-guard and was knocked out of the way as the person jumped out of the doorway and tried to bolt across the lawn. They did not get far, because Clara and Tommy had been poised just to one side of the doorway. The hoe had missed them by a mile and when the person sprung out, they were ready for them.

Tommy raced to tackle the figure, catching the person by the arm and for a second stumbling along with them. Then he lost his footing and the person managed to shove him away. He fell to the ground on his backside with a thud, gasping out a breath of air.

"Oof!"

Clara took up the chase. She was perhaps not the fleetest of runners, but she had always been a master of the running tackle during hockey at school. This was something of an illegal move, involving the shoving of one's hockey stick between the feet of an opposing team member, thus tripping them up. Clara had grabbed up the fallen garden hoe automatically and as Tommy fell to the side, she quickened her pace and thrust the end of the hoe's wooden handle between the legs of the fleeing figure.

The person was tripped by the hoe, made a desperate effort to save themselves and then fell forward with flailing arms, trying to save themselves from a nasty bump. They went down hard and there was a nasty crack as they hit the earth face first.

Groaning in agony, the person huddled up on the ground, unable to move. Tommy had righted himself and was now beside the figure, with Clara standing over him, pleased with her quick thinking. O'Harris joined them a second later.

The huddled figure on the ground was wearing a dirty old coat and shabby trousers. They had a cap on their head and a scarf around their nose and chin making it hard to say who they were, other than that they were male. With one hand clasping at their nose, it was even harder to know who the man dressed like a tramp was, though Clara was prepared to hazard a guess. She grabbed the cap off the man's head and revealed light brown hair.

"You've broke ma noze," the forlorn figure mumbled through his hands.

"You tried to flee – again – Micah," Clara said.

The figure was distracted sufficiently from the pain to snap their eyes up to her face and stop groaning for a second.

"It's a good disguise," Clara acknowledged. "And a clever hiding place. Why should the police come back here to look for you? But you were forgetting one thing. Eventually the police were going to search this whole place for the bomb and then they would find you."

Micah narrowed his eyes, his brow furrowing.

"What bomb?" he said.

This was not the response Clara had expected.

"The bomb you had Mr Martin make," Tommy interjected. "The one you stole after you had killed him."

"What?" Micah turned his head sharply to Tommy and then closed his eyes and winced at the pain it renewed in his wounded snout. "I don't know what you are talking about."

"You are denying you stabbed Mr Martin?" O'Harris asked.

"Of course I am!" Micah snapped. "I have never killed anyone! At least, not outside of the war, but we were all turned into killers for that."

Micah shuffled himself so he was sitting on the ground rather than lying on his hip and tentatively pulled down his scarf.

"Is my nose bleeding?" he asked nervously.

"No," Clara informed him.

He prodded his nose tentatively, testing to see if it was broken.

"Micah, you do not seem to appreciate the seriousness of the situation. We have evidence to prove you stabbed Mr Martin and caused his death," Clara said to get back his attention. "We found a bloody pocketknife in your jacket pocket."

"I don't possess a pocketknife," Micah said quite calmly.

"What about the anarchist periodicals in your room?" O'Harris demanded.

Micah had the decency to flinch.

"Well, you saw me at the meeting. You know I am interested, though Eric and Victor have seen fit to stifle my voice!"

"Because your views are too violent for their brand of anarchism," Tommy said.

"My views are radical, yes, but not violent," Micah corrected.

"The periodicals you read suggest otherwise," Clara pointed out. "One had an article about using bombs to make political statements."

"It was metaphorical," Micah corrected. "An exercise in thought alone, not something to follow literally."

"The police are going to think otherwise," Clara persisted. "They have enough evidence to charge you with the murder of your brother and Mr Martin, not to mention conspiring to assassinate the King."

"What? No!" Micah seemed genuinely horrified. "I don't know what you are talking about, I swear!"

"Then explain the knife," Clara said. "And explain how your brother's car made its way back to your garage on its own, with a blood-stained blanket on the back seat, no less."

"I don't know!" Micah insisted. "Why would I do any of those things?"

"You argued with William about your plans," Tommy suggested. "Things became heated, and you pushed him. He fell and hit his head. You thought he was dead and so you set out to dump his body. Whether you stabbed Mr Martin before or after attacking your brother I can't say, but you stabbed him because you preferred to limit how many people remained alive and knew about the bomb plot."

"No!" Micah declared furiously. "I don't know what you are talking about! I did not touch either of them!"

"Then tell us where you were the night of the gala," Clara said, offering him a way out of his predicament.

Micah hesitated, his face falling.

"I don't know. I don't remember. I lose track of

things when I get drunk."

"You lost track of the fact you murdered a man and your brother," Tommy said bluntly.

"I would remember that!" Micah insisted. "I just lose track of dates and places. The times I was here or there. You have to believe me!"

He saw from their faces they did not.

"Come on, back to the house so we can call this fruitless man hunt to an end," O'Harris grabbed one of Micah's arms, holding it firmly so he would not bolt.

Tommy caught hold of the other and they lifted him up to his feet. Micah seemed deflated by everything and made no attempt to flee again.

"I don't understand any of this," he said as they escorted him back to the house. "I was just getting out of bed and dealing with my hangover when the police were in the house asking for me."

"Why did you run?" Tommy said.

"Because of the trouble last night," Micah said. "And I always run from the police. On principal."

He hung down his head.

"I am not a murderer," he whispered.

Chapter Twenty-Five

It was not easy to recall the inspector and his constables from their spread-out search across Brighton. After bringing Micah into the kitchen of the house and informing his parents of his return, it was necessary to devise a plan to round up the police. It was decided that the household maid would be sent out with a message she would deliver to the first constable she found, and then he would be responsible for spreading the word.

Micah sat forlornly at the kitchen table with a cold wet cloth pressed to his nose. He could not meet his parents' eyes when they came to see him. They looked at him as long as it took to decide the maid could go out with a message for the police, then they departed without saying a word to him.

Micah was stunned by their lack of response to him. It was slowly hitting home just how serious a matter this all was. He had been prepared for their anger – he was used to it. He was prepared for criticism and disappointment, but to receive nothing, to be treated as if he did not exist, chilled him.

Clara left him being watched over by O'Harris while she and Tommy went back to the shed to look for a bomb, or any traces of materials used for making one.

"It is all rather pathetic," Tommy observed as they crossed the garden.

"All crime is rather pathetic in the end. What people will do for money or jealousy, or some notion of glory is always going to seem hollow and ridiculous after the fact. At least to those of us picking up the pieces," his sister replied.

"I suppose, but I was thinking more specifically of Micah and seeing him sitting in the kitchen a broken man. Because he is broken. He wants his family's attention, but because he cannot get it through achievement or intelligence, he drinks and causes trouble instead."

"Do you think that is what it is?" Clara asked. "Not that he is a man depressed by his own personal failures and he drinks to try to forget, and the drink makes him act irrationally?"

"But why do his failures bother him so, if not for the fact it is because he is desperate for the attention and approval of his parents," Tommy countered. "We all have failures in our life. You can't live without failing at something, but most of us accept our failures and move on."

Clara considered this for a second.

"You suppose the pressure Micah always felt from his parents to achieve great things, and then his inability to do so, has resulted in this spiral of destructive behaviour," she said.

"That, and his experiences during the war. The war changed everyone who fought in it."

They were at the shed and Clara pulled open the door which had swung shut on itself.

"I can understand how that could lead to chronic

alcoholism, but it seems another step altogether to start building a bomb to blow up the King," she mused. "That is more about ideology, isn't it?"

"Well, maybe Micah found the anarchist cause something he could relate to and where he finally fitted in?"

"Except he did not fit in. Victor and Eric made that clear."

The shed was dark and dingy inside. Cobwebs littered the ceiling and covered the window. They were heavy with dust in many cases and accidentally touching one produced a shower of grey particles. The shed had been left to decay for years. Tools lay untouched and in many cases their metal components were rusty. Flowerpots, empty and abandoned, were stacked on top of a bench and along the floor. One had been recently knocked over and smashed, which explained the noise they had heard. Broken objects from long ago summers took up the remainder of the space – a deck chair that had a great rip in the seat fabric flopped against one wall, while a long-discarded set of wooden nine pins were clustered in a heap nearby.

The dust and decay allowed Clara to see what had been recently touched, and what had been left in peace for years. It was quite obvious that Micah had not touched anything on the workbench, for everything had a fuzzy grey film of dust upon it. The only area that was clear was against the far wall where a low stool with a wobbly leg had been placed. The floor had been walked across regularly, displacing the collected grime and dirt. There was a large cardboard box tucked behind the remains of a broken sundial and inside Clara discovered a dressing gown and pyjamas, along with a sodden pair of slippers.

"Looks like Micah keeps this shed as a little hideout," she said. "He can sneak here when he needs to get away, change into the clothes of a workman and then slip away again without anyone suspecting who he is."

Tommy came forward and glanced in the box.

"Ok, we have his hideout, but there is nothing here that suggests he was making bombs," Tommy looked around the shed for a second time, taking his time. "No chemicals. No work tools that had been recently used. I don't think Micah was building anything here."

"I agree," Clara said, sighing as she stood up. "There is nothing here to suggest he made a bomb or was even involved in a bomb plot."

"Yet we have the bloody knife and his brother's car," Tommy pointed out. "Maybe Micah was not involved with the bomb plot directly but was convinced by someone to murder his brother and Mr Martin."

Clara was frowning.

"Micah does not strike me as a person you could hire to kill someone. Especially not his own brother," she paused. "Quite frankly, if I was someone working on a secret plot with such great care, I am not sure I would want to hire a man like Micah to do my dirty work. He is not exactly reliable."

"Good point," Tommy nodded. "Where does that leave us?"

Clara considered for a moment.

"Supposing someone is trying to distract us with Micah? All this attention being paid to him means that whoever is really responsible for all this is able to keep hidden."

"They could not have known we would catch Micah in his brother's car," Tommy pointed out.

"But they would have known that the police would start looking for the missing car and when it turned up in the Hershels' garage, then attention would have been switched to the brother who was known to be a wastrel and always in trouble. Even if we had not connected Martin's murder with the death of William, finding the bloody knife in Micah's pocket would have given us a good nudge in the right direction," Clara was becoming more certain of her theory. "The real killer knew that Micah would bolt at the first sign of the police, making it seem he had a guilty conscience, and the anarchist journals in his room would have just confirmed our suspicions. It was a great cover just in case the bomb plot was discovered. Whoever is behind this, is trying to cover all their bases."

Tommy was listening carefully, but he was not convinced.

"Why murder Mr Martin?" he said. "He seems to have been at the heart of things. A fellow conspirator, so why murder him and risk alerting the police to the matter?"

"Perhaps it was a calculated risk," Clara suggested. "Maybe, after all he had done, Mr Martin started to reconsider. Sometimes people get so far and then reality sinks in, and they realise that what they planned on doing is not something they are prepared to do. Maybe he wanted to back out or stop the plot altogether."

"The remainder of those involved in the bomb plot could not risk Mr Martin going to the police, so they stabbed him near the music hall, not expecting him to make it all the way home before he died," Tommy carried on. "If he had died in the street, then we would be considering the incident a mugging gone wrong and no one would have taken a close look at his home."

"I think you have hit the nail on the head. The killer was unlucky Mr Martin made it to his own bed, which meant we wondered if his killer had attacked him in his home and so we looked around his house."

"That does not explain why William had to die," Tommy added.

"Maybe Micah knows more than he realises," Clara pondered. "Who would have the opportunity to put this bloody knife in his pocket, for a start?"

"We should ask him," Tommy said, following her train of thought. "No one wants to be wrongly accused of a crime, maybe the possibility will focus Micah's otherwise vague thoughts?"

"Agreed," Clara nodded and so they headed back to the house, where Micah was still sitting in the kitchen.

Someone had made him a black coffee and he was sipping it with a tortured look on his face. Micah usually drank to overcome the hangover he had induced in himself from the previous night's overindulgence. Without his 'hair of the dog' remedy, he was feeling decidedly ill. Worse, he felt alarmingly aware of his situation, his thoughts unhappily sharp as he contemplated what was going on around him and being accused of double murder.

He looked grey and sick when Clara walked into the kitchen again.

"Becoming sober?" Clara asked him nonchalantly.

Micah pulled a face.

"You should have let me runaway," he muttered. "It is all I am good for."

"Micah, from my perspective it seems to me you gave up on life a long time ago. You decided you could not be what everyone wanted you to be and so you stopped trying to be anything," Clara sat down in a chair opposite him at the kitchen table. "You are already running away from life; you just do it by drinking from a bottle."

A sad smile tipped up the corners of Micah's mouth.

"Probably you are right," he nodded. "But I have not run far enough away."

"Why are you running at all?" Clara asked him.

Micah shrugged his shoulders.

"Sometimes I am not sure myself. Then I see the

expressions on my parents' faces and I remember. They hate me and yet I am too much of a coward to just up and leave. I suppose that is my story all along. Too cowardly and too lazy to actually do something with my life. I would rather stay here and drink myself to death, even with my parents' disapproval, than try to make it on my own."

Micah did not seem disheartened by his self-deprecation.

"You have given up on wanting to be something other than a drunk?" Clara asked bluntly.

"I guess," Micah answered without ire at her words.

"Are you happy to be framed for murder and building a bomb too?" Clara persisted.

Micah hesitated, some spark of resilience appearing in his eyes.

"I am not a murderer, and I would not make a bomb. I wouldn't know how for a start."

"Your brother William would," Tommy pointed out.

"Just having the knowledge does not mean you have the inclination to do something like that," Micah replied. "William was not the sort to hurt others. Of that I am certain. He was gentle and kind. It is nonsense to think he built a bomb."

"Maybe you did not know him as well as you thought," Clara said. "You have not been in the best frame of mind these last few years to make a judgement about someone."

Micah was unperturbed.

"I knew my brother," he said. "I don't care what you imply. I knew him. He would not make a bomb, just like I would never kill someone."

"Unless it was while driving a car drunk," O'Harris said sternly. "Or maybe if you got into an argument with them and pushed them."

"This again?" Micah huffed. "I have never done

either of those things. I don't care what you try to say. That is not me."

Clara turned to O'Harris and held out her hand to him. He fumbled in his pocket and produced the bloody pocketknife. She took it from him and set it on the table in front of Micah.

"We found that in the pocket of one of the dinner jackets on your bedroom floor."

"It is not mine," Micah shrugged.

Clara used the edge of the handkerchief to carefully unfold the blade.

"It is covered in blood. I think this is Mr Martin's blood."

"Whether it is or isn't, I did not use that knife," Micah said with his first hint of anger. "I don't even know Mr Martin, except in passing. Why would I hurt him?"

"Someone might have paid you to do it," Tommy said, repeating the theory he had proposed to Clara.

"No one has paid me to do anything," Micah replied.

"You don't recognise this knife at all?" Clara asked.

Micah shook his head.

"You know, this could all be cleared up if you just could tell us where you were the night your brother died," Clara pressed on.

Micah paused, hesitant.

"I don't think I remember," he admitted.

"It is to your own benefit to try," Tommy reminded him. "It might be the only thing that saves you from being tried for double murder."

Micah looked between the siblings and O'Harris with bleary eyes. Slowly he realised something.

"You don't think I did it," his eyes widened at the notion.

Clara sighed.

"I have to say you do not strike me as someone a person would put faith in to commit two murders. Nor do you have the knowledge or ability to make a bomb, and to consider you a mastermind behind a bomb plot rather beggars' belief."

Micah started to laugh.

"You mean, being a drunken wastrel has finally paid off?"

"Just because we are uncertain does not mean the police will be," Tommy reminded him.

This brought Micah soundly back to earth.

"I am really in a pickle," he mumbled.

"You are," Clara told him. "Unless you can tell us where you were the night your brother died."

A panicked look came into Micah's eyes. His memory was hazy at the best of times, but under the pressure of potentially being accused of double murder, his mind had almost shut down. There was a big blank where his memory of that night should have been.

"All right, if you cannot remember, someone else might," Clara said, seeing she was not going to get anything from him. "Where do you normally go to get drunk?"

"Oh, that's easy," Micah said, almost grinning. "That I remember."

Chapter Twenty-Six

Micah gave them a list of five different places he frequented. Three were pubs, one was a gentleman's club that he admitted he tended only to visit when he was briefly sober, and one was a house of very questionable repute. It was potluck which one might offer them an answer and so they randomly selected one by the process of Clara closing her eyes, holding her finger over the paper, and pointing at something.

Somewhat inevitably, her finger landed on the house of questionable repute. Tommy grinned. O'Harris wanted to do the same but was not sure it was wise. He could not quite help a smirk, however.

"Honestly you two," Clara said to them with mock disappointment. "We are professionals. Besides, Tommy, Annie would be most displeased to know where you are about to go."

This information took the smile right off Tommy's face.

"Are you not displeased with me?" O'Harris asked. "I smiled too."

Clara turned to him, amused.

229

"For a start, I am not Annie, and it does not concern me if you get excited about the notion of scantily clad, scandalous ladies. That is rather natural, and as long as you only plan to look and not touch, I am not going to be silly and jealous."

O'Harris thought about this a moment.

"I cannot decide if that means you care about me so much you completely trust me, or that you are not terribly taken by me at all and so it does not matter what I think about going to a house of ill repute."

He looked hurt, which surprised Clara. Perhaps she had been too nonchalant.

"John," she said firmly, taking his hand. "There is no one I care more about than you, but I also trust you completely. Please take my words as a sure sign of my deep affection for you."

She winked at him.

"I would just go with it, O'Harris," Tommy remarked. "Most women would make your life a misery if they knew about what we are now going to do. Trust me, it is much more refreshing to have someone who is rather more rational."

O'Harris' smile returned. Clara was pleased to see it and reminded herself to be a little more forthright with how she felt about him in future, rather than just supposing he would know. Then she registered what Tommy had said.

"Thomas Fitzgerald, are you saying that most women are irrational?"

Tommy winced.

"Is that how it sounded?" he said weakly.

"It sounded rather like you were calling Annie irrational," Clara pointed out.

"You referred to her as silly and jealous," Tommy reacted, remembering Clara's words.

"That is different," Clara said primly. "I did not make a direct reference, I merely stated what I was not going to be like."

"Isn't that the same?" Tommy said, feeling he was caught in an ever-tightening net.

"Not at all," Clara replied.

"We best get moving," O'Harris interjected. "We still have a bomb to find."

Deflecting attention back onto their task at hand worked to stop the siblings bickering and they all bundled into the car.

"So, where is this house of ill repute?" O'Harris asked when he was in the driver's seat.

"I can give you directions," Clara assured him.

Tommy shot a look her way.

"I happen to have been there once," Clara answered the unspoken question. "On a previous case."

Tommy gave her a funny look but said no more.

They arrived half an hour later at a Victorian townhouse, set back from the road between a coachworks and a grain wholesaler. The sort of businesses that closed at night and did not pay much heed to what was happening at their neighbouring property. Nothing about the outside of the building suggested it was a house where ladies made their livings on their backs. There was a neat front garden bordered by a brick wall, and a discreet plaque attached to the bricks read – Windmill House. There was nothing to make a casual observer suppose this was anything but a very ordinary domestic residence.

"Go on, Clara, tell us how you came to be here once before," O'Harris said after they had left the car on the opposite side of the road and wandered across to the garden of the house.

"A couple of years ago I was hired to look for a young lady who had run away from her family. I am always cautious about such cases, as sometimes the person in question has good reason to run away. I tracked the young lady to this house, where she was working informally at what classes as a reception just inside. She had done nothing sordid other than walk through the front door," Clara elaborated. "After discussing the situation with her and asking what she would like me to do, we agreed I should inform her family she was safe and well but needed time before she returned. The family was not ecstatic about the news, but I was able to persuade them it was for the best. She ultimately went home before another month had passed."

"You do get around," O'Harris remarked.

"You are only just coming to that realisation?" Clara chuckled. "This has to be one of the more genteel establishments I have gone to in my line of investigation. Certainly, I did not have to fear being stabbed, shot, or threatened as has been the case with other places I have visited. Hopefully the proprietor will remember me and will be amenable to questions."

Clara headed towards the front door, her companions following her. She rang the bell as if come to sell raffle tickets, and the door was opened by a young lady dressed rather frumpishly for such an establishment. She wore thick stockings, heavy, practical shoes, a dress that went down to her ankles and hung loosely like a smock, and over her shoulders was a thick pink cardigan. She had the thickest pair of glasses Tommy had seen on a woman and with her hair cut severely short as was the fashion, she had a rather austere appearance.

"I was hoping to have a chat with Miss Pennington," Clara said to her. "Can you tell her it is Clara Fitzgerald, and I am not here to cause any trouble?"

The girl looked a bit bemused by this speech. She nodded her head and disappeared back inside, leaving the door open so that Clara and the others could step into the tiled hallway. Clara closed the door behind them, and they were cocooned in a gentle silence, the sort that descends on a busy household when everyone is asleep or at least engaged in quiet activity. There was a pleasant smell of perfume in the air.

"This is not what I was expecting," O'Harris confessed.

Clara leaned back against the wall opposite him and raised an eyebrow quizzically.

"What were you expecting?"

"Oh, you know…" O'Harris looked sheepish now. "There were places like this dotted along the Front, well behind the fighting line of course. Back in the areas where men went to rest and recuperate. They were somewhat shabby, a lot of them had suffered from shelling or gunfire."

O'Harris hesitated, waiting for a response from Clara. She simply smiled.

"I might have visited one or two," he added, because if one is to make a clean breast of things it is best to do it swiftly. "I was rather more reckless in those days."

"I have heard about the brothels in Belgium and France that kept our soldiers' spirits up," Clara remarked with a straight face. "I am not naïve."

O'Harris relaxed.

"They were nothing like this," he said, feeling encouraged in his talk. "In fact, it was all rather business-like and depressing. I am not even sure it was terribly enjoyable."

O'Harris frowned at his own perplexing memory of that time.

"It was complicated," he concluded.

He fell silent after that and before anyone else could speak, an older lady appeared in the hallway.

"Clara!" she opened her arms wide to greet Clara.

"Miss Pennington," Clara responded by slipping into the woman's embrace and hugging her back. "How is your niece doing?"

"She took your advice and is studying to be a

doctor," Miss Pennington said proudly. "It is a challenging business of course, lots of resentment from the male students and even some of the tutors, but she is tough."

"Send her my regards," Clara added.

"I shall," Miss Pennington promised. "Now, come through to my parlour and explain how I can help you."

Miss Pennington escorted them through to a room at the back of the house which was furnished with Victorian furniture. The colour scheme was dark green and plush red, offset by dark wood panelling on the walls. Miss Pennington told them to take a seat anywhere and offered them tea. Clara declined as they had a long day ahead of them.

"I am here because I need to determine where Micah Hershel was on the night of the twenty-fifth," Clara began. "He cannot remember, but it is important we discover where he was. It is not too dramatic to say his life will depend on it."

"Oh dear," Miss Pennington said, mildly alarmed. "What happened on the twenty-fifth?"

"Micah's brother was murdered," Clara said. "Along with another man. Evidence is pointing towards Micah, but he claims he would never do such a thing and there is something about all this that does not sit right with me."

Miss Pennington listened carefully, then nodded.

"Micah is not a person I would consider violent or dangerous," she said. "Even when he is drunk, he is very respectful to my girls."

"He threw a punch at me," Clara said plainly.

"Well, that does rather change things," Miss Pennington nodded. "Look, I would not be happy to say for certain Micah was here that night without checking with both the girls and my records."

"You keep records?" O'Harris asked in surprise.

Miss Pennington gave him an amused smile.

"This is a business. I keep strict records about how long people spend here and when they have or have not paid for the privilege. Not to mention keeping track of any of the extras I sell. You might be surprised to learn I am very respected with the tax authorities for my thorough record keeping."

O'Harris was surprised. Though he doubted very much any of the records sent to the tax office specified the services Miss Pennington offered.

"I run a tight ship here. I do not even supply alcohol to my guests, as I do not have a license do to so, and it keeps things more harmonious for everyone if the drinks are kept alcohol-free."

Miss Pennington was a sensible woman, and she knew what she was doing. O'Harris found he was impressed. Many a legitimate businessman did not keep everything so organised.

"Now, back to Micah. He does visit often, but whether he was here that specific night I am not certain," Miss Pennington was talking to Clara again. "I won't keep you a moment while I fetch my records."

She departed the room, leaving them alone to consider what they had just learned.

"I will say this is nothing like I expected," Tommy spoke first. "It is actually rather… respectable."

"Miss Pennington treats her girls well and keeps them safe. Some of them would be on the streets selling themselves if it was not for this place," Clara said. "Personally, I would prefer to live in a world where no one found it necessary to sell their bodies to make a living, but I also know that is far from the case and this is the lesser of a number of evils."

"How does she keep the police at bay?" O'Harris asked.

"She keeps her head down and makes sure neither her clients nor her girls cause trouble. You may have noticed we are not in a residential area, so once the businesses are shut for the day, there is no one around to see people coming here," Clara explained.

Tommy would have asked more, but Miss Pennington was returning with a large, black ledger. She settled herself back in a chair and opened the book on her lap.

"The twenty-fifth was the night of the Royal Gala at the music hall," she said casually.

"Yes, it was," Clara said. "How did you know?"

"One of my regulars is a member of the Friends of the Performing Arts and he always asks one of our girls to accompany him to events. He is a widower, you see, and he gets very lonely," Miss Pennington was turning over pages carefully.

"Two people who were at the music hall that evening died in mysterious circumstances." Clara said.

Miss Pennington looked up sharply.

"The same two people who Micah Hershel is accused of murdering?"

Clara nodded. Miss Pennington thought about this a moment and then she found she was at the page she wanted.

"Here we are."

She ran her finger down the page and came to an entry that made her stop. There was a noticeable look of relief that came over her face as she read the entry.

"Micah has here from eleven o'clock on the twenty-fifth until four the following morning," she said, turning the book around to show Clara the entry.

"That seems like a very long time," O'Harris remarked, curious.

"If I am honest with you, Micah quite often falls asleep in a girl's bed. He is a sad creature, and we all feel rather sorry for him. He always pays up for the time he spends here, so it matters little that he is just sleeping."

"Could I speak to the girl Micah was with that

night?" Clara asked. "Just to confirm he was with her the entire time."

"You certainly can," Miss Pennington agreed. "We have nothing to hide, and we do not want to get caught up in some murder case."

"Unfortunately, that may be inevitable as you are the only people who can confirm Micah was not at the music hall," Clara reminded her.

"Ah, but Clara, I only need provide an alibi if Micah is taken to trial for this crime, and as I am sure you will do all in your power to find the real killer, I have no concerns that will be necessary," Miss Pennington radiated confidence.

Clara was flattered by her praise, but she tried not to show it.

"We best speak to that girl, now."

Chapter Twenty-Seven

Describing Mandy as a 'girl' was to omit certain key facts, such as that she was well past fifty and had probably not been called a 'girl' by anyone other than Miss Pennington in a considerable number of years. She looked her age, even with the heavily applied make-up she wore. She had her hair scraped back from her face, which made her look even older, and it was somewhat difficult to know quite what her allure was to the paying gentleman.

Mandy had been with Miss Pennington virtually from the start of her enterprise and seemed content to remain there until she slipped from this mortal coil. According to Miss Pennington, Mandy still garnered a great deal of attention and was rarely without a gentleman for the night. She clearly had some hidden appeal Clara was not seeing.

"Micah is a good lad," Mandy said as soon as she sat down before them. "He is misunderstood. His parents do not give him the credit he deserves."

This was an unexpected pronouncement.

"Sounds like you know him well," Clara said.

"I know him very well," Mandy nodded. "He has been coming here for the last few years and I am always the girl he visits. He likes to talk, and I am happy to listen."

"On the night of the twenty-fifth, do you remember what time he arrived here?" Clara asked.

Mandy thought for a moment.

"It was around eight. I recall the clock we have in the upstairs hall chiming the hour just as he knocked on my door. He looked more depressed than usual, so I asked him what was wrong. He said he had argued with his parents again about his lifestyle. It was always worse when his younger brother came home from university. They would hound poor Micah about what they deemed his failings," Mandy folded her arms across her chest, radiating righteous fury over the way Micah had been treated. "I have a good mind to tell his mother that it is her badgering him that has caused him to fall into drink. He needs understanding, not to be torn apart and told he is a failure."

"Micah was here most of the night?" Clara went on, avoiding getting into a conversation about Micah's family relations.

"Yes. We talked for hours. It must have been past midnight when we finally stopped. He was resting on the bed and suddenly he fell asleep," Mandy explained. "He does that. Talks himself out and then just falls asleep."

"Did you leave him sleeping?" Clara asked.

Mandy laughed.

"No, of course not," she said. "I was being paid to keep him company in whichever way he required. If I left, I would be neglecting my duty. Suppose he woke up and wondered where I was? No, I stayed and read a book."

Miss Pennington came forward now.

"There is only one way in and out of the house for

clients," she said. "I have someone stationed at our front desk all night, so they can see who comes and goes and keep track of how long they stayed. To avoid someone neglecting to pay."

"You are saying there is no way anyone could have left this house without being seen?" Tommy cautiously asked.

"The only other door is at the back, through the kitchen, which is busy all night providing food and drink for the clients. Non-alcoholic drinks, of course," Miss Pennington elaborated. "I suppose someone could try to exit via a window, but all the downstairs rooms are busy overnight and such an antic would have been noticed. And the upstairs rooms are also occupied at all times."

"You must have some rooms that are unused at night," Clara said. "Do you not have your own private rooms?"

"I do, and they are kept locked during business hours," Miss Pennington promised them. "It is not that I distrust our clientele, but we get a lot of new faces from out-of-town, and you never can be quite sure if they might try to run out without paying, or even attempt to steal something. That happened a few times in the early days, didn't it, Mandy?"

"We learned by our mistakes," Mandy agreed. "We are much more security conscious now."

It was a strange statement to hear coming from the mouth of a lady of the night. Clara was starting to think Mandy had undersold herself. She seemed intelligent and sensible, why had she not pursued a more respectable career? She supposed that was a question with a complex answer.

"What is this all about?" Mandy now asked, looking to Miss Pennington for an answer.

"Micah has been accused of committing a double murder on the night of the twenty-fifth," Miss

Pennington explained.

"Micah?" Mandy said in astonishment. "Preposterous! He is a church mouse."

Clara refrained from pointing out she had seen his violent side, she sensed this would not go down well with Mandy. In any case, they had their answer and Micah had an alibi. He was not responsible for the death of his brother or of Mr Martin. It was also looking less and less likely he was involved in a bomb plot. That meant there remained a bomber on the loose.

"Did Micah mention his anarchist beliefs?" Clara asked Mandy.

"Some nights that was all he talked about," Mandy rolled her eyes. "He was quite boring on the topic. I told him that it was all too much and that a world without a government would end up crashing into chaos. He would not listen."

"Did he ever talk about the more violent side of anarchism, such as bomb plots?" Clara asked next.

Mandy snorted.

"Oh, yes, he talked about that. About a fortnight ago he came here very upset because someone he knew had been talking about blowing up someone important. It was all twaddle, of course. The sort of thing people talk about when they are riled up without really meaning it. But he had upset himself over it and I had to convince him it was just someone letting off steam."

Clara was listening intently now.

"Did he say who this person was who had been talking about blowing people up?"

"Just that it was an old friend and he had been upset hearing them talk that way. You know Micah served in the war? He was with the artillery, responsible for the gun carriages. He saw enough people and animals blown up during that time to last him a lifetime. He hated explosives," Mandy was firm about this. "He found it all very distressing that someone would even consider such a thing. Funnily enough, Micah does believe in anarchism. I think it might be the first time he has found himself a cause he can cling to. Though he doesn't do a very good job because of the drinking."

"Micah did not mention to us anything about an old friend with an interest in explosives," Tommy remarked.

"Micah forgets things," Mandy shrugged. "The day after he told me all about the blowing up plot, he was back to his usual self, and you would never know he had been so upset."

Clara was not convinced Micah would completely forget something so important. They would need to ask him again. But, for the time being, they had what they needed.

"Thank you both for all your help," Clara said, rising to leave. "I think Micah will be heartily relieved."

"Do you think someone is trying to frame him for murder?" Miss Pennington asked.

"It looks that way," Clara replied. "We just don't know who. If we did, we would have an answer as to who committed these murders."

"You best find out who is doing this to Micah before I do," Mandy said, angry again. "Because I shall give them a piece of my mind, and a kick from my boot if I discover who they are. My poor Micah."

She shook her head, saddened at the predicament.

"I shall see you out," Miss Pennington said, escorting her guests towards the front door.

"You know, I don't think you will need to look far outside Micah's circle of friends to find the person behind this," Miss Pennington said in a soft whisper as they were about to leave. "Micah does not have many true friends, and some of those he is regularly with are perhaps not there for his best interests, but rather because he has a deep purse and is too generous with his money."

"We shall bear that in mind," Clara nodded. "I don't suppose you have ever had Mr Martin from the music hall visit here?"

Miss Pennington shook her head.

"I know him. I have been to a few events at the hall, but he has never come here. He probably does not even know my name."

Clara made no mention that Mr Martin was dead. She thanked Miss Pennington and headed off back to the Hershels.

They found Micah where they had left him, in the kitchen. Except now there was a police constable stood over him, scowling as if he anticipated Micah jumping up and making a run for it at any moment. The remainder of the police force, along with Inspector Park-Coombs, were tearing the house apart looking for a bomb – much to the distress of Mr and Mrs Hershel. Clara could have told them it would prove a fruitless search but doubted she would be believed.

Micah looked up hopefully when they entered the kitchen.

"You have an alibi," Clara told him.

He breathed a sigh of relief.

"I knew I didn't do it," he said, almost laughing. "Who remembers me?"

"Mandy," Clara said, careful about the details in front of the police constable.

"Of course!" Micah said, delighted. "I went to her that night because I was feeling so despondent about everything. My parents were going on and on about how well William was doing at university and how, if I had just applied myself, I could have done the same. I was feeling very miserable."

"Now we know where you were," Tommy said, "we

need to work out who would want to frame you for murder. Someone planted evidence on you and did not expect us to come along and provide you with an alibi."

The joy drained from Micah's face.

"That's true," he said, rubbing at his pounding forehead and wishing he had a drink to hand.

"You have to think hard, Micah. You told Mandy that someone you knew had been talking about blowing up an important person. Who were you referring to?" Clara added.

Micah frowned.

"Who was I referring to?" he said, dredging back into a hazy memory. "I remember being upset about something like that at the time."

He was scratching at his head when the inspector walked in.

"I heard your voice," he said to Clara. "Do you come bearing good or bad news?"

"I take it you have not found a bomb?" Clara answered with a question.

"I haven't," Park-Coombs grimaced. "You are going to tell me why that is?"

Clara aimed not to smile at the statement, it seemed uncouth, but he was right.

"Micah was with a woman all night on the twenty-fifth and could not have murdered either his brother or Mr Martin. More to the point, Micah is not a person who keeps secrets well or could be considered reliable in a bomb plot."

"She is right about that," Micah nodded. "No one wants me to help them."

He frowned as he realised what he had said.

"Someone is trying to frame Micah," Clara continued. "They brought back William's car because it would make it look as if Micah had killed his brother and driven home. They also planted evidence on him. We have been keeping it safe."

Clara motioned to O'Harris who produced the bloodied pocketknife.

"That is not mine!" Micah said quickly as the knife was placed on the table.

"I think this is the weapon that killed Mr Martin," Clara told the inspector, ignoring Micah's comments. "If we can discover who this knife belongs to, I think it will lead us to who is behind the bomb threat."

"You should have turned that evidence over to me at once," Park-Coombs said crossly.

"We had no idea where you were," Clara reminded him. "It did not seem wise to leave it lying around. We found it in Micah's dinner jacket pocket."

"And you are sure about his alibi?" Park-Coombs pressed.

"Positive," Clara nodded.

Micah was staring at the knife, his brow creasing deeper and deeper.

"Which dinner jacket?" he asked.

Clara had been distracted talking to the inspector. She glanced back at Micah.

"What did you say?"

"Which dinner jacket?" Micah repeated the question.

Clara glanced to O'Harris because he had been the one to find the knife.

"It was in a bundle of clothes on the floor," he said.

"Show me," Micah insisted and there was now a new determination to his tone and demeanour.

Clara was curious at the change in the man. He suddenly did not seem the wretched drunk but showed a glimmer of the man he must have been at the Front when he had served so valiantly.

"We best go upstairs," she suggested, and so they all marched up to Micah's bedroom.

It was difficult to say if the police had searched the room or not, because it remained in a state of dishevelment. Fortunately, the pile of clothes containing the dinner jacket where O'Harris had found the knife had been hardly touched. He went to the bundle and dug around until he found the item of clothing.

"It was this one," he said. "I remember the lining of the pocket."

He showed them the patterned inner lining of the jacket pocket.

"I was looking for signs of blood on it, but saw none," he added.

Micah was looking at the jacket with a smile on his face.

"That is my second-best jacket," he explained. "I only wear it when my best jacket is being washed. It is a little bit tight around the shoulders and I do not care for it all that much, which is why I only wear it occasionally. I also happen to recall when I last wore it, because that evening I had a mishap and tripped off the pavement on my way home, wringing my ankle. In trying to save myself, I put out my arms and I heard a rip. I tore the right shoulder seam."

O'Harris examined the shoulder and found the rip, poking his fingers through the hole.

"You can remember all that, but not where you were on the twenty-fifth?" Park-Coombs said in exasperation.

"I happened to not to be very drunk that night," Micah confessed. "I was on my best behaviour because I was invited to a dinner party with an old friend. I was on my last warning with him, because of previous occasions and so I made an effort."

Micah's jubilation faded.

"I know who put that knife in my pocket," he groaned. "It all becomes clear now."

Chapter Twenty-Eight

Asher Lightman opened his front door when the bell summoned him. He was irked to see Micah on his doorstep.

"Let me in Asher," Micah pleaded. "The police are hunting me!"

"I wonder why," Asher said drolly. "What did you do this time?"

Micah did not respond, other than to push his way through the door and half stumble into the front hall.

"I have to hide," he hissed. "You will hide me, won't you Asher?"

Asher glared at him.

"If you have struck a police constable when you were drunk, I want nothing to do with it. You got yourself into trouble, you can get yourself out of it!"

He pointed out the open door, his message clear.

"That is not it at all," Micah winced. "They say I killed my brother, and another man. They say they have proof. Asher, they say I am a murderer!"

Micah broke down and slumped to the floor sobbing hysterically. Asher cast his eyes up heavenwards, wondering why he had the misfortune of knowing this idiot, and then he shut the front door and went to Micah's aid.

"Come into the sitting room," he said, grabbing Micah by an arm and helping him through to the next room. "Is this the dinner jacket you wore to my dinner party?"

"Yes," Micah mumbled through tears.

"You have a rip at the shoulder," Asher said lightly.

Micah did not respond, but he was sobbing less as Asher helped him onto a sofa.

"Thank you, Asher," Micah said weakly. "I didn't do it, you know?"

"Tell the police that," Asher answered, folding his arms.

"I did! But they won't believe me! I was lucky to give them the slip," Micah rubbed at his nose with the sleeve of his jacket. "They kept asking me about a bomb. I don't understand."

"Why don't you just tell them where you were the night they claim you did these things?" Asher suggested.

Micah shook his head.

"That's the problem. I don't remember where I was."

He sighed and slumped back on the sofa.

"It is odd, you know, Asher. Because, I recall that William was mumbling something about a bomb too. He thought he was alone in the house, and he was muttering to himself. I should have told the police that."

"Best you didn't," Asher said. "They might have thought you and your brother were working together on a bomb plot."

Asher took a step away from Micah.

"Why would they think something like that?" Micah frowned.

"You know how the police think," Asher shrugged. "And you haven't been terribly subtle about your anarchist leanings."

"You encouraged me," Micah declared. "You gave me that journal."

"Yes, but I didn't expect you to go about plotting to blow someone up!"

"I have plotted nothing!" Micah yelled. "You don't believe me, either?"

"I just think you don't know half of what you get up to when you have had a gallon of drink," Asher said. "Just think about it, really think about it. Can you be sure you have not done these things the police say you have? I'll go get you a glass of water while you consider."

Asher left the room. Micah sat in silence, avoiding letting his mind think of anything at all. Asher returned after a while with a glass of water for him.

"Micah, you always knew something like this could occur," he said.

"What?"

"Well, your drinking makes you irresponsible and temperamental. Sooner or later, you were going to hurt someone."

"I didn't Asher!" Micah declared adamantly, then his face fell. "Did I?"

"Tell me about the proof the police say they have?" Asher pressed him.

"William's car was back in the garage at home. How was I to know the police were looking for it? I went for a drive in it. They say there was a blanket on the back seat covered in blood, probably my brother's."

"That is pretty damning Micah."

"I didn't do it!" Micah insisted. "I wouldn't hurt William. I wouldn't hurt anyone."

"Oh, you have thrown your fists around before now, Micah," Asher shook his head. "You could have done it."

Micah fell silent. In the distance, the doorbell rang, and Asher excused himself. Micah carefully put the glass of water to one side. His hands were trembling, and he felt sick. His heart was racing in his chest, and he was scared he would never feel well again.

Asher returned. Behind him were two police constables and Inspector Park-Coombs. Micah jumped up from the sofa.

"You betrayed me!"

"Micah, it is for your own good," Asher said gently. "A man has to own up to his crimes."

Micah shook his head.

"I didn't kill them!" he insisted.

"The police have proof," Asher said calmly.

"Thank you, Mr Lightman," Inspector Park-Coombs moved forward. "We have been wanting to ask Mr Hershel a few more questions."

"You are going to arrest him," Asher said sadly.

"No, actually, Mr Hershel is correct. The evidence we have is circumstantial at best. It is not enough to charge him with anything."

Asher stiffened.

"I thought Micah said you accused him of murdering two men?"

"We have been asking him about it. He is a suspect. But I would need something more concrete to be able to arrest him. Still, thank you for letting us know where he is," Park-Coombs nodded to Micah. "We can ask you a few final questions here, Mr Hershel, then we shall let you alone. No need to panic."

Micah relaxed his shoulders.

"Thank goodness you are not arresting me," he groaned. "Isn't that good news Asher?"

Asher's face had flushed, as if he was holding his breath.

"He has to have done it," Asher declared. "If not

Micah, then who?"

"Well, that is what we are continuing to investigate," Park-Coombs said casually. "Mr Hershel does not strike me as a killer, if I am perfectly honest."

Micah grinned broadly. Asher glared at him.

"He said something about a bomb plot!" Asher persisted.

"We have concerns that Mr Hershel's late brother may have been involved in plotting something," Park-Coombs admitted. "However, we do not believe Mr Hershel was also involved. We are trying to locate anyone who recently spoke to William Hershel. Which reminds me, we were told you and William argued on the night he died?"

Asher looked startled and he suddenly pointed at Micah, his calm gone and his voice high-pitched.

"Look in his right jacket pocket!" Asher said. "You will find the knife that he used to kill Mr Martin. I saw it, just now!"

Micah stared at his friend, his smile fading as a look of sadness overcame him.

"You would be referring to this knife?" Park-Coombs produced the bloodied knife from his own pocket, still wrapped in a handkerchief. "Now, how could you have known about this?"

"You already have the knife," Asher's face was now haggard as he realised what had occurred. "But… you said you had no proof…"

"We found the knife, yes," Park-Coombs said. "But Micah has a cast-iron alibi for the night of the murders. Therefore, he could not have committed the crimes."

"I was not wearing this jacket the night of the murders," Micah added, pulling at his lapel to emphasise his words. "I was wearing my best dinner jacket. This jacket I did not wear until the day after the murders when you invited me to dinner here."

Asher just stared at him, realising he had been had and contemplating his next step. He abruptly turned and made to bolt. The police constables dived and grabbed him.

"Asher Lightman, I am going to get this knife checked for fingerprints," Park-Coombs said. "I am hopeful I will find yours. Not on the hasp, because I think you are smarter than that, but on the knife blade itself."

Asher shut his eyes as he realised his mistake.

"Would you care to tell us where the bomb is?" Park-Coombs asked.

Asher opened his eyes and gave the inspector a sinister smile.

"What bomb?" he said, before laughing.

"We shall search this whole house," Park-Coombs informed him, trying to keep the urgency out of his tone. "We shall find it!"

"No you won't," Asher told him coldly. "You will never find it."

There was a flicker of satisfaction in Asher's eyes.

"You will hang for your crimes," Park-Coombs snapped at him. "It will all have been in vain!"

"Revolutions are cast in blood," Asher said darkly. "I wasn't expecting to live past this weekend, anyway."

"Take him to the station, lock him up," Park-Coombs growled, knowing when he was defeated.

Asher would give him nothing, but he would enjoy taunting the policemen. Park-Coombs did not want to see the man's smirking face anymore.

Asher was led away, as Clara, O'Harris and Tommy entered the house.

"I take it our ploy worked?" Clara asked.

"To a point," Park-Coombs nodded. "He revealed himself as the killer of Mr Martin. He planted that knife in Micah's pocket. He knows about the bomb too, but he won't tell us anything. We need to search this house from top to bottom."

Park-Coombs motioned to his men who split up to search.

"I am going to call the army and have their bomb disposal people come and take a look too. I don't think the bomb is here, but they may find more evidence we can use against Asher."

The inspector walked off solemnly. Clara glanced at Micah, who was looking exhausted by his performance.

"You did well, Micah," she told him.

"I did it for William," Micah replied. "I don't know why Asher killed him, but he didn't deserve to die. That, I am sure of."

"If he was involved with the bomb plot…" Tommy began.

Micah cut him off with a grin.

"William was not a bomb maker. He knew the science of it, but he was too peace loving. Besides, he and Asher detested one another. They could not have worked together."

"Are you sure?" Clara asked.

Micah nodded his head.

"They have never gotten along. Asher felt that William was too nice, too kind. You should have heard some of the vitriolic things he said about William. I am certain they were enemies, not friends."

"They were seen arguing the night William died," O'Harris reminded them. "William would not tell Miss Addison what the argument had been about. Could that argument have been the reason William died?"

"We have no evidence that Asher attacked William," Clara pointed out. "If someone had seen him in William's car, then we might have something, but we only have proof he killed Mr Martin."

Micah was thinking hard, trying to activate his fuzzy memory and recall something he felt was important. He hit himself in the side of the head.

"Remember!" he scolded himself. "Remember!"

"Micah?" Clara glanced his way.

"I told Asher I had heard William muttering about bombs," Micah said. "I was stringing him along, like you told me, but now I think about it, I don't think that was just something I made up."

Micah started to pace back and forth.

"You know, William was always being helpful to Stacy – Miss Freeman. He was desperate to marry her," he continued. "I was only paying limited attention, but I do recall that before the Royal Gala, William went to the music hall to help set up the decorations. It was that same day, after he got home, that I heard him muttering. I am sure of it. He was sitting up the dining table with his head in his hands. He looked upset about something, but I was not listening properly."

Clara considered what he was saying.

"Mr Martin was having secret meetings with a mysterious plumber at the music hall," she said. "Presuming that plumber was Asher Lightman, it might have intrigued William that they were having a clandestine conversation?"

"Maybe William overheard something he should not have," Tommy concurred.

"Or he saw something that bothered him," Clara was thinking fast. "He confronted Asher at the gala. Probably he didn't mean to, but they bumped into one another, and the matter cropped up. They were rivals and William had no reason to view Asher favourably."

"Bit risky, confronting a man about a bomb plot," O'Harris said.

"People do not want to believe the worst of others," Clara replied. "Maybe William was unsure of what he had heard and wanted to have Asher laugh it off to make him feel better. No one wants to suppose a person in their social circle is capable of something so drastic. From what we have learned about William, it seems he was a little naïve."

"He was too quick to give people second chances," Micah interjected. "I told him, some people are not worthy of them. Myself included."

Micah clasped his hands together; it helped stop them shaking.

"It should have been me who died that night," he said. "No one would have missed me."

"Micah, that is too harsh," O'Harris told him. "I think you would have been missed."

Micah shrugged his shoulders.

"My brother had so much life ahead of him, so much future. Not like me. If I had paid more attention to his muttering, maybe we could have done something, together."

"You are not being rational," Clara told him.

"But Asher was my friend," Micah persisted. "At least, I thought he was. I knew about his anarchist leanings. If I had just listened more, maybe I would have picked up something about this bomb plot long ago. Before my brother had to die."

Micah fell back onto the sofa. There was no consoling him. He felt he had failed and that was that. Clara was distracted from his dark mood by the return of Park-Coombs.

"Look at this," Park-Coombs showed her a set of workman's overalls and a flat cap. "Just like the description of the mysterious plumber. I am going to take a photograph of Lightman and show it to the people who met the plumber and see if they recognise him."

"Any signs of a bomb?" O'Harris asked.

Park-Coombs shook his head.

"We have found a stash of anarchist periodicals beneath Lightman's bed and there is correspondence between him and some people using codenames who vaguely discuss things such as blowing up the Houses of Parliament," Park-Coombs elation at finding the disguise had disappeared. "Asher is our man. The more we search, the more we will find, but the bomb is not here."

"There is only one place it could be," Clara said. "I think they planted it at the music hall."

"Why would Mr Martin risk destroying the place he had devoted himself to?" Tommy asked.

"Maybe he wouldn't and that was why he had to die," Clara replied. "In any case, we have to search the music hall for that bomb."

"And we better hurry," Park-Coombs groaned. "The King arrives tomorrow and will be expecting his dinner."

Chapter Twenty-Nine

They headed straight to the music hall, feeling the
pressure of the mounting urgency weighing them
down. Park-Coombs sent a message for the army bomb
squad to meet them at the music hall rather than
Lightman's house. The bomb had to be there –
somewhere.

Mr Mitchell looked surprised at the number of
vehicles pulling up outside the hall. There was the
single police car, and then a police carriage containing
extra constables, next came two army lorries and, of
course, there was O'Harris' car. An air of trepidation
came over Mr Mitchell and he trembled as he watched
the assortment of official looking people converge
outside his building. It was not long before people
from the neighbouring buildings were stepping
outside to see what was happening. Even though most
of them knew little about the death of Mr Martin, it
was plain to see something peculiar was happening at
the music hall and they were all curious.

"Mr Mitchell," Clara approached the worried
caretaker with the picture of Asher Lightman Park-

Coombs had found. "Do you recognise this man?"

The caretaker had become ashen in his alarm. He looked at the picture, at first not really taking in what he was seeing, then his gaze focused, and he started to return to himself.

"Why that looks like…" he frowned, studying the photograph harder. "I would almost say that was the man Mr Martin employed as a plumber."

"Why only almost?" Clara asked.

"Because… well… he looks too posh to work as a plumber," Mr Mitchell scratched at his head anxiously.

"Aside from him looking 'too posh', would you say this is the man you saw having secret meetings with Mr Martin?" Clara pressed.

Mitchell took his time before replying.

"I would say it is, but why would this man be here working as a plumber?"

"He was not working as a plumber," Clara explained. "Mr Mitchell, do you know anything about the arrangements for the royal visit tomorrow?"

Mr Mitchell managed to go even paler than he had been before.

"I didn't know anything until after Mr Martin died, and now I have people talking to me about the matter," he said. "I was scared to answer the telephone at first, seeing as it is not my place. But when Mr Martin was not going to come back, well, I had to. Someone from the Trustees' committee came to see me and told me I was in charge until they arranged a replacement and I had to make sure all the prebooked engagements went ahead as planned."

Mr Mitchell was despairing at his new role which was completely beyond him. He could fix things, sweep floors, lock doors and deal with any general maintenance required, but talking to people and making arrangements for functions was another thing entirely.

"Talk me through the arrangements for the royal visit," Clara said, trying to make things as easy for him as possible. "I imagine all the details have already been worked out by Mr Martin?"

"Yes," Mitchell nodded. "I found the paperwork after looking for ages. The King is coming here at noon. He will be in a plain car, so no one ought to realise who he is. He will exit the car right by the entrance and I shall show him through to the main room which will be arranged for dinner."

"How many people will be present?"

"The King and Queen, and about a half dozen staff, such as the King's secretary and his personal physician," Mitchell told her, sweating as he recalled the details and thought about the prestigious nature of the guests he had to deal with the next day. "I am not supposed to tell anyone these details."

The caretaker looked faint, having spilled out the details of the event far too willingly.

"It is no matter, Mr Mitchell. I need to know these things. Let us go inside and talk further."

With everyone arrived, it was a simple matter to usher the trembling caretaker into the hall and into the main room where the fateful royal gala had taken place.

Mr Mitchell paused before the large fireplace and suddenly realised he had quite the audience. Aside from Clara, Tommy and O'Harris, there was Inspector Park-Coombs with numerous constables lining the wall and waiting for orders. Then there were the army men, in their khaki uniforms, looking stern and fearsome. Mr Mitchell decided this was swiftly becoming the worst day of his life – he had no way of knowing how much worse it was likely to get.

"Mr Mitchell, this is the room the King will dine in?" Park-Coombs asked when everyone was gathered.

Mitchell nodded his head.

"The tables over by the wall will be moved into the centre of the room," Mitchell explained, indicating the tables that on the night of the royal gala had been used for the buffet.

"Will the King be given a tour of the music hall?" Park-Coombs continued.

Mitchell shook his head.

"There is not really much to give a tour of. This is the main room for events, the rest of the building is purely functional, such as Mr Martin's office and the kitchens."

"Then, if a bomb has been placed it must be either somewhere in this room or beneath it," Park-Coombs said to the army fellows.

Mr Mitchell could not fail to register the word he had just heard.

"A bomb!"

"Mr Mitchell do not panic," Clara came forward and clasped at the man's forearm as he looked about to sway backwards into the ornate fireplace. "We believe that Mr Martin and Asher Lightman plotted to blow up the King and placed a bomb somewhere in the music hall. We have to keep clear-headed to find it and avoid a disaster."

"But... but a bomb would destroy the music hall too!" Mr Mitchell said in alarm.

"Yes," Clara told him. "And that has caused us concern because it would seem to go against everything Mr Martin worked for. But then Mr Martin was murdered, by Asher Lightman, possibly because he did not like the idea of the music hall being used in the plot."

Mr Mitchell was struggling with the notion that his employer had been involved in a bomb plot. A lot of information had just been thrown at him and little was making any sense.

"Mr Mitchell, just concentrate on helping us, the

rest we can discuss later. Does the basement run under this room?" Clara asked.

The caretaker nodded his head.

"I am not sure how far under it goes, I have never taken much notice, but there is a space beneath this room."

Park-Coombs was listening in to the conversation.

"Right, we need to search the basement from top-to-bottom. Show me how to reach it, Mr Mitchell," he waved at his constables and then followed the dazed caretaker to the basement entrance. The army men went along too.

"What should we do?" Tommy asked his sister.

Clara looked around the room for a moment. Something felt odd. Lightman had seemed so confident they would never locate the bomb and that suggested he had avoided hiding it somewhere as obvious as the basement.

"I think we should look around here," she said. "Maybe the bomb is not below us."

O'Harris looked around the room, his gaze going from floor to ceiling, then to the windows. He frowned.

"There are lots of potential hiding places for a bomb here."

"We take our time, and we are thorough," Clara replied. "We have to think like Lightman, think about where he would choose to hide a bomb."

They split up and began to circulate around the room. Clara began near the windows, looking behind the large curtains, though she knew that was too obvious a spot, and then gazing up into the pelmets which were a solid wooden structure that hid the curtain rail. She could not see well into the shadows of the pelmets, but she rather doubted there was a bomb in there, because it would be less effective above the King, than if it was either level or below him. However, if they could not find the bomb, she would suggest getting a ladder and searching the pelmets thoroughly.

Tommy was examining the vast fireplace in detail, trying his best to see up the chimney and determine there was nothing hidden within. O'Harris was knocking on the panels of the wall, hoping to find a hollow space where a bomb could be hidden.

Clara tried all the windows and discovered they were locked. She had vaguely wondered if the plan was for another accomplice to come along and lob the bomb through the window. The locks on the window would prevent that. The glass panes were split into multiple small squares by wooden cross pieces, and it would actually take some force to cast an object straight through. She doubted Lightman would take such a chance.

"Ah, anyone, could you, perhaps…?"

She turned around at the voice of her brother and saw a sight that would normally have amused her. In his efforts to search the chimney, Tommy had clambered up as high as he could and had now wedged himself. All they could see were a pair of legs dangling into the fireplace.

"I appear to be stuck," Tommy said, trying not to sound as helpless as he felt. "I might be suffocating, actually."

"You are not suffocating," O'Harris said, chuckling as he went to his aid. "There is plenty of air coming down that chimney."

Clara left them to it, the bomb her priority. As she turned back from her brother's predicament, her eyes landed on the clunky radiators that had been installed beneath the windows. The radiators were not original, but had been added to this room just before the war to try to alleviate some of the damp issues and also because guests had complained how cold the room became, even with the fireplace lit.

The radiators would be linked to a boiler, Clara

mused, and boilers and pipes are the sort of things plumbers would look at without anyone paying heed. She went to the nearest radiator and looked behind it. She could see between the bulbous pipes of the radiator and the wall behind, but there was nothing there. She checked all the radiators with the same result. She was disappointed. For just a moment, she had been convinced she had found the solution.

O'Harris extracted Tommy from the chimney, producing a cloud of soot in the process. Tommy was coughing and spluttering, his face blackened. Mr Mitchell wandered back into the room, and stared first at Tommy, then at the soot on the clean floor.

"Now I shall have to wash the floor again and put more polish down," he groaned.

"We were just trying to find the bomb," Clara rebuked him as gently as she could, thinking he was rather missing the point.

Mr Mitchell turned her way and spotted her as she was crouched down by the middle radiator, the last one she had searched. A puzzled look came onto his face.

"I wondered if the bomb might be behind the radiators," Clara explained to him. "I theorised that Lightman would have placed the bomb somewhere it would not seem odd for a plumber to be working."

"Yes," Mr Mitchell said, still with that odd look on his face. "That is why I paused, because you reminded me of the other day when I came in here and found the plumber crouched by the same radiator. He said he was looking for a leak, but here is the thing, I emptied those radiators myself just the other week because the boiler was going to be replaced. We have been making do without heating ever since. I couldn't see how the radiators could be leaking, but I was so busy at the time I forgot all about it."

Clara gingerly tapped her knuckles on one of the upright tubes of the radiator. It made a hollow sound.

"What exactly was Lightman doing to this radiator?" she asked Mr Mitchell.

The caretaker walked over.

"He had this end cap off the pipe here," he pointed. "And he had been looking inside."

Clara started tapping on the radiator again, but this time following the bottom horizontal tube at the base of the radiator, where it linked to the pipe from the boiler. As she tapped, suddenly the sound beneath her fingers changed and it was no longer a hollow response, but a dampened, dull noise.

"He put something inside the radiator," O'Harris said in astonishment. "We would never think to look inside."

Clara very carefully took off the end cap. As she removed it, something pulled away and a ticking noise began. She glanced inside the pipe and saw there was a wristwatch – a good quality one – now starting to tick.

"It's a time delayed bomb," Tommy winced. "Removing the end cap began the timer."

"We need the bomb disposal team right now!" Clara said urgently, not sure how long they had.

She grabbed Mr Mitchell's arm and hastened him out of the room. O'Harris was already running to the basement door to call for assistance. Tommy hesitated just a moment, to glance at the bomb mechanism, then he hurried to follow.

The bomb team rushed back to the main room and took one look at the device, before shouting at Park-Coombs he needed to evacuate the building and the street.

"This brings back memories of a couple of days ago," Park-Coombs muttered forlornly, before he gave orders to his men to clear the road.

Clara was keeping close to Mr Mitchell, who was looking extremely upset and might do something reckless if they were not careful. She encouraged him into the back yard with O'Harris and Tommy's help.

"Someone would have needed to come in and trigger the timer like you did," Tommy mentioned to his sister as they were moving through a back street to get as far away from the building as possible. "Lightman seemed quite confident that despite being arrested the bomb would go off, which must mean there is another accomplice."

Clara agreed with him.

"Mr Mitchell, who else was going to be at the dinner tomorrow?"

"I told you already," Mr Mitchell huffed, angry at being dragged from the music hall.

"I was referring to kitchen staff and other such people," Clara persisted.

"Well, not many," Mr Mitchell replied. "I was in charge of arranging the room. Then there would be the cook preparing the meal and a waiter to serve it."

"Someone would be coming to bring the ingredients and other supplies," O'Harris pointed out.

"Oh, yes, I forgot about that. There was something in Mr Martin's paperwork about a delivery coming first thing tomorrow morning."

"Who was to bring the delivery?" Clara asked.

Mr Mitchell shook his head.

"I don't know," he groaned.

Chapter Thirty

They waited across the road in anxious anticipation, the minutes ticking by.

"How long does it take to defuse a bomb?" Clara asked her brother.

He shrugged his shoulders.

"Depends on the device and it doesn't help it has been activated, that makes it more dangerous."

"I did not know that would happen," Clara said, aggrieved.

"I was not blaming you," Tommy hastened to add. "I was just explaining how much harder this potentially could be."

They fell silent again, aside from Mr Mitchell who was making odd mumbling noises to himself and pacing back and forth in agitation. Clara was finding his fussing movement grating on her nerves. She had to distract him.

"Mr Mitchell, did you ever suppose Mr Martin would consider the destruction of the music hall?"

Mr Mitchell turned to face her in alarm.

"No!"

He was angered by the question, but then he hesitated.

"He always said the music hall would be nothing without him. I thought it was a touch of pride and rather unbecoming. But once he stated that if he had to leave the music hall, it would be finished," Mr Mitchell paused as the words hit home. "It seemed rather dramatic at the time, and I assumed he was just angry, but in hindsight you start to wonder if he meant something more… literal."

That did cross a person's mind.

Clara was about to probe Mr Mitchell further on the subject when she saw the inspector on the opposite side of the road waving at them. He looked relieved and that filled her with newfound hope.

"It took them forty-five minutes," O'Harris commented. "Must have been fiddly."

They headed back to the music hall. Park-Coombs was looking quite chipper now the bomb was found and safely defused.

"They checked all the other radiators too, to be sure," he said. "But there was only the one bomb. They have put it in a box for me, so I can present it to Asher Lightman. We will rattle a confession from him."

"What about the last accomplice?" Tommy asked. "The one who would have started the bomb ticking."

"I shall leave a couple of men here tomorrow. They will dress as if they are workmen helping Mr Mitchell and will keep an eye out for anyone tampering with the radiator. Then we shall have our final plotter," Inspector Park-Coombs was on cloud nine at his success. "Want to come to the police station and see me take that smug smirk off Lightman's face."

"Absolutely," Clara nodded. "I want to know why he killed Mr Martin and if he also did away with William Hershel."

"And once that is done, I shall report to my Chief

Constable how I caught a traitor and saved the King from assassination," Park-Coombs continued.

"Just you?" Clara raised an eyebrow at him.

"I meant 'we', Clara, of course I did," Park-Coombs chuckled, a little abashed. "We were in this together."

Clara rather fancied she had done a good deal of the heavy lifting in this case, but she was gracious enough to not say so and to be satisfied with getting due credit for her actions.

"Shall we head to the police station now?" Park-Coombs asked sheepishly.

"That sounds a good idea," Clara agreed.

At the police station, Clara was allowed to sit in with Park-Coombs as he interviewed Asher Lightman. The man was brought into an interrogation room looking cocky. He was still under the impression he had won. He sat at the table in front of them and simply smiled.

"I know nothing about a bomb," he said, spreading out his hands in a gesture of polite defiance.

"We are not here about the bomb," Park-Coombs told him. "That matter is resolved."

Lightman laughed.

"Oh, is it?" he chortled. "If you think you can trick me…"

Before he could finish his statement, Park-Coombs produced the wooden box he had stashed beneath the table when they arrived in the room. He placed it before Lightman. Inside was a metal cylinder, probably a section of pipe. There were copper wires poking out of the end and attached to a wristwatch.

"Was it vanity that caused you to use one of your own watches as the timer for the device?" Park-Coombs asked Lightman. "It is an expensive time piece and I intend to trace who made and sold it, so I can determine it was yours."

Lightman was staring hard at the bomb and the

watch attached to it, but he was not about to be cowed by the sight.

"I know nothing about it," he declared.

"Once I prove the watch belongs to you…"

"When you do that, come back and see me," Lightman folded his arms defiantly.

Park-Coombs was amused.

"Within your house we found a curious set of workmen's clothes," he continued. "We also showed your picture to various people who all confirmed you were the mysterious plumber who regularly had surreptitious meetings with Mr Martin."

"I did a bit of plumbing work for him," Lightman shrugged. "I was helping him out."

"What exactly was this plumbing work?" Park-Coombs asked.

"I fixed a leak," Lightman shrugged.

"It took you several months to fix a leak?" Clara asked in mock surprise.

"It was more than one leak," Lightman replied fast.

"You were also seen 'fixing a leak' in the very radiator that this bomb was found in," Park-Coombs commented. "Mr Mitchell thought it very odd you were attempting to fix a leak in a radiator that had already been drained of its contents. Rather awkward to determine where it was leaking with nothing inside it."

Lightman stayed silent, though Clara was sure he seemed to have tensed up as the evidence was laid out before him.

"The men who removed this bomb wore gloves," Park-Coombs continued. "They are professionals, you see, and they know how important it is to avoid removing any fingerprints from the bomb. How confident are you that in the process of handling this device you did not leave a fingerprint? On the watch, perhaps? After all, it was going to blow up, wasn't it?

So why worry about fingerprints."

Lightman had grown very still.

"We know who your last accomplice is," Park-Coombs continued. "We shall catch them tomorrow as they go to start the bomb's timing device and then it is over for you. Honestly, I have enough evidence already, especially with the anarchist papers we found in your house."

Lightman had his lips pressed together in a thin, tight line.

"I am curious about why you killed Mr Martin," Clara said when the inspector asked no further questions.

Lightman flicked his eyes to her, though his head remained still.

"We have all the evidence we need to prove you did that too," Park-Coombs informed him.

"Did Mr Martin really want to blow up the music hall?" Clara asked Lightman.

Something glimmered in Lightman's eyes, a final, desperate way to shift the blame for the bomb plot off himself and maybe avoid a firing squad.

"It was Martin's idea," he said quickly. "He was always going on about such things. I am more of a pacifist, truly!"

Park-Coombs and Clara were not about to believe that. Lightman continued talking, trying to turn things around.

"Martin was angry that the board of trustees was going to remove him as manager of the music hall. He felt betrayed. He said if he was to be removed, then he was going to take down the music hall with him so no one else could have it. That place was his pride and joy. It was his life," Lightman spoke in a rush. "I didn't take him seriously. I thought he was letting off steam. We did share some political leanings, that is true, but not to the point I wanted to blow up the king. In any case,

I knew nothing of this bomb business until last week when I was at Mr Martin's house, and he showed me the device he had made. I was truly shocked! He had been working on it in secret for months. It was to be his revenge on the trustees for the music hall and taking out the king at the same time was just the icing on the cake."

"What about William Hershel?" Clara asked. "How was he involved?"

"He wasn't," Lightman shook his head. "I couldn't stand him. But he had been going to the music hall to help set things up for the gala night and he happened to come down into the basement when I was talking with Mr Martin. He was looking for a new fuse, or something. Anyway, he overhead me trying to dissuade Mr Martin from his bomb plot before we realised he was there. He argued with me on the matter the night of the gala, saying he was going to tell the police about what he had heard."

"That was when you decided to kill him," Park-Coombs said.

"No! I never touched him. He confronted Mr Martin in his office. They argued and somehow William fell and hit his head. Mr Martin panicked and summoned me. He said we had to do something, hide the body. He was off his head, and he scared me, so I agreed to take William away."

"Mr Martin scared you?" Park-Coombs said in amazement.

"He did," Lightman said firmly. "He had this violent streak. I was too nervous to refuse. So, I took William in his own car and dropped him in a ditch. Then I needed to get rid of the car and it just seemed to make sense to drive it back to his home and put it in the garage. It was never locked. I thought William would not be found for a while, especially with his car in the garage, and I could deal with Mr Martin."

"By murdering him?" Clara asked.

"I was trying to stop the bomb plot, don't you see?" Lightman snapped at her. "That night, after I went back, Martin was ranting and raving. He was quite mad. He was talking about letting off the bomb there and then. He would not tell me where the bomb was, and I believed he was going to explode it! In my desperation to stop him, I stabbed him!"

Lightman came to an abrupt halt, as he finished his statement.

"You want us to believe you are actually a hero in all this?" Park-Coombs asked. "That you were trying to save the King?"

"Yes!" Lightman said earnestly. "I was trying to prevent a tragedy."

"Then why not come to the police and tell us everything?" Park-Coombs tilted his head to the side as he asked this logical question.

Lightman breathed in deeply, his mind working fast.

"I did not think you would believe me," he said.

Park-Coombs nodded solemnly.

"Well, you are right on that front. I don't believe you."

"You have to!" Lightman's desperation had turned to fury.

"You were seen planting the bomb," Park-Coombs informed him. "You kept the truth hidden from us. You tried to frame Micah Hershel and you left William Hershel to die in a ditch rather than seek medical attention for him."

"He was dead," Lightman barked.

"No, he was not," Clara replied quietly. "He might have lived had you not left him in a ditch. However, then he could have revealed how fictious your whole story is, and you could not have that."

"No!" Lightman yelled. "I was trying to help!"

"The evidence speaks rather loudly against that," Park-Coombs informed him, rising and taking away the bomb in its box.

"You see? This is why I did not come to you in the first place! You don't believe a man telling the truth!"

He was still shouting at them as they left the room and stood in the corridor outside.

"Not quite a confession," Park-Coombs said, a little disappointed.

"But we now know that William Hershel was not a conspirator," Clara reminded him.

"Do you believe Mr Martin killed him?" the inspector frowned.

"I am not sure. I think Lightman had a good reason to be rid of William. If only William had come to you immediately, but I suppose he doubted himself. It is quite a thing to say someone you know is building a bomb."

"His hesitation cost him his life," Park-Coombs nodded. "We shall probably never know who truly killed him, but sometimes that is the way things go."

"If you do not mind, Inspector, I would like to take the information we have learned to the Hershel family. It is time they had some answers."

Park-Coombs had no reason to disagree.

Clara headed back to the front of the police station and found O'Harris and Tommy.

"I'll update you on what we learned as we head to the Hershels' home," she told them.

Around an hour later, they had gathered the Hershels in the sitting room of their home. Mr and Mrs Hershel were sat side-by-side on a sofa, clasping hands. Annabelle was stood to one side, leaning against the fireplace. Micah sat in an armchair, looking pale and sober. He had not had a drink in some hours, and it was taking its toll.

"Thank you for letting me interrupt your day again," Clara said to the family. "I have news about the death of William."

Slowly and steadily, she told them about Lightman and the bomb plot, how it had involved Mr Martin and how William had learned of it and tried to prevent tragedy occurring. She revealed how Micah was wholly innocent in the matter but had been framed by Lightman. As she spoke, she knew there was little in the news to make the family feel better about their loss, though at least they now knew that William was not plotting to blow up the King.

When Clara finished, Mrs Hershel choked on tears.

"My William was always thinking of others," she said. "He was trying to do the right thing."

She burst into tears and was comforted by her husband.

Clara stood uncomfortably before them, wondering if it was advisable to leave. It was Micah who distracted her by standing up and walking towards her.

"You have done me a good service," he said, holding out his hand for her to shake.

Clara took it. His palm was cold and clammy.

"My little brother deserved a lot better than this, and I will be glad when Lightman goes before the firing squad," Micah pulled a face. "This has made me think about a lot of things. Actually, I still have a lot of thinking to do, but, thank you, Clara Fitzgerald."

Micah turned around and left the room. There was nothing more to do but leave the Hershels' to their grief. Annabelle saw Clara and her companions to the door.

"Mr Martin was always so quiet," she said as she showed them out. "To think he was building a bomb in his spare time."

"It is sometimes hard to know someone truly,"

Clara said,

Annabelle nodded.

"Perhaps that is true of my brother Micah, as well?"

"Perhaps," Clara smiled.

Annabelle sighed.

"Things need to change in this family," she said. "Thank you, Clara."

They shook hands.

~~~*~~~

The following day as arrangements were being made to set up the music hall for the King's arrival, a lone delivery boy appeared. He had a box of special goods for the occasion, including some expensive blooms of flowers. He suggested to Mr Mitchell that he place these immediately in the dining room. He had been instructed by the florist who had sent him to arrange the flowers in a certain way. He insisted he must place them himself.

Mr Mitchell, pretending he had no knowledge of a bomb, left him to do so. The young man closed the door behind him as he entered the main reception room and set his flowers on the table. He was not to know there was a constable quietly watching from behind a screen in the room. At first the young man seemed just interested in the flowers and ensuring they were correctly placed on the table. Then he glanced over his shoulder, paused to listen, before walking directly to the middle radiator and pulling off the end cap.

He was confused when he saw nothing there. He swore quietly. Then he felt a heavy hand fall on his shoulder. The game was up.

The young man proved to be one of the members of Eric and Victor's anarchist group who had grown tired of talk and wanted action. He had met Lightman by chance. Sometimes life threw up flukes like that.

The young man was quick to confess when confronted with Inspector Park-Coombs and he, metaphorically, drove the final nail in Lightman's coffin.

The King arrived later that day and dined at the music hall, unaware of the danger he had been in. Clara later heard from Mr Mitchell that the King had enjoyed his meal greatly, so much, in fact, that when he learned of the music hall's plight, he agreed to donate money from his personal purse to assist in its restoration.

Everything had worked out well, in the end. Except for the death of William Hershel, which could be considered nothing other than a tragedy. If only he had gone to the police immediately instead of confronting Asher Lightman, but what was done, was done.

Clara concluded the case by writing up some notes for the files she kept on every investigation. She was sat alone in the parlour of her house, listening to a crackling fire in the grate and sipping tea. She was thinking that when she started as a detective, she had never imagined she would be trying to save the King from a bomb. A smile curled up the side of her lips.

No one would ever know what she had done and the disaster she had averted. She rather liked having such an impressive secret.

Still, she would be quite glad to never have to deal with a bomb again.

We hope you enjoyed this book.
You might also like

The Gentleman Detective
by
Evelyn James

Norwich 1898.
Colonel Bainbridge has spent more years than
he cares to consider as a private detective, but
the unexpected death of fellow detective,
Houston Fairchild, has left him wondering if it is
time to retired. His niece, Victoria Bovington,
has her own ideas about what the future might
hold for them. When a pugilist dies
unexpectedly, and an innocent man is accused of
his murder, the unlikely pair find themselves
investigating the murky world of street fighting
and match fixing. Can they find the real killer
before it is too late?

Available on Amazon Kindle
(Paperback coming soon)

Red Raven Publications
was founded to bring great stories to
life through digital and traditional
publishing.

The majority of our books are
exclusively published through Amazon.
For more information on our titles,
authors, and forthcoming releases,
go to our website!

www.redravenpublications.com

or find us at
Facebook.com/RedRavenPublications

Printed in Great Britain
by Amazon

19936410R00164